KEITH THOMAS WALKER

● ● ● ● ● ●

"You got my mama's house shot up!" Shaun yelled.

"Wha-what?" Mike was having a hard time understanding things. His brain was dizzy from the punch in the jaw, but fear pumped enough adrenaline to keep his eyes open.

"What you doing? What's wrong?" he pleaded.

"My *mama*, nigga!" Shaun growled. He enunciated the last word with a solid thump to Mike's skull. "My *mama's* house! Them niggas shot up my mama's house 'cause of yo dumb ass!"

"Wha? *When?*" Mike stalled.

He didn't think Shaun's fit of rage could get any worse, but it did. A new look took over his face. "What, you think it's funny?"

Mike had no idea what he was talking about. He didn't think he was smiling, but he couldn't be sure what expression his face was making. He couldn't feel anything on the right side, where the two blows had landed.

Shaun reached under his Polo and pulled out a .38. He shoved the pistol in Mike's face.

"What he doing?" Spider cried.

Killa Karl cut off his noise with a mean blow to the choppers. "Shut up, nigga."

Karl was twice his size. Spider cowered and began to cry.

Passion took that as her cue to vacate the premises. With nothing on but her panties, she stood and headed for the door. Shaun either didn't notice her or didn't care about her leaving.

Mike pleaded with his mentor, "*Don't do it, Blood! Don't do it!*"

Before the whore could make it out, Mike saw a figure appear in the open doorway and block her path. The new arrival belonged to the blue side. Mike was sure of this, even though the man was wearing all black. He had seven cornrows braided tightly. His skin was dark, his face emotionless. He held a Tec-9 with a banana clip. Mike knew this was the second, and now *only* leader of the fagg land crabs.

"Which one of y'all niggas is Mike?" Kody asked. He didn't raise his voice, but his words were enough to shut. down. everything.

● ● ● ● ● ●

1

COLORED RAGS

COLORED RAGS

KEITH THOMAS WALKER

KEITHWALKERBOOKS, INC
This is a UMS production

COLORED RAGS

KEITHWALKERBOOKS

Publishing Company
KeithWalkerBooks, Inc.
P.O. Box 331585
Fort Worth, TX 76163

All rights reserved. Except for use in any review, the reproduction or utilization of this manuscript in whole or partial in any form by any mechanical, electronic, or other means, not known or hereafter invented, including photocopying, xerography, and recording, or in any information retrieval or storage system, is forbidden without written permission of the publisher, KeithWalkerBooks, Inc.

For information write
KeithWalkerBooks, Inc.
P.O. Box 331585
Fort Worth, TX 76163

All characters in this book have no existence outside the imagination of the author and have no relation whatsoever to anyone bearing the same name or names. They are not even distantly inspired by any individual known or unknown to the author and all incidents are pure invention.

Copyright © 2016 Keith Thomas Walker

ISBN-13 DIGIT: 978-0-9967505-1-6
ISBN-10 DIGIT: 0996750517
Library of Congress Control Number: 2016903803
Manufactured in the United States of America

Second Edition

Visit us at www.keithwalkerbooks.com

KEITH THOMAS WALKER

This book is for Fort Worth's South Side legends

MORE BOOKS BY
KEITH THOMAS WALKER

Fixin' Tyrone
How to Kill Your Husband
A Good Dude
Riding the Corporate Ladder
The Finley Sisters' Oath of Romance
Blow by Blow
Jewell and the Dapper Dan
Harlot
Plan C (And More KWB Shorts)
Dripping Chocolate
The Realest Ever
Jackson Memorial
Sleeping With the Strangler
Life After
Blood for Isaiah
Brick House
Brick House 2
One on One

NOVELLAS

Might be Bi Part One
Harder
Primal Part One
The Realest Christmas Ever

POETRY COLLECTION

Poor Righteous Poet

FINLEY HIGH SERIES

Prom Night at Finley High
Fast Girls at Finley High

Visit keithwalkerbooks.com for information about these and upcoming titles from KeithWalkerBooks

ACKNOWLEDGMENTS

Of course I would like to thank God, first and foremost, for giving me the creativity and drive to pursue my dreams and the understanding that I am nothing without Him. I would like to thank my wife for being my first and most important critic, and I would like to thank my mother for always pushing me to be the best I can be. I would like to thank Janae Hampton for being the best advisor, supporter and little sister a brother could ever have.

I would also like to thank (in no particular order) Beulah Neveu, Deloris Harper, Denise Fizer, Michele Halsey Hallahan, Priscilla C. Johnson, Tia Kelly, Melissa Carter, Cathy Atchison, Lanita Irvin, Ramona Weathersbee, Jason Owens, Chanta Rand, Ramona Brown, Sharon Blount, BRAB Book Club, and Uncle Steven Thomas, one love. I'd like to thank everyone who purchased and enjoyed one of my books. Everything I do has always been to please you. I know there are folks who mean the world to me that I'm failing to mention. I apologize ahead of time. Rest assured I'm grateful for everything you've done for me!

COLORED RAGS

KEITH THOMAS WALKER

PROLOGUE

*The gutters take your blood and bile
These gangstas with those sinful smiles
With colored rags spread country miles
Tec-9 is Dad to the bastard child
And so a grin streaks your face while
The bullets buck from kids gone wild*

*And then you spoil the walls with paint
When your locs meet their destined fate
Of bars that are their pearly gates
Or muddy holes where fat worms mate
Hospital beds where flat lines skate
Morticians drive nice cars and wait*

*For customers when handguns blast
For gangstas with those grinning masks
For you to cock yo .44 Mags
And smoke some leaves, and start to laugh
And give your nose a crystal bath
Then pump some lead in his bitch ass!
Yeeeah!
I guess you got revenge at last
Our caps get peeled for colored rags*

"See. *Looka here.* It's shit like this that piss me off."
 William Broadnax sat up in his Cutlass Supreme and surveyed the block. His younger brother Andre sat in the passenger seat gnawing on a greasy burrito. Will's shiny .45 automatic sat between them. Hearing Will's displeasure, the pistol wanted a taste. But this predicament required no firearms.

COLORED RAGS

They sat in the parking lot of Rainbow Gas and Grocery. The convenience store was not the safest place to get hot foods, but Dre was a fat kid, so that didn't matter. Rainbow was a great place to park and sell dope, and Will's old school Cutlass, sitting on twenty-inch rims, was like a magnet for fiends. Will had conducted four transactions in just thirty minutes but still found something to get bad-tempered about. He never went too long without bunching his eyebrows over something.

"You know who that is, don't you?"

Dre looked up from his meal but didn't see anything out of the ordinary. It was Sydney. Sydney was light-skinned, wore dirty clothes and was addicted to crack cocaine. He walked by with the same worried, hesitant look he always had. There was nothing in his hands. That was *kind of* odd, because Sydney usually had something to barter with rather than actual cash, but that was the only thing Dre could point out.

"That's Sydney. What about him?"

"That's *Sydney*," Will agreed. "Where he going?"

Dre hated these pop quizzes. How the hell was he supposed to know? Will had them backed into the parking spot, so Dre had a good view of the neighborhood, but it always looked the same to him. Sydney was on the sidewalk headed east, towards Riverside Dr. Other than the fact that he was not coming towards them, Dre had no idea what Will wanted to hear.

"I don't know," he said. "He gon' score from somebody else?"

"Yeah," Will said. "And why he gon' do that?"

Dre grew a little warm. His first guess was correct, but it wasn't hard to figure out what was on his brother's mind. "He owe you some money?" he queried.

Will nodded, his eyes on the offender. "You see he ain't looked over here, don't you?"

Dre saw that Sydney was looking forward, walking stiffly. The fiend's eyes usually darted around a lot, because when you're an addict *anything* had the potential to make a profit. Dre turned and watched his brother closely.

Will didn't close his mouth when not speaking, so his bottom lip hung. A little spittle glistened on it. He was still handsome, though. He had a strong jaw-line, dark skin and serious eyes. Just six months back on the streets after a two year bid, Will was cut; big chest, big arms, big shoulders and no gut. Hoochies fought over who got to braid his hair.

At thirty-two, Will was considered *old school*. He led a rough group of Crips who had developed a nice stronghold on the city's south side. Fresh out of the pen, Dre thought Will should be happy. He had his health, his freedom, a pocket full of money, a whole gang to command and all the power and perks that came along with it.

Sydney was a two-bit hood with no more than five dollars in his pocket on a good day. But Dre knew his brother wasn't going to let it slide. Will was teaching him about the streets, and there were such things called *principles*. Whenever principles were involved, his big brother usually kicked some ass.

"I'ma get him," Will decided as he hopped out of the car like a jump-out boy.

Dre was left with his burrito and the .45. He preferred the burrito. On the CD player, Tupac had advice for brothers being pursued by their local law enforcement.

Open fire on them busta-ass bitches! Lord knows!

Will had to march a good twenty paces to catch up with Sydney. Dre watched stoically. He couldn't hear their conversation, but there were only two answers you could give when someone demanded their money.

Dre chewed slowly. His stomach grew a little queasy. Will was talking to the transient rather than hitting him. That was good. But Sydney made no attempts to reach into his pockets. He held his hands to his side, then outstretched in a *Who me?* gesture. And then he pointed down the street to where his pot of gold was buried perhaps. Will's arguments grew louder, and a few curse words made it back to the Cutlass. Dre turned the radio down and took a deep breath just as Sydney took a right cross to the jaw and promptly crumpled as if he'd been shot.

Dre sighed. He didn't know what to feel. On the one hand, Sydney was a loser; a drug addict who only exacted tolls on society. But he was still a *person*. He had relatives who loved him and was born beautiful, just like everyone else. On the other hand, watching Will in action was something wonderful. He may not have gotten his GED while locked up, but he certainly got his *ass-whooping-degree*.

COLORED RAGS

     He had told Dre that things were primitive in the pen. With no guns, you had to get good with your fists. You had to get better than inmates who'd been in there practicing for twenty years. Will was *really* good. You couldn't even see his hands move. He bobbed and weaved like a prairie dog with a hawk on its ass.
     Sydney's mistake was popping back up like a jack in the box after every blow. Dre wondered why he didn't just play dead. The cocaine in his system made him either numb or dumb. With the radio down, Dre could hear them now.
     "C'mon, Will, I-"
     WHAP!
     "I swear I'ma get it, man. I got-"
     WHAP!
     "*G*! Hey. Listen! *Please*, Will! I ain't lying! If you just let me make it over here, I got-"
     WHAP!
     Sadly, Will wasn't even really fighting. He had a good thirty pounds on the dopefiend and could have easily knocked him out. He toyed with him instead; hitting him with open handed smacks. Will feigned like he was going to throw a right hook, then clocked him with a left when Sydney tried to block. Will hunched his shoulders, making Sydney react for a jab, then pummeled him with an uppercut to the gut.
     "Where was you finna go?"
     "*Nowhere, G. I swear man!*"
     "You was finna score from Reggie and them?"
     "*Naw, Will. No I wasn't! I ain't even got no money!*"
     "Where my money, man?"
     "G, I got you. Please! I-"
     WHAP!
     "You said you was coming back Tuesday!"
     "I *tried, Will. I came. You wasn't here, man. I swear*!"
     "Fool, you know where I be at!"
     WHAP!
     And this was broad daylight. Dre marveled at his brother's daring. At eleven in the morning, Will stood on one of the busiest corners in the city and whooped the tramp like Sydney was his child. He looked back to the Cutlass and yelled something to his little brother.

Dre pretended not to hear. Sydney took this moment to flee, but Will kicked his legs from beneath him almost nonchalantly.

"C'mere!" he yelled again. "Hurry up, Dre. Come whoop this nigga for me!"

Dre hoped Will didn't say that, but he knew he wasn't mistaken. This would be the third fight Will tried to get him involved in since he got back from the joint. Dre kept telling him fighting really wasn't his thing, but Will said that was akin to *homosexuality*. He assured Dre that "*Everybody in the pen with nonviolent tendencies get dealt with.*"

"C'mere, nigga!"

Dre reluctantly got out of the car. He didn't rush to the foray. He didn't have to. Will had Sydney by the collar. He dragged the hobo back to the Cutlass almost effortlessly. Sydney reeled like the scarecrow from the *Wizard of Oz*. He fell, was drug on his knees, made it to his feet, rode an imaginary bicycle and then fell again.

"Come on, man. *I can get it!* If you just, if you just. *Hey!* Let me go, Will. I'll pay you. *Don't do me like this.*"

Will threw the dopefiend at Dre's feet.

Sydney didn't know who to plead to, so from his knees he begged both brothers for leniency.

"Just let me go around the corner, y'all. I can get it in *five minutes*. I swear. I got a dollar fifty right here. *Take it*. I can get you eight-fifty more, right around the corner. I can, I could get you ten. *Ten* more! *Fifteen* more! Just let me go, man. I don't want no more." He spoke quickly, rambling and drooling.

Sydney's eyes bugged. He looked like the LAPD had been at him. In just one minute, Will had given him nasty bruises about the lips and eyes. Blood flowed from his mouth. Dre thought he might have lost a tooth, but there were a few missing already, so it was hard to tell.

"Dre, you heard me calling you. Whoop this nigga for me."

Will was breathing a little heavy. He stared at his brother with contempt but not serious anger yet.

Dre tried to back away from them but found his rump on the car.

"Naw, man. *Please* don't hit me no more." Still on his knees, Sydney turned to Dre. His big eyes sought compassion. He held his hands up, and his fingers trembled. "I can't get no money looking like this, man. I *steals* for a living. I can't go in no store. They call the police. *Stop, man.* Listen. I got you. Let me make it, lil' homey. Don't hit me, man. *Please* don't hit me."

    Will kicked him in the side. Sydney fell flat on the pavement.

    "Shut up, cuz! Say, you better hit this nigga, Dre!"

    "Will, I..." Dre's heart was like a speaker box in his chest. His mouth was dry. Will saw this, and his eyebrows knotted over his nose.

    "Dre. Hit this nigga."

    "Don't hit me man, I-"

    "Shut up, cuz! Kick him or *something*, Dre!"

    "Will, I don't wanna..." Dre squeezed his burrito so hard the innards spilled from it.

    "Don't kick me, man!"

    "*Shut up, I said*! My little brother *is* gon' kick you. Either that or I'ma knock yo ho ass out. Which one you want?"

    "Don't kick me in the face then. *Please.* I gotta go in stores. Get some money."

    "Dre, if you don't kick this nigga *right now*, I'ma *beat yo bitch ass*. Quit acting like a goddamned *mark* all the time. You make me sick with that shit, cuz. I *swear* you make me sick."

    Dre kicked and caught the junkie on his shoulder. It wasn't very hard, but Sydney was a good actor.

    "*Oww*! Man, *that hurt*! He got me! See? He did it! He *got me*. Let me go, Will. I'll, I'll go get yo money-"

    "Kick him again, Dre. That didn't hurt."

    "It *did hurt*, G. I ain't gon' lie to you. I never lie to you. I done learnt my lesson, Will. You ain't gotta do me like this in front of everybody like this."

    "Kick him again!"

    Dre booted harder this time and tagged him on the same shoulder. Sydney squealed and got his whole body into the act. He fell onto his side and grabbed the injured arm.

    "*Oww*! He got me, man. He got me *good*, Will. It *hurt* too. Let me go, G. He got me!"

    "Kick him in the *face*, Dre."

    "*No*! Not in the face, man. I gotta go in the store!"

Dre's face twisted with emotion. He felt his eyes watering and knew Will would hit him if he cried. If he cried, Will would have *him* on the ground, and he might make Sydney take a few kicks himself. Dre dropped the burrito and balled his fists. It was never going to be enough. He drew back, and when Dre kicked this time, he seriously tried to punt Sydney's head from his body.

It was a perfect shot; right on the temple. Upon impact Dre felt like he jammed his big toe. There was a funny sound, somewhere between a *crack* and *squish*.

Sydney didn't have to feign injury. His head snapped to the side, and his body followed, sending him spiraling into a roll that looked like break dancing for a second. He wobbled to his knees, rubbed his head, asked his mother for fifteen dollars please, then fell spread eagle. He looked dead, but his breath stirred the dirt around his mouth.

Dre's heart tried to squirm up his throat. Will hadn't seen anything greater since Tyson took a piece of Holyfield's ear. He laughed and pointed.

"*Hell yea, cuz*! That's what I'm talking about! You shut that nigga up, Dre. Look at him, man. *He gone*. That the first nigga you knocked out?"

Dre nodded numbly.

"Look at 'em, cuz! That don't make you feel *good* – to see you can shut a nigga down like that? That don't make you feel *good*? Quit looking like that, nigga. You can't be looking like a ho when you fuck somebody up. You still look *soft*, like you finna cry or some shit. We gon' get that bitch up outta you, Dre. Get in, nigga."

Dre stared at the body for a moment longer and didn't notice his brother was ready to pull off.

"Get in, *cuz*. Somebody gon' call the law. Can't have nobody laying in the parking lot like that. Somebody gon' think he dead."

Dre's legs were wet noodles, but he managed to get back into the car. Will exited the parking lot without speeding and turned the radio back up. Six blocks down the road, Dre told him his foot hurt.

"That's the dumbest shit I've ever heard," Will replied. "Out of all the things you could've said, you pick some punk-ass shit to complain about. You know what, nigga, you just lost all the

COLORED RAGS

respect you earned from knocking that nigga out. You gon' have to knock out somebody else to get it back."

Dre didn't have anything to say about that. He wiped his hands on his pants leg nervously, hoping to avoid getting burrito grease on his brother's seat.

KEITH THOMAS WALKER

CHAPTER ONE
COLLEGE BOY

My friend wants me to smoke some weed
And kick it with his gang this week
In my hood you can't be cool
If you not faded off pills and brew
I see commercials on TV
Telling me to "Say no to guys like these"
They tell me, "Saying no is cool"
But they're not here to tell this fool

    Chris crossed the main lawn of Texas Lutheran University with a deliberate strut. He wanted to look menacing and confident. He had no friends there but wasn't uncomfortable at all. A detailed search was not needed to conclude he was one of a very small number of black faces on campus. But it was summertime. He figured there would be more students of color come fall, though he doubted the ratio would ever be more than ten percent. By the time he made it to the administration building, he caught himself subconsciously playing *Count the Black People*. His high number was two.

    The July afternoon was hot but not unseasonably so. The heat index would rise to 110 degrees later in the week, and August would be like a fart from hell. So today's high of 94 degrees was actually nice. The students Chris encountered wore shorts and sandals. Only a few were carrying books. Most of them lived on campus with little care about anything going on past the school's perimeter.

    Chris grinned at them and judged them. He knew a lot of them had big dreams that would never be accomplished. He

COLORED RAGS

stereotyped his peers, thinking he could tell their whole life story by how they dressed. He figured they were doing the same to him.

Chris wore a blue tee shirt that hung midway down his thighs, where a pair of black Dickeys emerged. His pants were too long. They made neat puddles that sat atop his blue Chuck Taylor's. The shoe strings on the Chucks were also blue.

His skin was dark, his hair cut short. Despite the clean cut, Chris knew his appearance conjured the word *THUG*, which was fine with him. At first glance, one wouldn't think he was an exceptional student who could count the C's he made in high school on one hand. His scholarship to the university was *not* athletic, and he was a pre-med major.

When he handed his registration papers to the clerk in the admin building, he thought she would second-guess him, asking if he'd filled it out correctly. *Pre-med major? Nah, not you.* He actually hoped she would say something along those lines, but she simply typed the information into her computer. That irked him a little bit.

Chris had a bad habit of wanting to rebel against authority figures. *You been reading too much Huey Newton*, his mom told him on more than one occasion. *You keep running around thinking the white man trying to keep you down, and you gon' end up **letting** him keep you down.*

"Looks like your financial aid packet is complete," the clerk told him, handing his papers back with a smile. "See you in the fall."

And that was it. He had signed up for five classes and was officially a college student. He left the building with his spirits high. He still wanted to look tough, but he couldn't stop smiling as he skipped down the steps.

• • • • • •

Chris exited the parking lot and headed south on Lutheran Road. He drove two blocks and made a right on Rosedale. Rosedale Avenue, like the whole neighborhood, had once been beautiful. Back in the 50's, if you were lucky enough to have a business on the thoroughfare, you were almost guaranteed success. Nowadays there was more graffiti than entrepreneurs on the decaying strip. The only businesses that thrived were the churches and liquor stores.

Rosedale's potholes were big enough to qualify as manholes, and Chris' car had bad shocks. The combination was anything but fun. He tried to slow down at the mouth of each crater, but the posted speed limit was forty. He needed to get closer to 10 mph to minimize the damage the street inflicted on his hooptie. Drivers passed him and complained that he was a Sunday driver. At the tender age of 18, this was *big-time* embarrassing. Chris kept his head down and turned off the busy street as soon as possible.

A few turns later, and less than five minutes away from the university, he arrived at Evergreen Terrace Apartments. The complex was a sprawling 90 unit catastrophe enclosed by a length of fence that was ten-feet-tall and topped with razor wires. The razor wire was stretched, compromised, and completely removed in several sections, and the natives had cut a number of holes in the fence at strategic locations. These holes were so regularly traversed, there were trails leading to and from them.

Chris never understood whether the fence was to keep the residents safe or to keep the city safe from the residents, because anyone breaking into Evergreen Terrace had better pack a lunch, an Uzi and a platoon if possible.

Sadly, the fence was only the beginning of the apartment's disrepair. The lawn hadn't been mowed all season. The grass stood high enough to conceal a legion of snakes. Abandoned units were either left open or broken into, usually by prostitutes or crackheads looking for a safe place to get high.

Apartment management at the Evergreen was nonexistent. Technically, they'd been between managers for the last two months. There were no maintenance personnel to call for leaky faucets or regurgitating toilets. When the last owners abandoned the venture, most of the residents who were seriously concerned about their safety left shortly afterwards. The ones who stayed stopped paying rent because there was no one there to collect it. For the most part everyone was waiting for the city to show up and shut the place down.

In the meantime, Evergreen Terrace was run by a gang. Crime was always the order of the day. The *AGG Land Crips* had renovated the place to better suit their needs. The *AGG* stood for *aggravated.* Any knucklehead bold enough to roll past the front gates was guaranteed to find exactly what he was looking for, whether that be dope, guns, a good high, or a good fuck. The AGG Land set was run by two individuals, both of whom were ruthless and a clear hindrance to Overbrook Meadows' Gang Unit. OG Will was dark and menacing. OG Kody was well-educated, but equally evil.

No pre-med student (or any student for that matter) would find comfort or safety at the Evergreen, but Chris was an exception to many rules.

He pulled up to building F and parked next to a Fleetwood that had shiny twenty-inch rims. From his car, he could see a crowd hanging out on the breezeway upstairs. There was always a lot of activity in or around apartment 4F. The whole complex belonged to the gang. This unit was considered their headquarters.

Chris only recognized one of the four men on the breezeway. Dante was Kody's right hand man. He was overweight at 240 pounds, but he was more stout than fat. Chris got out of his car and slowly climbed the stairs. He had known Dante for years, but the bigger man's greeting was not always welcoming.

"What you doing here, nigga?"

"Nothing."

"Ain't nobody in there but Trez," Dante told him.

"That's cool."

Like most gangs, the AGG Lands Crips used a specific handshake for a greeting. Chris passed the four goons on the breezeway without giving them dap because, despite his dress, he was not a member of their gang.

Dante's depiction of the residents inside the apartment was not accurate. At first count, there were at least eight people in the living room and kitchen area. Chris suspected several more might be lurking in the bedrooms. Three of the occupants were women who appeared to be high off unknown intoxicants. Dante most likely only mentioned Trez because he was the thug Chris hung out with most often.

Deuce, the youngest member of the gang, held most of the crowd's attention as he played Call of Duty on the room's only television. The thirteen year old had a huge afro that was admired by all. Anyone could grow hair, but his mother was Hispanic, so he had the always-popular *good* hair.

In the kitchen, two angry-looking men cut a large slab of crack into chocolate chip-sized morsels that would go for ten dollars a pop. A couple of the females looked on with obvious interest. Trez sat in the apartment's only love seat with a baking sheet on his lap. He was in the midst of his favorite activity, which was something Chris rarely saw him go more than a couple of hours without doing: The baking sheet was covered with marijuana, and five fresh blunts were already assembled.

Trez looked up and spied Chris with a delightful twinkle in his eyes. The weed-roller was tall and thin. His skin was fair enough to pass for Hispanic. His long, curly hair furthered this illusion, but it was actually a German grandfather that infiltrated his bloodline. He had a long, slightly pointed nose that made his thin face look even skinnier. Overall, most people thought he resembled a rodent. The struggling whiskers sprouting under his nose furthered this comparison.

"What up, *my nigga*? Say, come here, boy!" Trez smiled brightly as he waved Chris over. He was in his early twenties, but he looked like a child sitting there, with his thin legs meeting at the knees to support the baking sheet.

Chris found a metal folding chair and set it up close to his friend. As psychotic as Trez was, he was Chris' favorite person there. Trez was the joker of the crew. He couldn't fight and wasn't very menacing. But no matter how bad you felt, if Trez was around, he would try to cheer you up.

"What's up," Chris said, his eyes on the marijuana. "I see you still at it."

"*At it?* What, *this*?" Trez held up a blunt and stroked it under his nose like an expensive cigar. "Nigga, this shit ain't no hobby. This my motherfucking life! I thought you was starting school. Didn't you say you was going today?"

One of the boppers closest to them was eavesdropping. She grinned at Chris. He smiled back, but he would never go out with her. Most of the girls who frequented that apartment would go down on you for a twinkie of raw (aka a twenty dollar bag of powder cocaine).

"I only had to register for classes today," he told Trez. "School don't start till August."

COLORED RAGS

"You my motherfucker," Trez said. "Say, y'all," he called to the crowd in the living room, "this fool going to *college*! This nigga finna be somebody! Ain't you, Chris?"

Chris' smile faltered as the Crips turned and gave him a once over. He had too much melanin to blush, but his face grew warm.

One of the girls said, "For real?" and a few others told him that was, "Tight," but mostly, they didn't give a damn about his aspirations. If Trez announced Chris had just robbed a bank, he would have garnished a lot more praise.

"Say, Chris, watch me bust this rocket launcher at these ho ass niggas," Deuce yelled over his shoulder. The crowd erupted in approval as his video game character took out a couple of noobs in a fiery explosion.

Glad the attention was off of him, Chris looked back to his friend.

"So, what you gon' major in?" Trez asked.

"I told you I was pre-med, nigga. You didn't believe me?"

Now the bopper was really interested.

"I thought you was bullshitting, nigga." Trez traced the length of a sixth blunt across his tongue. "So you really gon' be a doctor? Cuz, you that smart? You know them Chinese motherfuckers got that shit sewed up."

Chris downplayed his intelligence, as he often did when he hung around this apartment. "I'm smart enough."

Finished for now, Trez placed the last blunt on the baking sheet and leaned forward in his seat. He presented the cigars to Chris. Each one was rolled perfectly.

"Get one. I *know* you gon' get high today." Trez's grin was maniacal.

Chris made it all the way through high school without ever touching the wacky tobacky. But two weeks ago, after much prodding from the likes of Trez, he finally took a few puffs from a blunt. Much to his amazement and Trez's disappointment, he didn't get even a little high. A few days later he tried again with the same results. Trez told him a lot of people didn't get high off weed until their third or fourth experience.

"Say, nigga, you through with them?" a cocoa-colored hazard named Croc wanted to know.

Croc was one of the roughest members of the set. Although he was a ruthless adversary and always down for mischief, he was not well respected in the gang. He was the only member Chris knew of who had to be reprimanded for wearing dirty Dickeys and scuffed sneakers too often. Croc was also gaining a reputation for being untrustworthy because he sometimes came up short on his drug peddling. This was most likely due to his increasingly destructive *boy* habit, but snorting heroin recreationally was not frowned upon in the gang.

"Hell naw, cuz," Trez told him. "The first one going to *college boy*! This nigga finna be a *doctor*! Get you one of these bitches, Chris." His eyes were nurturing as he held the tray out to his friend. He could have been Grandma offering a fresh platter of peanut butter cookies.

"Hell yea," someone piped in.

"Celebrate that shit, nigga!" another said.

"Chris finna get *blowed*!"

The room filled with adulation for the corruption of the one pure homeboy they had left. Croc was the only one who wasn't in a festive mood.

"Man, fuck that ni-" He stopped short and looked around to see if anyone heard him. Croc, as well as everyone else in the room, knew that disrespecting Chris would bring swift and deliberate consequences. They didn't have to like him, but they were required to tolerate him when he came around.

With all eyes on him, Chris selected one of the skimpier blunts from the baking sheet. Trez caught the move and wasn't having it.

"Hell naw, nigga. Get that fat one!" Trez motioned with his nose, which was more pointy than wide.

Chris replaced the skinny and took the fatty. He held it awkwardly and looked around. Everyone looked on with amusement – everyone except Croc. Croc looked like he wanted the fatty.

Embarrassed again, Chris said, "I ain't got no..."

"Here you go." One of the hoodrats produced a lighter.

Chris accepted it and looked to his mentor. Trez nodded, his smile big and toothy. Chris lit the tip of the blunt and sucked until an ember manifested. A racket of coughs immediately erupted from his lungs as his body rejected the foul smoke. With

COLORED RAGS

tears in his eyes, he looked around and saw that everyone was pleased with him.

With the formalities over, a horde of Crips rushed forward to snatch up the remaining cigars. Chris ducked to avoid the arms reaching around his head. Trez was the only one who sat motionless.

"Yo, hit that shit again, nigga," he urged. "You finna get high for real! This some corn, my nigga!"

Chris inhaled again, slower this time, and managed to hold most of it in. He winced at the smoke drifting towards his eyes as he wondered what the hell *corn* weed was.

CHAPTER TWO
TALES FROM THE HOOD

*Mostly I do it for the clothes
True Religion and Polo's
I want a fat ass stack to fold
I like to drape myself in gold*

*Really, I do it for respect
Blasting on fools has its effects
I'm keeping all these punks in check
Niggas is scared of my whole set*

*Them police ran up on my spot
They put my ass on this cell block
It don't matter what high bail they got
I'm gon' get out and sell my rocks*

The third time proved to be the charm.

With the blunts gone, the atmosphere in apartment 4F shifted from energetic to the nonchalant boredom that sometimes led the gang to commit acts of violence, just for the hell of it.

Deuce traded exploits on Xbox battlefields for a far more comfortable fetal position on the floor. He snored softly and looked younger than his thirteen years. The sofa was filled with people, and Chris noticed it was a really *nice* sofa, considering the environment. It was new, black, and leather. It could go for $2,000 at Haverty's, but a desperate dopefiend sold it for three dime rocks four days ago.

Trez lounged so deeply into the cushions of the loveseat, he appeared to be in danger of breaking his neck. He used the cap of a discarded Bic pen to dig wax out of his ears. He looked down his

COLORED RAGS

nose and studied each clump he excavated with keen interest. Chris couldn't help but laugh at him.

Trez eyed him lazily. "Man, yo eyes red than a motherfucker," he noticed.

Chris squinted at his friend. "Nigga, you got a long ass nose," he said and chuckled.

Trez shook his head. "Aw, fuck you nigga. You high, cuz. I told you that shit was some–"

"No, I'm for real," Chris insisted. "That long nose and them beady eyes make you look like a rat."

"Chris–"

"And your teeth, they like–"

"Chris–"

"They like – what man?"

"Nigga, you *high*," Trez told him. "You high as hell, cuz."

"I'm not." Despite his denial, Chris took a moment to assess his faculties. "Well, I'm..." Slurred speech, eyes wanting to close though not really sleepy. "I guess I..." Looking around, the room swam in a slow-motion fashion that was not indicative of sobriety. "Yeah, I might be..."

"Fuck that *might be* shit. You is high, nigga."

"A'ight," Chris conceded and laughed.

"Shit's funny, ain't it?"

"Man, I don't know. It just seem like..." He giggled.

"Yeah. That's how it be when you first start smoking." Trez was an expert on the subject. "You be like, thinking everything funny and shit. And sometimes you be getting paranoid; thinking everybody trying to fuck with you. But then, after you been smoking that shit for so long, you just be like, *cool* with that shit. Shit still be funny, but not like when you first started."

"I guess so, 'cause right now you starting to look like a rat."

"Nigga, that's that corn talking. I don't look like no damned rat."

"Damn, Trez, you do kinda look like a rat," a female voice said.

Chris didn't know the girl was still there until she spoke. Her eyes were low and bloodshot, like theirs. She sported a smile for Chris that was almost *wicked*. He hadn't noticed before, but she had a lot of ass stuffed in her jeans. He suddenly found her very enticing.

"Ho, I don't look like no damned rat." Trez's smile was gone now. A homey clowning him was one thing, but he'd be damned if he'd take it from some skeezer.

"But you got those little whiskers," she said, happy that she'd gotten a rise out of him.

Chris cracked up. He couldn't help himself.

Trez looked at Chris with a flicker of resentment, and then he sneered at the bopper.

"Fuck you, bitch. You look like a damned *drive through*. You know how many niggas done ran through this bitch, Chris? It's like, all yo fingers and toes, and that's just last week! She don't even know they real names. *Boon. C-Loc. Tay. Mack.* What's Mack's real name, bitch?"

She twisted her lips but didn't respond.

"It's *Daryl*, ho! *Daryl Jeffries*. If you gon' fuck a nigga, at least ask him his name. We gon' start calling yo ass *Stop N Go*."

Chris laughed.

"Fuck you," the girl said. She tried not to let on how embarrassed she was, but Chris could tell her ego was wounded.

"Say, Chris, you hungry?" Trez sat up and stretched. "Let's go get something to eat. You want some chicken wings, or something?"

Chris rolled his eyes dreamily. "Nigga, I ain't going *nowhere*. I ain't hungry."

"Yeah you is, cuz. Get up, ol' lazy ass nigga." Trez stood and kicked his foot as he passed.

"Alright, but I ain't trivin' – I mean, *driving*. I ain't driving nowhere."

"Fool, you can't even talk right. I sure as hell ain't finna get in a car with yo crazy ass. You want something, Stop N Go?" Trez asked the girl on the way out.

"Nigga, fuck you."

● ● ● ● ● ●

Outside, the balmy sun felt good for the first few seconds, as it warmed their bodies. But by the time they made it around the side of the building, Chris felt beads of sweat forming on his forehead. Trez marched ahead of him and was already ducking under one of the holes in the fence as Chris hurried to catch up. It was 3 pm, and the temperature was at its peak. Chris felt like this was the absolute worst time to be walking anywhere. Trez noticed him lagging and stopped to wait for him.

"Nigga, what's wrong with you?"

"Man, it's hot out here. Why you wantsupposed to go now?" Chris stumbled over a protruding root and nearly fell.

"What nigga?"

Chris grimaced as he ducked through the hole in the fence. "How I'm supposed to enjoy this shit, if I'm trekking all over the damn city?"

"What, cuz?"

"I said, how you niggas be getting high and going all over the country and shit?"

"Chris," Trez put a hand on his shoulder and stared into his eyes. "You know you sound retarded right now, don't you?"

"I'm just saying, if you be getting high all the time, why you wanna be going all across the country if you already got you an established high spot?"

Trez grabbed him by both shoulders. "Cuz, I'm really gon' have to ask you to think about what you saying before it get out yo mouth."

"Cuz, I told you I was messed up."

"I know," Trez laughed, "but you done took it to another level. What the fuck you talking about *Star Trek* and shit for? You done got on some ol' *science fiction* shit!"

"Man, I didn't say nothing about *Star Trek*."

"Yeah you did. You said we was *Star Trekkin*!"

"No I didn't, fool. I said we was *trekking* to this dumbed, I mean damn store."

"That still sound like some *Star Trek* shit to me. That's the only time I done heard that word."

"To *trek* means to travel, Trez." Chris smacked his lips. He didn't remember wringing all the moisture from his tongue and then sucking on cotton balls, but apparently he had done so at some point.

"Like when you be taking hikes through the woods and shit," he continued. "And I'm just saying, we giving, I mean, we going a long way to this damn store." Chris tried to stay focused.

"I'm asking how the hell do y'all be getting high, then go on hikes and shit? That don't make sense to me. The air conditioner in the apartment works just fine..." He wiped his brow.

"The store is right there, Chris." Trez pointed to a building no more than fifty paces away. "You high for real, nigga. Try to cool that shit out before we get in there."

How does one cool out a high? Chris pondered this as they walked, but he didn't get it. He knew he failed to pull it off when they entered the store and Sam, the owner, eyed him with much amusement.

"Trez, this nigga's fucked up, man. What you do to him?"

Sam was of Arabic decent, but he grew up in the States and had absorbed a good deal of black culture since he opened the store. He talked and dressed like he was from the hood and even dated black women.

"Just a little smokey smoke," Trez called over his shoulder. He disappeared down one of the aisles, heading for *Sam's Famous Diner*.

On the south side, nearly all of the corner stores were capitalizing on the Negro's love for salty, greasy foods and their willingness to purchase these rations from anyone. Only in the hood can you get gas for your car, malt liquor, jewelry, CD's, DVD's, Robitussin, diapers and a pork chop sandwich all in the same place. At Sam's you could also get Salisbury steaks, sausage on a stick, collard greens and even pig's feet.

"You been smoking that kill?" Sam asked.

Chris stared at him and shrugged.

Sam wore a Polo golf shirt with baggy jeans. His platinum necklace drew attention, but not as much as his Movado watch. Sam's bling might have made him a target in this neighborhood, but his demeanor warranted respect. Everyone knew he was down for the hood. He let vagrants clean up his restrooms for beer money, and dope boys could duck inside the store if the police were on to them.

"You know, I just got out of jail two days ago," Sam hollered at Trez.

Trez ambled over to the counter and leaned on it with both elbows. "Yeah, I heard you shot somebody, Sam. What the fuck?"

"You remember that motherfucker I told you was stealing 40's?"

COLORED RAGS

"Yeah."

"The motherfucker keeps coming in here. I see him. I'm watching him. *Every day* he comes in here and don't buy shit." Sam looked from Chris to Trez.

"So the other day I'm waiting on this motherfucker," Sam told them. "And he comes in and does the same shit. I'm busy with customers, so I don't watch him the whole time. But when he gets ready to leave, he *don't buy shit*! I'm pissed off 'cause I missed him, but later that day, he comes in *again*. This time, I watch him go to the beer. I open the register and start counting money, like I don't see him, but out of the corner of my eye I'm watching his ass the whole time. He takes out a forty, looks around, and then put that shit under his shirt." Sam looked from Trez to Chris again.

"A forty, you know, ain't shit," Sam said. "Just a dollar-fifty, right? But I don't really make nothing in this motherfucker. I buy that forty from the vendor for a dollar and get fifty cents profit. That's it. He steal one, that's a dollar-fifty gone, so I don't get no profit off the next three I sell. I got bills man. My electric bill last month was twenty-three hundred dollars!"

"*Damn!*" Trez said. "Just from the lights?"

"Well, I got all the signs and shit. Plus I leave the coolers and the lights on overnight. Then I got the kitchen – but that ain't the real problem. The problem is this motherfucker's stealing from me every day. Two, three, four times a day. So, I'm watching this asshole."

Chris wanted Sam to stop looking at him.

"I wait for him to come to the counter. He walks up. I give him a chance to pull that shit out and pay for it, but he don't. He just keeps walking. So when he gets to the door, I pulls out my shit. You know I keep this motherfucker right under the counter." Sam produced his hand-cannon and showed it to them.

"Shit!" Trez shrieked and backed away from the counter.

"I don't even say shit to him, just **BAM!**" Sam pointed the gun as if shooting.

This totally unnerved Chris, who happened to be standing in the imaginary line of fire. He ducked, drawing a chuckle from the storekeeper. Sam put the gun away.

"I ain't gon' shoot you, motherfucker. Anyway, the first bullet went in the wall over there by the door. I shot again and hit him in the shoulder. He fell into the door and pushed it open. I ran around the counter and caught up with him in the parking lot, and I beat the hell out of him!"

"You whooped him?" Trez asked; eyes wide. He loved violent endings.

"Hell yeah!" Sam's eyes were big and frenzied too. "Then I looked up and saw this *other* fool in the car waiting on this idiot. So I'm thinking, *You been driving this motherfucker to my store to steal? And you drinking my beer too?* So I got off the one I shot and ran over to the other one. I reached in his car and tried to drag the motherfucker out, but he holding onto the wheel too hard. So I started beating his ass too."

Chris' mouth hung open. This shit was impossible to believe.

"Man, I fucked up my knuckles in that nigga's mouth!" Sam held up his fist and showed off the fresh bruises. "By then, the first motherfucker done managed to get in the passenger side, so the driver starts backing up with me still hanging on his car. I said fuck it, and let them go. They take off down the road. You wanna know the *fucked up* part about it?" Sam asked Chris directly.

Chris shrugged, and Trez said, "What?"

"Them niggas get to the hospital and call the police on *me*! They wanna press charges on me! Can you believe that shit?"

It made perfect sense to Chris, but he didn't say so.

"The police come over here and arrest me," Sam complained. "I had to close the store and everything. They were talking about charging me with attempted murder. You know the only thing that saved me?"

Chris had no idea.

"You paid 'em off?" Trez was the king of ignorant responses.

"The one I shot was still inside the store," Sam explained. "If he was outside, I'd be fucked. Ain't that some bullshit?" The Arab was seriously annoyed that he couldn't defend his fifty cents profit with deadly force. "In *my* country, you steal from somebody, they chop off your hand. You rape somebody, they cut your dick off. They don't play that shit where I come from."

Chris laughed. Sam's accent only came out when discussing his roots.

COLORED RAGS

"They still charged me with assault on the guy outside, but my lawyer said I can get probation for that. Ain't that fucked up?"

Chris didn't know what to think. He was plenty uncomfortable, though. Trez was laughing like the Joker.

"Anyway, what y'all getting?" Sam asked.

The hell up out of here, Chris thought.

Trez paid for 24 spicy hot wings.

● ● ● ● ● ●

Back at the apartment, Chris didn't think he had much of an appetite, but boy was he wrong. Trez told him he had the munchies. Chris knew what the munchies were and didn't think that was it, but damn if those weren't the best hot wings ever. He ate twelve of them and then sat next to Trez on the couch and laughed his ass off as his friend regaled him with another tale from the hood. Chris knew a good deal of Trez's anecdotes contained more fabrication than fact, but that was okay. With an attentive audience, Trez could spin one hell of a yarn.

A couple of hours later, Trez stopped in mid-sentence to confront Chris.

"You sleep nigga?"

Chris mumbled that he wasn't, then politely succumbed to slumber.

KEITH THOMAS WALKER

CHAPTER THREE
OG KODY

Hot lead flies up and down my street
It wakes me from a peaceful sleep
Wailing sirens and flashing lights
Decorate the dopeman's night
A copter hovers overhead
Big floodlights shining on the dead
Yellow tape on dying trees
Chalk lines where he used to be
Gotta stay strapped on these streets
Or next time the grief might be for me

Chris awoke to the clamoring of seasoned thugs who usually achieved their greatest level of degradation after nightfall. No one was in the same position they were in when he fell asleep. Disoriented, he rubbed his eyes as he looked around the room.

The loveseat Trez sat in was now occupied by the thick girl who'd been smiling at him earlier. *Stop N Go*, Chris thought and grinned. Deuce was at the dining table bagging up more marijuana than Chris had ever seen. He scooped fistfuls from a garbage bag that was almost half full.

There were new arrivals too. Spooko, wheelchair bound from a baseball bat (rather than bullet) to the spine, was there, and so was Moon. Moon was older, at least forty, and recently back on the streets after a routine traffic stop went horribly wrong a couple decades ago. When the dust cleared, a deputy could no longer walk without a limp, and Moon lost the use of his right eye.

There were plenty of lively characters, but only one of them garnished the attention of the whole posse. People levitated to this guy. They surrounded him and exchanged greetings. They

COLORED RAGS

exchanged money with him and sought his approval. As he pounded fists with the crew, Chris saw the scar in the center of his left hand from where a bullet had gone completely through.

The man wore black and blue. His hair was recently braided into seven tight cornrows. They hung down his neck like mambas. He wore a neatly-trimmed goatee. The white of his eyes had a permanent crimson tint.

The man was short and stocky. He had the body of someone who'd been to the pen, where weightlifting and gorging oneself was the only activity to look forward to on most days. His skin tone was dark mahogany. On the streets, this man was known as OG Kody. He was the battle-proven, well-respected co-founder of the AGG Land Crips.

Kody scanned the room purposefully. His expression was bright and pleasant, for the most part, but when his eyes fell upon Chris, they grew cold for a moment. It was a quick look no one else noticed, but it kept happening. Each time his eyes returned to Chris, the flicker of anger was undeniable.

Kody wore a black tee shirt with blue Dickey pants. His blue Chuck Taylor's had thick, black shoe strings. On his right forearm, a bold tattoo announcing AGG LAND barely stood out against his skin tone. On the other arm were the initials *SCC; Southside Crip Cartel*. Chris knew Kody had more tattoos concealed under his shirt: On his left shoulder were four tombstones bearing the names of fallen soldiers. On his stomach, *NOTHING TO LOSE* circled two bullet wounds.

Chris loved to watch Kody interact with the people in the apartment. His exploits in the hood made him an icon, yet there he was. Tupac in the flesh. You could see him, talk to him, and even touch him. There were places in the city where saying OG Kody brought you into the gang would guarantee you respect. There were places where the same statement would guarantee you an ass-whooping. Chris knew Kody better than anyone in the apartment, but he still found himself caught up in the grandeur.

Kody finally broke away from his comrades and glared at Chris. "Come here, nigga," he yelled across the room. He turned and walked out of the apartment without looking back, because, when you're OG Kody, you know people are going to do what you say.

Chris got up and yawned. He stretched lazily, trying to give the impression that if he was leaving, it was because he wanted to do so. But a couple of thugs were already grinning at him. They knew better.

Outside darkness had set in. Time-activated bulbs glowed and hummed around the apartments. Moths and mayflies bounced off the dingy lamps. From the breezeway, Chris looked down on Riverside Dr. and he thought he could see for miles. It was like their ghetto version of the Las Vegas Strip. The breezeway was unusually deserted, except for Kody. He stared at Chris for a few long seconds before pouncing.

"Nigga, what you doing over here?"

"I came to see you." Chris looked away and couldn't stop a smile from creeping to his lips.

"You didn't come to see me. You would've left when you seen my car wasn't here. You came to see *Trez*, nigga."

"I didn't even know Trez was in there till I got here."

"Yeah, but you knew somebody was gon' be here to get you high."

Chris' eyes widened. Kody was like one of those nosey, helicopter parents. He liked catching his little brother off guard.

"Oh, you didn't think I knew about you smoking weed? What's wrong with you, Chris? Why you wanna fuck with that shit?"

"I was just–"

"Just what? Man, that shit ain't even you, cuz. You a nerd, Chris. You get all the way through high school without smoking, making straight A's and shit, and now you wanna experiment?"

"Weed ain't that bad. Everybody smoke weed."

"It's niggas in there snorting raw and boy too, cuz. You wanna fuck with that shit next? Plus, I keep telling you, 'This ain't no motherfucking hangout.'" Kody was serious now; stern eyes with lips curled. "It's all kinds of shit in there. It's *dope*, Chris. *Guns*. Everybody in there taking penitentiary chances, and they know it. What makes you think this is some place to go to chill?"

"I wanted to see you," Chris said, and there was some truth in that.

Kody softened a bit. "Yeah, but what if the laws run up in there while you sleep on the couch? What you gon' do then? You

COLORED RAGS

ain't going to college, if this motherfucker gets raided while you up in there. You know that, don't you?"

"I don't have no drugs on me."

Kody shook his head. "You think them white folks give a fuck if you got dope on you or not? Hell naw, cuz! They want *all* us motherfuckers doing life. When they come up in this bitch, they ain't gon' be like, '*Well, he had this much crack, and this one had this money, and he had that gun, but this one didn't have anything, so he can go.*' You think its gon' go down like that?"

Chris didn't say anything, because, in truth, that was exactly how he thought it would go down.

"When they ran up in that house on Jessamine, they found two ounces of crack," Kody informed him. "Wasn't nobody around that shit. That dope was in a bedroom by itself, and everybody else was in the living room. Everybody said it wasn't theirs. You think they let them go?"

Obviously not, Chris thought.

"Hell naw! They divided that shit up four ways, and all of them got charged with half an ounce. All of 'em caught a case, and one of 'em really didn't know that crack was in the house. He still caught a case. You don't think that shit can happen to you?"

Chris believed any half-decent attorney could parade his high school transcript before a judge and get charges like that thrown out, but he didn't say anything. It was trivial, and besides, Kody was right.

A breeze rustled the leaves of a nearby tree. The dry branches clicked together. They sounded like bones. The scent of something dead drifted up from the fence line.

"I don't hardly ever get to see you no more," Chris said. He was glad they were alone, because comments like that could set you up for a season of ridicule, even if you were talking to your brother. "You never come by the house anymore. Them niggas be around you all the time. You even spend the night over here."

Chris lowered his eyes for effect, and it almost worked. But Kody followed his gaze.

"What the fuck you doing with that shit in yo shoes?"

"They just shoe strings."

Kody was flabbergasted. "Chris, what the fuck is wrong with you? You wanna get shot? You can be–" He paused, then snarled. "You better take them shoe strings off! Soon as you get home, boy. Don't *never* wear them shoe strings again. You a school-boy, Chris. You ain't even gon' know what to do when some niggas roll up and wanna know what set you claiming. We got *enemies*, cuz. Niggas wanna kill us. I don't know what part of that you don't understand, or what you think is cool about it, but you..." He shook his head. "Go home, man. Just, go home."

    Chris sighed. Kody was right, as always. He never passed on an opportunity to push Chris away from his lifestyle. Chris knew that what his brother was doing was a good thing, but he would never stop wanting to be around Kody. As much as the thugs in apartment 4F loved their leader, they would never adore him more than his little brother did. Chris turned and headed downstairs to his Plymouth.

    "Say," Kody called after him.

    Chris glared over his shoulder.

    "You need to chill with that weed for real."

    "It's just weed," he replied without stopping.

    "Alright then. On the way out, ask one of them crackheads what drug he started off on. For real. Ask 'em."

● ● ● ● ● ●

    Chris didn't encounter any crackheads on the way out. But he did pass OG Will as he exited the complex. Will drove a black Cutlass with dark windows and shiny, black rims. Most debates about who the tougher leader of the AGG Land Crips was ended undecided, but Chris always gave the edge to Will. Both leaders were tough, resilient, and pretty damned ruthless, but Kody had a heart, and it was common knowledge that Will didn't.

    Because of the Cutlass' tint, Chris could barely make out the occupants, but he thought he saw Dre's afro in the passenger seat. If ever an apple fell far from the tree, it had in the case of OG Will and his little brother Andre. Will stood 6'2, while Dre mustered a mere five-foot-seven. Will was fresh out of the pen and cut-up like Evander Holyfield in his prime. Dre was chubby with plump cheeks, wide hips and a round belly.

    Their personalities were flagrantly different, too. Will was at the top of his street game, revered by friends and enemies alike. Dre was the quiet type – the perpetual benchwarmer; last to be picked for basketball or drivebys.

COLORED RAGS

A few months ago, without the use of any psychology handbooks, Will decided he could fix his little brother. The course was called *Get That Bitch up Outta You*. OG Will was the only teacher. He began to take Dre with him everywhere he went. Dre didn't like apartment 4F, but he had to spend time there. And Dre didn't want to do drivebys, but Will made him ride shotgun, literally. Any deviation from Will's perception of *macho* resulted in discipline.

Will tongue-lashed his brother in public for small infractions. He slapped the back of Dre's head more times than Chris could count. Chris saw Will fight his brother a couple of times, delivering blows to the arms and chest rather than the head. And he was there when Will pushed Dre down the second half of a stairway.

Last Chris heard, Dre was struggling mightily with the course. That was probably because he was never given an option or a manual.

Anyone paying attention knew Will was getting nowhere, but no one counseled their OG. Ninety days into the experiment, Dre was still timid. Some would say he was even worse than before. But Will pressed on with dogged determination, constantly pushing and applying pressure. At this point, everyone was waiting for one of them to snap.

Chris made a left onto Riverside Drive and headed home.

CHAPTER FOUR
MIKE & SPIDER

I cussed and punked my teacher
Check it, I'm too cool
Principal straight up told me, "Get out my school!"
So it's they fault if I don't graduate
I guessed they expected me to beg to stay
And it's also they fault I can't read
School damn sure wasn't the place for me

No more school, so I roll with a gang
I'm called Lil' Spider where I hang
Somebody stole all my OG's weed
Since I'm little, them fools blamed me
Now I can't kick it on my own street
I'm still looking for a place for me

    Dre wondered how everyone in the world could love his brother so much, while he, flesh of Will's flesh and blood of his blood, absolutely hated him. Actually, *hate* was probably not the right word. Deep inside, Dre knew he harbored *some* feelings for his brother that were not totally negative. He didn't wish Will was dead, for instance. Whatever it was, Dre was certain he did not love his big brother. There was no doubt about that.

    And it wasn't so much the *Get That Bitch up Outta You* course he'd been forced to enroll in. The course sucked, but that wasn't it. It wasn't the constant pestering to W*ear this*, or *Lose some damned weight*, or *Walk like a man*, and *Don't be saying no ho shit like that*. It wasn't the way Will would ridicule him in public about his many personal flaws.

COLORED RAGS

The reason Dre had feelings about his brother that *might be* hate was because everyone knew Will wasn't doing any of this nonsense to help Dre. Will was doing it all for Will.
And that sucked.

• • • • • •

Will turned into the Rainbow's parking lot and pulled in front of the entrance. The place was nearly deserted on Thursday night. On the weekends, the store became a happening spot for players, hoes, and thugs with blue flags. They flooded the lot and cranked their systems up. The air would be thick with weed smoke. Dre used to think it was odd that people hung out at a corner store, but he was beginning to understand gang members did a lot of things that didn't really make sense.
But on this night, all was quiet. The only other vehicle in the parking lot was an old El Camino occupied by a Mexican gentleman who sat behind the wheel in a daze; either too drunk or confused to remember what his next action should be. He stared at the steering wheel for thirty seconds before shifting the vehicle into reverse and backing out of his spot.
Not that Will minded if he had an audience. He calmly cracked open his boy pill without spilling any of its contents. He looked around for a moment, and then handed one of the pill halves to Dre.
"Hold this."
Dre took it carefully. He had once expressed revulsion for the damned thing and let it fall from his clumsy fingers. When he looked up and saw the expression of rage filling his brother's eyes, Dre barely had time to brace himself for the blows that ensued. He never dropped one of Will's pills again.
Will made a fist with his free hand and deposited a small pile of dust on his thumbnail. He lowered his head over the powder and snorted quickly. He looked up at Dre and snorted again.
"You want something outta here?" he asked, his voice as normal as ever.
Dre shook his head.
Will handed him the other pill half and rubbed his nose. His eyes were a bit low, but not what Dre would expect. In the

movies, heroin users closed their eyes and drifted to unknown places. Will nodded sometimes, but he never seemed too far gone.

With dope in both hands, Dre was at the hard part. Combined, the pill halves contained 2/3 the original amount. It was his job to unite the two and make one pill again. Will would want to snort the rest later. Dre's fingers were already starting to sweat, but luckily his big brother didn't stick around to watch.

Will got out of the car moving slowly, Dre noticed. One leg. Then the other. An arm on the door. Then he stood. Before closing the door behind him, he looked back at his brother.

"Say, you can get a taste if you want, nigga." He smiled wanly.

As if, Dre thought, thankful that he didn't utter the phrase out loud. Not only would refusing the drugs make him a *pussy ass nigga*, but *As if* sounded white. Will's rebuke would have been especially stinging.

The older brother closed the car door, and Dre reunited the pill halves quickly, spilling only a small amount. He brushed the evidence from his pants and watched his brother enter the store.

● ● ● ● ● ●

The owner of the Rainbow was a middle-aged man named Oscar. Dre didn't think that was his real name, but he responded to it eagerly enough. Whenever he wasn't manning the register, either his wife or his only child had to take shifts. To Oscar's chagrin, 23 year old Lisa had become a much-admired Asian beauty. She was thin with long, dark hair that inched midway down her back. For a Vietnamese girl, Lisa had a nice backside. Her breasts were mentionable as well.

She smiled and tolerated a ton of flirting, but everyone knew she wouldn't have anything to do with the customers outside of financial transactions. OG Will knew this too, but he never passed on an opportunity to pull off what no other thug in the hood could. If he could get Lisa in bed, he'd be considered the player of the year. He leaned on the counter and grinned at her. Dre watched the *mack attack* for a minute before losing interest.

Dre lifted the armrest that divided the front seats and gazed at Will's .45 magnum. It was the biggest handgun he had ever seen. Bright chrome, the pistol had a long, almost comically

COLORED RAGS

exaggerated barrel that reminded Dre of the piece Dirty Harry had shoved in that guy's face.

Do you feel lucky? Well, do you, punk?

Dre once hefted the gun and whispered that phrase as he stared at himself in the mirror. Dre sneaked a peek at the gun often and liked how heavy it was. He never told Will about his fascination, although he knew the OG would have no problem with it.

Will would be tickled pink.

● ● ● ● ● ●

Michael Hammonds hit a dip at the intersection of Hemphill and Berry with a vengeance. The dip was notoriously brutal. Commuters on either side of him slowed to as little as ten miles per hour to ease through the fault. Mike plowed through the center of them doing a hardy forty-five. The front end of the Impala crashed into the recess producing a hearty *CRUNCH!* before the following incline launched the vehicle into the night. They slammed back to earth with a solid, but less damaging *WHOMP!*

Mike knew he would be admonished if he was chauffeuring his OG or one of the elders from his set. There were plenty of reasons to drive safely. The Impala was, first of all, hotter than a Mexican lunch plate. Neither driver nor passenger had a license. There were open containers of alcohol in easy reach, and both occupants were a little twisted from a concoction of Thunderbird mixed with unsweetened Kool-Aid. Even worse, there was a stolen .25 automatic under the passenger's seat. And of course there were drugs. Always drugs.

One of the gang's elders would've told Mike to pull that shit over *right fucking now*, and get from behind the wheel – and never get behind the wheel again while *he* was in the car.

Mike considered this as he checked his rearview mirror. No grinning police officer swooped behind them with the cherries blaring. Mike disciplined himself anyway and applied the brakes a little. His passenger laughed so hard, Mike could see his cavities. Spider thought they were playing *Dukes of Hazard*.

The juvenile bounced in his seat like a happy cricket. "Damn, nigga! You hit the hell outta that shit! This motherfucker was *flying*, dog!" Spider's squeals were deranged. His glossy eyes danced as he rocked a small fist in the air. "That was the *shit*, nigga! *That was the shit!*"

"Yeah," Mike concurred, "that was *wild*." But he kept his eyes on the road. At thirteen, Spider sometimes didn't understand the full impact of their actions. Mike was sixteen, so he had to be the responsible one, or as responsible as their lifestyle required them to be.

But going to jail wasn't necessarily a bad thing. Mike and Spider were young and dumb – ranked as BG's in the Tate Street set. They were *baby gangstas*; up and coming. They sold dope, ran errands and carried weapons for the homies. They spray-painted a lot of walls and made a lot of noise. They were a necessity because they got less time for serious offenses. They were too naïve to understand that BG's were often disrespected and misused by seasoned criminals.

The next step up the gang ladder was the G's, or *gangstas*. These men were older, a little wiser, and known to have put in work for the set. They might have a couple of bodies under their belt. G's only took orders from the set's OG; the *original gangsta*.

Reaching OG status was every BG's dream, but Mike and Spider had more realistic ambitions. They wanted to be G's. The stolen Impala was one rung on their ladder to success.

The Tate Street Bloods was a humble set. They only had twelve members who were not incarcerated; making them the smallest gang in Overbrook Meadows. Their leader, OG Shaun, kept a tight leash on his ragtag band of hoodlums. Under his guidance, they maintained a steady flow of income from two dope houses. One sold crack. The other offered boy and girl to fellow gangstas in the city.

● ● ● ● ● ●

Mike slowed to a stop at a red light and eyed his crazy friend. Spider was small and caramel-colored. He was trying to grow an afro but so far had only managed an impressive collection of naps. A recent growth spurt added noticeable inches to his arms, legs and neck, but it was all length. Spider was a skinny kid, gangly even. He could never be counted on if they were fighting grown men, but his reputation for carrying weapons usually helped him avoid fisticuffs.

"Man, you know we ain't gon' get shit for this motherfucker," Mike told him.

"Naw. It's still good." Spider giggled. "Coon say he was looking for an Impala like this. This a *bad* ride! Hit that bump and took off!"

"*Man*," Mike was not impressed. "But look at this shit. Seats fucked up. Cracks and shit in the dash. Radio don't work. Ain't even got no rims on it."

"He just want it for the engine and some more parts," Spider told him. "He ain't never said he want a *pretty* car."

Spider sounded sure of himself, and Mike had no choice but to trust him. The hustle was Spider's idea. Mike only went along because the five-hundred dollar payday was more than he made pedaling dope all week for Shaun. A brother had to get his come-ups somewhere.

"Well, *somebody* better get this motherfucker, or I'm kicking yo ass, dog." Mike waited for Spider's asinine response, but none came. "You hear me, nigga?"

The light turned green, and Mike proceeded east on Berry, towards the relative safety of Stop Six. The Stop Six neighborhood was home to most of the Bloods in the city, Tate Street included.

Mike looked to see why Spider wasn't responding. His friend's attention was fixed on a convenience store across the street. As they passed it, Spider did a full 180 in his seat to keep his eyes on it.

Mike looked back but didn't see anything. "What, nigga?"

"You see that?" Spider's wide eyes snapped back in his direction.

"What?" Mike tried to sound calm as goose bumps birthed on his arms.

"Mike, *go back*!" Spider turned in his seat again.

"*What*?" Mike felt his heart thumping as he applied the brakes. *Why the fuck am I slowing down?* But he couldn't help it.

"It's *Will*! That OG nigga!" Spider screamed in Mike's face and pointed back towards the store. "That crab nigga! You know, them *fagg land* niggas! He right – they OG! *Them*!" He shook his head in exasperation. "They *OG*, dog! He right there! I saw him. Go back! *He right there!*"

"Nigga, what the hell you talking about?" Mike had no intention of going back, but he made the first right turn anyway. The street lights on this road were pretty much nonexistent. Spider looked ghoulish in the dark, like one of Satan's minions.

"He right back there! You didn't see him?" Spider's voice squeaked. He kept looking back, as if the crip had followed them.

"Naw, I didn't see him." Mike executed a three-point turn until they faced Berry again.

"He right back there, Mike."

"So what, Blood?" What the fuck?"

Spider looked him squarely in his eyes. "We gon' get him."

Mike's heart was pounding now. He sneered at the child. "Fool, you bumped yo head. What the fuck you talking about?" The Thunderbird was fucking with Mike too, but not like that. He had to piss more than anything.

Spider reached under his seat and fumbled around before he came up with the .25. The pistol was petite and black. It was small enough to conceal in his front or back pocket. Every thug in the world knew a .25 caliber weapon was not preferred for what Spider was suggesting. A .25 would do in a crowd, where people would hear it and not see it. Empty the clip at a club, and you'd cause a stampede for sure. But for OG Will?

The sight of the puny piece made Mike turn right on Berry. Fuck what Spider was talking about. They were going home.

To his surprise, Spider reached and grabbed the wheel. He jerked it to the left, and the headlights swam in that direction.

Towards destiny.

"Nigga, what the fuck you doing?!" Mike knocked Spider's arm away, but their course was set.

Spider stared at his mentor with confusion distorting his features. "What? You *scared*?"

"Naw, I ain't scared. But you don't know what you talking about. You know who that nigga is?" The bright lights of Rainbow Gas & Grocery came into view.

"Yeah, I know who that nigga is. Everybody know who he is." Spider scanned the parking lot. "See!" He pointed with a stiff finger that didn't shake. "See! There his car go right there. I saw him when he was going in the store. He still in there, Mike."

And Mike did see.

COLORED RAGS

The black Cutlass Supreme parked near the entrance sported black rims. Black tint furthered the impression that this was not a car, but a shadow floating down the road. A black plague. To his own dismay, Mike made a left into the parking lot.

"You seen him?" he asked.

"Yeah, I seen him!" Spider focused on the store. "He got out the car and went in. He still in there. He – *there* he go." Spider's voice dropped to a whisper.

Mike parked four spaces down from the Supreme, though no other cars were in the parking lot. His heart pounded against his sternum. Through the windows of the store, Mike saw him too. OG Will, the most notorious gangsta in the city and the leader of the fagg land crabs, leaned on the counter next to the cash register, making small talk with a woman who appeared more frightened than flattered.

Mike kept the car idling because there was no key to turn it off. The steering column was a battered, mangled thing with its innards exposed. He held onto the steering wheel for dear life and looked at Spider. Spider finally looked away from Will and met his gaze. Mike's mouth was very dry.

"So, what we gon' do?"

"You gon' *shoot* 'em," Spider said and licked his lips.

"M-me?" Mike expected more participation from his feral friend. "Ain't we both gon' do it?"

"We only got one gun."

"But, you can still go in there with me."

"I'ma be in the car, so we can take off fast. I'ma be the *driver*." Spider was whispering. Mike was too.

"Nigga, you can't drive!"

"I *can* drive!" Spider watched Will again. The infamous thug walked away from the cashier and headed towards the beer section.

"What if he got a gun?" Mike felt no shame in seeking counsel, felt no shame in allowing a nappy-headed thirteen-year-old to convince him. This would be the biggest atrocity the south side crabs had ever experienced.

"That's why you gotta get him while he still in the store." Spider was suddenly an expert on these matters. "If you let him get to his car, *we fucked*." He held the diminutive firearm out to his friend. Mike stared at it for an enormous amount of time. "If you let him come out, when he see us, he gon' kill us," Spider pleaded.

Mike liked that. Spider made it a matter of *him or us*. That was cool, but Mike knew it wasn't really like that. He could easily put the car in reverse and drive away without OG Will ever knowing these two misfits were plotting his demise. They could drive back to Shaun's boy/girl house and repress the memory in a thick cloud of marijuana smoke.

But what would the others think? What would they do if they had the chance to kill the most famous crab in Overbrook Meadows? What if they found out Mike had an opportunity but didn't seize it?

"Here, Mike," Spider whispered. "You *got* to."

Mike agreed. He *had* to. He accepted the piece from Spider and took a deep breath as he stepped from the security of the bucket.

"Get him," Spider whispered as Mike closed the door behind himself.

CHAPTER FIVE
BLOODY MURDER

You wanna see my ghetto groove?
Well, first take off yo red and blue
Now come on, jump inside my ride
First we rolling to the south side
You see that nigga wearing blue?
He 'bout to blast on them red fools
You see the way he pulls his gun?
You see the way them bullets jump?
They jerking now, blood in they shoes
Them boys got the ghetto groove!

    The night air was cold.
    That was odd, because it was 90 degrees a few minutes ago.
    Mike took several unsteady steps away from his banged-up Impala and ignored a maddening urge to hop back into its safe confines. He walked past Will's car on rubbery legs and eyed the cashier through the window. She was pretty, about 25 years old.
    There were a lot of stickers on the glass door. Mike saw that she was looking past the cigarette and alcohol advertisements. She was looking at him, and there was suspicion in her eyes. Mike looked down and realized he was holding the .25 in plain view. He quickly tucked it under his shirt.
    Damn. You fucking up, nigga. Quit being stupid. Get in the car. That was good thinking, but Mike didn't listen to that voice. Spider was his best friend, but he had a big mouth. If he went back and told everyone that Mike got this close and chickened out, he might be labeled a coward. No gangsta wanted that.

An engine roared briefly, but loudly. Mike turned quickly, half expecting to see his ride fleeing the scene. Spider lost his nerve and left him to fend for himself. But the Impala wasn't moving. Spider had accidentally stomped the gas pedal as he crawled over to the driver's seat. Spider saw that Mike had stopped. He held up a small hand as if to say, *Sorry, dog. My bad. Go 'head and kill that nigga.*

Mike shook his head and took a couple of deep breaths. He turned back to the store, opened the door and stepped inside.

There was something wrong. He looked around frantically and figured it out. The pretty cashier was not behind the register anymore.

She's calling the police.

This thought was as clear to him as any revelation he would ever receive. His mouth dropped open, and Mike stood there wasting precious moments; moments in which he should flee the scene.

She saw you with the gun, stupid. She went to call the police. She went to get her own gun, which is much bigger than that damn .25. Get the hell outta there!

This time, Mike *did* listen. He executed an about-face and pushed the door with his free hand. Fuck Spider. Fuck OG status. Fuck all of that. That bitch was up to no good, wherever she had gone, and that was important. Nothing was more important than that. Fuck OG Will too. Someone else could kill the bastard.

Mike froze. Out of the corner of his eye, he saw the worst thing he'd ever seen in his sixteen years on earth. OG Will stood less than 15 feet away with a Colt 45 in one hand and a 40 ounce of Bud Ice in the other. Both looked pretty damned refreshing. Mike noticed perspiration sliding down the side of one of the bottles.

"What the fuck you doing in here, *slob*?" Will's voice boomed like a cannon.

Mike pissed his pants.

Calling a Blood a *slob* is akin to asking if he wants to fight. But Mike was by no means inclined to reprimand Will for the slight. He stumbled over a few incoherent words meant as apologies for infringing on the crip's turf.

How he know I'm a Blood? Does he know me? Mike wondered. But he remembered that he was flamed up, as usual. He wore khaki Dickies with red and white Jordan's and a red tee shirt that was currently bulging as it concealed his fist. Mike's fist, in turn, concealed an itty-bitty .25 automatic.

He had forgotten about the gun. Just as he remembered, Will noticed the lump in his stomach. Will noticed that Mike's right arm disappeared under his shirt at the exact spot of the bulge. He cocked his head to the side as dogs do when you ask them to perform a task they're not familiar with. A second later confusion was replaced with understanding, and Will bared his teeth.

"What the fuck you got up under yo shirt, nigga?"

Mike was fundamentally aware that what he had under his shirt would not be enough for this imposing figure. Will stood unarmed and caught with his guard down, but he was still the more menacing of the two.

Mike couldn't respond. He wanted to whip his piece out and tell Will he was a *dead ass crab*, and he'd better show some fucking respect to the Grim Reaper. He wanted to ask him *Who the fuck you calling a slob? My niggas killed all yo dead homies, and you about to be with 'em! What you think about that shit?*

Mike wanted to say a lot of things, but he could barely breathe, let alone talk. Instead he just stood there, feeling his warm urine soak into his pants.

"You coming to rob this motherfucker or what?!" The possibility that this pipsqueak had come there to harm him had the OG incensed. "You better take yo ass back to Stop Six with that shit!" Will took a step forward and broke the spell that held his nemesis paralyzed.

Mike tried to jerk the gun from under his shirt, but it got snagged on his tee. As he struggled to free it, Will took two more steps – two *quick* ones – in his direction. The OG raised his arm. Mike looked up frantically and saw that the Bud Ice was in throwing position.

"Bitch ass nigga," Will spat.

Mike winced from the blow he expected to receive just as the pistol came free. It looked small in the car. Now it looked like Mike pulled a magic marker from his belt. He pointed it at Will, and damn if the little motherfucker wasn't bouncing all over the place. Mike couldn't steady it. His whole arm shook, all the way up to his shoulder.

Will looked down at the firearm. His face strained with a glimpse of fear, but only for a moment. He snarled and looked down on Mike with anxious eyes that belied his courage.

"What the fuck you gon' do with that cap gun? Don't you know who I am, nigga? *I'M OG MOTHERFUCKING WILL! SOUTH SIDE CRIP CARTEL! AGG LAND, CUZ! YOU CAN'T KILL ME WITH NO–*"

Mike raked his left hand across the top of the gun and managed to cock it with the awkward motion. He began to pull the trigger, though his hand was still not steady.

POP!POP!POP!

The shots were loud, but to Mike, they sounded like mere firecrackers going off in the store. They weren't going to do it. He knew they wouldn't be enough. Maybe it was only a cap gun. His whole body trembled as the kick from the pistol radiated through him.

A wet spot emerged on the stomach area of Will's tee shirt, and he dropped his Bud Ice. His face did not register pain or shock. It registered hate. His eyebrows furrowed, nostrils flared.

"*You motherfucker!*" He lunged at him. He came with one arm outstretched, his hand twisted like a claw meant to wring the life from a skinny punk.

Mike raised the barrel and tried his best to aim this time.

POP!POP!

The gun suddenly went silent; not even producing clicks.

Damn, Spider, why you didn't fully load this thing?? Mike grimaced, on the verge of tears. *Only five shots from a .25 for a nigga like this?*

But the damage was done. Will dropped his other beer and groped at the new hole in his throat.

He tried to say something, but the air wasn't making it to his mouth. Most of it squirted through his fingers along with the bright red blood of an arterial bleed. Will sounded like he was drowning.

Mike took a half-second more to marvel at his accomplishment, and then he turned tail and ran. OG Will, one of the leaders of the AGG Land Crips, a menace to society since his first arrest at the age of eleven, dropped to his knees amidst broken glass, beer, and his own warm blood.

Mike never saw him fall. He slammed through the doors of the convenience store like a full back and rushed to the Impala. It was still there, but it appeared to be floating. The whole parking lot was askew.

"Come on, nigga! *Come on!*"

Spider screamed at the top of his lungs, but Mike couldn't hear anything over the blood rushing past his ears. It was hot now. Even as the night air contacted his pants, which were matted to his thighs by his own urine, it was hot as hell.

Mike dove, headfirst into the open passenger window. Spider slammed his foot on the gas immediately, and Mike's body lurched backwards rather than forward. He knew this was wrong, and as he tried to make sense of it, the Impala bounced hard and jumped a parking block. They were going forward. Spider had to stomp on the brakes with both feet to avoid plowing through the front windows of the store.

Mike was right; his homey couldn't drive for shit.

Spider was panicked, but he managed to get the stolen bucket into reverse. Again he stomped down on the gas. The Impala hopped the curb and shot backwards at an outrageous speed. The tires squealed when he applied the brakes, and Mike felt the car spinning. Spider righted the vehicle when they faced Berry again.

Smoke and the stench of burning rubber filled Mike's nostrils. He wanted to tell Spider to *Slow the fuck down!* before they had a wreck, because Mike had his eyes closed, and in that darkness he had a vision. OG Will was still alive, and he'd managed to make it to his car. Will was bleeding from the neck and gut, but he found the strength to retrieve a .45 magnum from his ride. Mike and Spider were unarmed. If they wrecked, Will would walk up and deposit fiery lead into their skulls.

But Mike couldn't speak. He grunted as his groin area scraped the door frame. His legs flailed like a rag doll's as Spider began to accelerate again, this time without speeding.

"You get him, Mike? You get 'em?"

Mike's face was planted in Spider's lap. He thought he was having a heart attack, and at some point he was going to have to explain how he managed to piss his pants. But he still had enough sense to fix Spider's statement.

He pulled himself to a sitting position and reached for his seatbelt with trembling fingers.

"Yeah, we got him, dog. *We* got him."

CHAPTER SIX
SUPER CRIP

The next morning Chris woke up at 7:32 a.m. His mother stood over him wearing a pink scrub suit. She wore the uniform well, but the way the fabric stretched over her thighs and ample hips garnished way too many gazes from wily old men – as far as Chris was concerned. She worked as a secretary for an ICU unit at Jackson Memorial. Chris knew that she had just gotten home from her graveyard shift.

Theresa wore her hair in a bun. She had smooth, dark skin, like her sons. Chris thought she was beautiful. She had kind eyes that were only a little weary from her work at the hospital.

"Mama, what you want?" He rolled over and buried his face in the pillow, more to hide his smile than to escape the sunbeams that were invading his room.

"Boy, why haven't you told me what happened at the school?"

She threw a stray pillow that hit him in the back of the head. Chris grumbled and kicked weakly with one leg.

"Oh, you trying to kick me?" Her voice was closing in. "Boy, don't make me—"

Chris didn't plan on *making her*, but apparently he already had. She grasped his ankle in her strong, single-black-mother hands and began to pull. If she gave it her all, he knew she could snatch him out of the bed, despite the fact that he had a height advantage and youth on his side.

He rolled over to his back and managed to free himself in the process. He looked up at her and grinned. She smiled down at him with pride lighting her features. Despite being disheveled, un-bathed, and ungrateful, Chris was the apple of her eye. He was the *white* sheep of the family.

She sat on the bed and repeated her question. "Why you didn't call to tell me how it went?"

He sat up lazily. "You know I don't like to call you at work. I don't wanna get you in trouble."

"Boy, you know I answer the phone. Who am I supposed to get in trouble with?"

He shrugged.

"So, how'd it go?"

He brushed the sleep from his eye with a bony shoulder. "It went alright."

Theresa smirked. "What that mean?"

He sighed, feigning exasperation. "All I did was register for classes."

"And..."

"And, you know..." He looked away. "They set up my schedule for the fall."

"*And?*..." Theresa's eyes glistened.

Chris met her gaze and beamed all thirty-two. He knew what she wanted to hear, and it felt good to say it again. "I'm a *pre-med* student."

"Oh, baby!"

Chris didn't have time to brace himself before she wrapped him up in a big hug.

"*Mama!*" he yelped. "I can't breathe!"

"My baby gon' be a *doctor*!" she squealed. Up close, she smelled like cocoa butter.

"Mama, you knew what I was majoring in. You knew since high school!"

"I know, baby, but now," she sniffled, "you done registered. Now you a college student for real. It's *official*."

Chris stiffened. He felt moisture on his neck. Theresa backed away, and he stared into her big, wet eyes. Sunrays dappled her features, making her appear radiant.

"I love you, baby," she said and embraced him again.

"I love you too, Mama." Chris held onto her as tightly as she held him.

● ● ● ● ● ●

COLORED RAGS

He managed to fall back asleep after his mother retreated to her own room. When he woke up again, it was 10:52. This was a more appropriate time to start off his day during the summer, but it still took a few minutes to crawl out of bed.

He took a shower and dressed in the same clothes he wore yesterday. He didn't have any plans, so it didn't matter what he looked like. When he put on his shoes, he considered changing the shoestrings, as his brother requested. But even that was too much trouble. He only had 30 days to chill before school started. He planned to exert as little energy as possible in that time.

He made sure to keep quiet as he got ready to leave the house. His mother was sound asleep. He knew she wouldn't wake up until 3 pm. She left him a serving of leftover spaghetti for lunch, but it didn't look appetizing. Chris exited the house with an empty stomach, knowing his friend Jason would have something to eat.

Jason Moore was the closest Chris had to a best friend, though time and separate paths in life had altered their relationship. They were as thick as thieves when they met in the fifth grade. This was around the time the school started testing them, to see who should apply for the magnet program next year. When the results came back, Chris was bussed to another district, so he could learn with other "gifted" students, while Jason remained at their home school.

The friends only lived a few blocks away, so they continued to see each other regularly, but things were never the same. When it was time for high school, Chris elected to go to the north side of town, where the magnet program focused on science and medical professions. Once again, Jason attended their home school.

Chris pulled up to his friend's house and parked in the driveway. By the time he got out of the car, Jason stood in the backdoor toting a breakfast plate. Jason never had to be summoned to the door. The sound of a vehicle in the driveway was enough to warrant investigation. From behind the screen, Jason eyed his friend warily as Chris ambled up the steps.

"What's for breakfast?" Chris asked as he pulled unsuccessfully at the screen door.

Jason continued to stare at him, now with one eyebrow raised.

Chris tried the door again and confirmed it was locked. "You gon' let me in?"

Jason kept two mongrels in his back yard. They were familiar with Chris, but they still viewed him as a threat, especially since the man of the house wasn't letting him in. They rushed to the fence; one growling ferociously and the other in full bark mode.

"What?" Chris asked his friend with outstretched arms.

Jason shook his head, flipped the latch on the door, and walked away. Chris wore a look of confusion as he followed him inside. The house was dimly lit and smelled of bacon. Chris' mouth began to water. His friend headed to the den without looking back.

Jason was a big guy – not sloppy fat, but his waist size had been over 40 since middle school. His den was filled with electronics, which was a rarity in that neighborhood. Jason didn't usually make him feel unwelcomed, but Chris got those vibes today.

Jason returned to his spot on the loveseat, with Chris' eyes glued to his plate. He still had a few strips of bacon, a hash brown and scrambled eggs with cheese and salsa. Chris' stomach let out an audible roar for sustenance. If Jason heard, he ignored it.

Chris took a seat on an adjacent couch and waited for his friend to say what the problem was. Instead Jason cracked a smile and then laughed. Chris didn't get the joke, but he was pretty sure he was the butt of it.

"What's so funny?" He leaned forward, rubbing his hands together. He didn't think he'd ever wanted bacon more than he did at that moment.

Still laughing, Jason pointed a beefy finger at him and shook his head. Chris wondered if he'd committed a fashion faux pas. He looked down at his outfit. His shirt was a little wrinkled, but his pants were still creased. He had bathed, so he knew he didn't stink.

Growing annoyed, he stood and looked himself over in a large mirror mounted above the couch. He never considered himself an overtly *handsome* man, but he was no ugly duckling either. He turned back to Jason who had made the hash brown disappear. Jason continued to laugh around a mouthful of food.

COLORED RAGS

Chris sat down again. "Nigga, what you laughing at?" He sneered at him, but his aggressive tone had no effect on his longtime friend. Everyone knew Chris wasn't violent, prone to violence, or a friend of violence.

"*You*, man!" Jason chuckled and managed not to choke on his meal. He inhaled a strip of bacon and burped pleasantly. "Man, why you got that shit on? What you supposed to be, *Super Crip* or something?"

The tension in the room was replaced by embarrassment, and Chris' sneer fell away. "What you talking about?"

"Don't play that shit with me. Why you got that shit on? I know Kody ain't put you down."

Jason was right about that. Under no circumstances would Kody allow his little brother to become a member of his gang. Whenever the subject came up amongst the crew, Kody squashed it immediately, sometimes with malice.

A year ago when Kody was in jail, Croc had brought up the fact that Chris was the only one hanging around them who wasn't down. He wanted Chris to get initiated. He even threatened to do it himself, if no one participated. Initiation into the set, as in most gangs, required a new recruit to get *jumped in* by other members. The fighting was supposed to be done with love, but every initiation Chris witnessed looked like nothing more than an orchestrated beating.

Everyone told Croc he was crazy, and he backed down, but it was too little too late. He had already stepped to Chris with his fists balled. He had threatened the OG's brother. When Kody got out of jail and heard what happened, he called Croc to the square. He beat him bloody while the whole set watched. No one ever tried to get Chris to join the gang after that.

"What, because I'm wearing Dickies?" he asked his friend. "Just because I'm wearing these pants don't mean I'm in a gang. You sound like one of them white folks."

Jason wasn't having it. "It's only two kinds of people who wear Dickies around here; the ones who wear them to *work* and *gangstas*. You ain't at work. You ain't even got no job, fool! And it ain't just them pants, neither. Stop acting like you don't know what I'm talking about."

Chris lowered his gaze. "Say, can I have some bacon?"

"*Bacon?* Fool, we ain't talking about no damn bacon! Tell me why you got that bullshit on your shoes? I know you been hanging with yo brother a lot, but I thought you was gon' cut that shit out, now that you finna go to college."

"Man, why you tripping?" Chris expected another lecture, but Jason chose a different tactic.

"Oh. Okay." He looked away from him to a music video playing on TV. "You know they killed your homeboy last night," he said nonchalantly.

Chris had no idea what he was talking about. He leaned back and stretched his legs out. "One of my homeboys gets killed every day. That's what that C life is all about."

"Oh, you already knew?" Jason kept his eyes on the television.

Chris didn't know where he was going with this. "Which one, Jay? I told you, my homeboys get smoked all the time."

His friend used a bacon strip to scoop up the remaining eggs on his plate. Watching him made Chris' stomach twist even more.

"You'd remember this one, if you heard about it," Jason said. "This one's *big time...*"

Chris began to feel uneasy. He leaned forward with his elbows on his knees. "What, you for real?"

"You said you knew about it." Jason was smiling a bit. He sucked his teeth noisily.

"Naw. I don't know nothing," Chris admitted. "If you for real, tell me what you talking about. Somebody got killed last night?"

"I just figured," Jason stalled as he set his plate aside. "Since you come in here like Super Crip and shit, I figured you knew about it already."

Chris felt anger rising from deep in his chest. But anger wasn't going to get any information out of his friend. "Cuz, if somebody got killed, you ain't gotta be sitting there laughing about the shi–"

"*Cuz?* Nigga don't call me *cuz!*" Jason snapped. He glared at Chris. "I ain't one of you and Kody's homeboys over there. If I *was* gon' bang, I'd bang *Blood*. All my niggas is Bloods. Don't come over here with that *cuz* shit."

COLORED RAGS

Chris didn't know if these were fighting words or not. The colors he wore set him up for battle, but he had to remind himself that he was not in a gang. He was not required to feel disrespected by what his friend said. "Look, man, I'm just trying to find out what you talking about. I ain't trying to diss you."

Jason's anger receded just as quickly as it had come. His eyes returned to the television.

"Did somebody get killed last night?" Chris asked as politely as possible.

Jason sighed loudly. The seconds ticked by slowly. Finally he said, "You know somebody named *Willie*?"

Chris knitted his eyebrows. Relief washed over him. There were plenty of Crips in the city. Jason had mistakenly assumed they were all associates. "Naw." He shook his head. "Ain't nobody named Willie in our set."

"*Your* set?"

"I mean Kody's set."

"I think they called him Will. Some OG nigga. *Big timey...*" Jason dropped the bomb as if it was a feather.

Chris' mouth fell open. His eyes widened. "*OG Will?* Somebody killed OG Will?"

Jason's eyes remained on the TV. The disrespect was infuriating.

"Somebody killed OG Will? Look at me!"

"Nigga, don't be yelling and shit in my house!"

Chris stood up. "Why you playing?"

Jason stared at him. "What you talking about?"

"I'm talking about you! Why you sitting there acting like this ain't no big deal? You won't even look me in my face!"

"I said don't be yelling in my house, fool!"

Jason's mother was at work and would be for six more hours. Chris knew the request for quiet was purely his need to exert control.

"I wanna know why you acting like this, cuz! How you gon' sit there eating and shit and tell me OG Will got killed? Are you serious or what?" His voice kept rising, despite his efforts to remain cool.

"How you gon' come over here wearing all that blue and shit, my nigga? You supposed to be going to college, and you rocking blue shoe strings and everything. You know why them niggas killed your homeboy? He ain't never fucked with them niggas. He didn't even know 'em. You know why they killed him? 'Cause he was a *Crip*, that's why! 'Cause they knew he was a Crip."

And there it was. Chris understood that Jason wasn't treating him differently because of any of the stupid reasons he suspected. Jason was tripping because he loved him. He knew that Crips got killed on a regular basis and went to jail more often than that. He was upset because the only homeboy he had with enough brains to do something great in life was fucking around with gangs. Chris took a deep breath and sat back down.

"OG Will got killed for real?" he asked, hoping the whole thing had been a scare tactic.

"I told you that."

Chris closed his eyes and allowed memories of the fallen leader to fill his mind. OG Will was dark and ruthless, but he had his redeeming qualities, didn't he? Chris tried his best to think of something good about him. He had to stop himself after awhile. What was he doing? OG Will was a hoodlum who preyed on the weak and broke laws wantonly. He dispensed death to his own people, in the form of bullets and drugs.

But couldn't the same be said about Kody?

Jason rose from his seat and took his plate to the kitchen. "You said you wanted some bacon?"

"Naw," Chris responded. "Who told you Will got killed? Do you know who killed him?"

He heard running water in the kitchen, but Jason didn't answer. He returned a few minutes later. He sat down and smiled at Chris.

"Say, what the hell is wrong with you? Some nigga got killed, and you think it's funny?"

"I ain't laughing about that nigga. I'm still laughing at you."

"What? My shoestrings?"

"Yepper. The whole get up. You know how silly you look?"

"Whatever. This still ain't no time to be laughing."

"Crips get smoked all the time," Jason said. "You said so yourself. I don't see why you getting so worked up about it. You need to let them niggas on the south worry about it."

That made a whole lot of sense, but Chris couldn't detach himself so easily. "Do you know who killed him?"

"Just some young niggas. Some nobody-ass niggas." Jason eyed him suspiciously. "Why? You wanna tell it on 'em? You wanna set 'em up for some retaliation?"

Chris didn't respond. That was exactly what he wanted.

"Don't worry about that shit," Jason advised him.

That was cool. Chris had enough info. He knew the murderers were slobs, and he knew they were young. Word traveled fast on the streets. By the time he got to the Evergreen, Kody would probably have their names already. He rose to his feet again. "I gotta go."

"Where you going? You finna play hero?"

Chris didn't respond. He headed for the door, growling under his breath.

"I thought you wanted to meet Tracy," Jason called after him.

That stopped him in his tracks. He turned and headed back to the den.

"You talked to her?"

"I called her while I was in the kitchen. Told her you was over here."

Chris was surprised to feel a slight erection growing. He had never met the girl before, but she looked fine in her Facebook pictures. He had been single for four months, which was an eternity for a horny boy his age.

"She wanna meet me?" he asked.

"She say she on her way over here, unless you wanna go play Super Crip..." Jason gave him a wry smile.

Chris did not feel bad about putting OG Will on the backburner. At this point in his life, getting some ass came way before the homies. "No, I'll wait on her."

Jason chuckled.

"You, um... You still got some more of that bacon?"

KEITH THOMAS WALKER

CHAPTER SEVEN
TATE STREET BLOODS

Have you ever heard a crack baby scream?
Already addicted to drugs she's never touched or seen
And her premature body, so tender and frail
Convulses reflexively with each one of her wails
Only a few minutes old, but already a fiend
Have you ever heard a crack baby scream?

Have you ever heard a dying man's last breath?
Soft as a whisper, already reeking of death
As he lies in a growing puddle of his own blood
And the shooter's still screaming, "Now what's up, cuz?"
And his heart pumps his blood through a hole in his chest
Have you ever heard a dying man's last breath?

Michael Hammonds caught a right hook to the side of the head that sent him reeling to the ratty carpet at Shaun's crack house. On some level he thought he heard Spider screaming, *"Leave him alone!"*, but that voice was drowned out by the pain and humiliation of being face down on that carpet. Crack crumbs were all over that dirty ass carpet. Spilled blood from crackhead beat downs stained that carpet. And now Mike was face down in it.

He spun over quickly like a pit fighter. With his back on the ground, he could mount some sort of defense. He began to kick wildly into the air, because he knew Killa Karl was coming fast. Killa Karl weighed 230 pounds. He wore a dirty tee shirt with dirty khakis. Karl had a torso the size of a log, and arms the size of thick branches. He was completely bald. He reminded Mike of The Rock.

COLORED RAGS

    Mike caught him on the shin with a solid kick and regretted it immediately.
    "Oh, you *motherfucker!*" Karl's eyes became like fire. His fists were like bowling balls.
    The whole side of Mike's head was throbbing where Karl had hit him. His ears were ringing, and his heart was tap dancing. He needed the .25 again. Actually, if no one was going to help him, he needed more than that. Jesus would be nice. Mike was relieved but also surprised to hear the leader of their set call for mercy.
    "Stall him out!" Shaun shouted. "Let that nigga make it!"
    Mike lie on his back with both arms and both legs sticking up like toothpicks. Through wide, unblinking eyes, he saw that Karl had no intentions of stalling him out. Killa Karl did not want him to *make it*. Karl's nostrils flared so big, Mike thought he could shove his whole fist in one of those holes. The gorilla advanced again.
    Mike let out a little prayer, braced himself for the onslaught and began to kick again.
    Intervention came in the form of a high-yellow brother tackling Karl from his blindside. Shaun shoved the big man into a wall and held him there with his reputation alone. Shaun gave up at least forty pounds to his subordinate. Karl could've easily flung him aside, but he respected Shaun's authority. He allowed the OG to restrain him.
    Spider rushed forward and put his tiny frame between Killa Karl and his best friend. Karl continued to glare at Mike over Shaun's shoulder. His big chest rose and fell visibly. Everyone else in the room looked on with confused loyalties. They too wanted Mike to pay for his transgressions, but their leader had chosen to give him a reprieve.
    Mike had to get off of that damn floor. He sprang to his feet and pushed Spider aside. It was suicide, but fuck it. If he lost any more face, he might as well go to the south side and tell the fagg land crabs that he was the one they wanted. For a gangsta, losing respect was a death in and of itself.
    "Fuck you, nigga!" he shouted to Karl. His face was hot. He tasted blood. "Bring that shit!"
    This brought a new wave of struggles from Karl, and Shaun was no longer able to contain him. But since it was clear their OG

did not want Mike dead, Skimo Blood rushed in to reinforce the barricade. Skimo was more overweight than muscular. But with two pairs of hands on him, Karl finally abandoned his efforts. Mike stood before them defiantly, but he was glad when the struggling subsided.

The set meeting was going a lot differently than he had expected. There were no cheers, no brownie points, and there damn sure weren't any congratulations. No one recommended a promotion from BG to G status. There were no smiles. Instead there was resentment and condemnation. And yes, if Mike was right about his perceptions, there was fear. There was plenty of that.

It was fear that led to the violent confrontation between him and Killa Karl. The gang feared OG Will's death would spark a short, yet brutal war that would bloody the streets of Stop Six. They feared the small Tate Street set could not possibly stand up to the retaliation that was sure to come from the fagg land clique. They feared crips from other sets in the city would join the battle because of OG Will's prominence.

None of this was voiced, but Mike knew what was going on. They were few, and they were outgunned. And because of Mike, they were now on the endangered species list.

"Kick 'em out the set!" Karl demanded. "We need to drag that motherfucker over there and turn 'em over. Wash our fucking hands!"

Mike didn't know if he was serious about that, but he dared not show uncertainty at this moment. He was young, but he couldn't start whining like a child. It only took one or two more hotheads to agree with Karl, and they would turn the tide again. Shaun wouldn't be able to broker peace if *everyone* was against the idea. Mike knew that no one in the room was prepared to give their life for what he did. Ten incensed faces stared at him with a myriad of emotions. It was do or die.

"Nigga, we all *Bloods!* What the fuck y'all tripping over killing an *ericket* for?" Mike voiced this plea from a sunken chest, but the power of his words kicked them all in the gut. With his fists clenched, his face swelling, and his pants stiff with dried piss, his words had to be bigger than the speaker. His eyes stung with tears, but he refused to let them fall.

COLORED RAGS

"Nigga, ain't nobody told you to be renegading on the south side." Copper sat in a corner caressing his favorite friend; a coal black m&m gun. "You ain't no damned G, fool! You–"

Rodney interrupted him. "You fucked up, Blood! You wanna bring this shit down on us. Who the fuck told you and this nigga to be over there in the first damn place?"

"We was just–"

Mike cut Spider off quickly. He couldn't risk the juvenile throwing a monkey wrench in his train of thought. "We *Bloods*!" he repeated. It seemed so fundamentally obvious. Mike couldn't understand why everyone didn't feel as he did. "*We Bloods*! That nigga a *crab*. What the problem is?"

"You don't know shit, dog!" Shaun's voice had more bass than the late Barry White's. He released his grip on Killa Karl and spun on Mike. To Mike's great fortune, Karl did not seize the opportunity to charge forward for another assault.

Shaun was so light-skinned, his thick moustache and eyebrows stood out against his skin like zebra stripes. He had long hair that was plaited into uniform cornrows. Shaun never wore tee shirts. It was always golf-shirts with Timberland or Polo boots. His appearance alone warranted attention, but it was his voice that made people shut up and listen.

"You can't be going around popping motherfuckers, like you Wyatt Earp or some shit! Who the fuck you think you is?" Shaun paused to give time for a response. Mike didn't have one. "You ain't *shit*, Blood! You's a BG-ass-nigga who done bit off some shit yo ass can't handle. You think we all wanna get shot over that shit? We finna roll with you for some shit we ain't even approve?"

Again Shaun wanted a response. Mike remained mute. Spider looked back at him feebly, pleading with his eyes that Mike say *something*. Mike loosened his fists and shook his head at his mentors. He scanned them all one by one. His lip curled.

"Nigga, when y'all put me down with this shit, what the fuck you told me? *Huh?* Y'all told me we was *Bloods*! We tagging *CK* on them nigga's set. We spraying *CK* on all them stores over there. What that mean? That mean we *crip killas*, right? Ain't that what you told me? '*Fuck a crab*,' right? '*Kill a crab when I see a crab*.' Y'all taught me that! Y'all the ones who put me down! You didn't say 'Kill *this* crab but not *that* one. Give that nigga a pass.' Naw, you didn't say that shit. You said we was CK *all day*! Even on a fucking *holiday*!"

No one could contradict that.

"We *Bloods*!" Mike continued. "Stop Six, nigga! Tate Street busting on they ho ass!" He threw up an array of gang signs that matched his words perfectly. "I ain't scared of them ho-ass niggas! I'm *real* about this shit! Them niggas wanna come get me, *fuck 'em*! I'll kill some more of them bitch-ass niggas! I ain't never scared! I ain't never tired! *Fuck 'em!*"

As his words danced in the air, Mike stood tall, daring anyone to call him a liar. Maybe what he did was wrong. On a basic level, there was no doubt that it was. But this wasn't going to be about right or wrong. He wouldn't allow it to be. It was going to be about truth. Everyone in the room had chosen to bang Blood, which meant they chose to be an enemy of the crips. That was a simple fact that Mike had to bring to their attention. If he failed, he knew he would die.

Shaun was the first to speak. "You know you fucked up, right?"

Mike didn't answer. He breathed through his nostrils and forced his bruised left eye to remain open.

Shaun continued to watch him. He stared at him for so long, Mike thought he could see his thoughts.

"But I ain't gon' leave yo dumb ass hanging," the OG decided. "We ain't gon' put you out like that."

Inwardly, Mike breathed a great sigh of relief. The rest of the set looked on coldly, but Mike would swear he saw something else in their infuriated faces. Something akin to respect.

With the matter settled, he relaxed a little. Adrenaline exited his pores in the form of a cold sweat.

"You said you saw some nigga in dude's car?" Shaun asked Spider.

It was back to business now. If the gang had no further punishment for Mike, then they needed to understand what they were up against. Everyone looked to Spider for a response – everyone except Killa Karl. Karl's eyes remained focused on the man who pulled the trigger. Mike matched his glare with the same hostility.

"Yeah." Spider looked around the room but avoided eye contact with everyone. "I saw him when Mike was in the store."

COLORED RAGS

"What he look like?" someone asked.
"Who was it?" asked another.
"You know who it was?" Shaun inquired.
"Nuh, naw. I ain't never seen him before," Spider replied.
"What he do when Mike was in there?" Shaun asked.
"He didn't do nothing. He was watching. I couldn't see good through the window. That nigga, he had a real dark tint on his windows. I couldn't really see the dude, but–"
"If you didn't see him, how you know somebody was in the car?" Skimo wanted to know.
Spider didn't look his way. "I saw somebody in the car. I couldn't see what he looked like is all. I saw his head and, like, his shoulders. He was moving. I *saw* him. He looked at me, and he looked at Mike too."
Spider had delivered this news to Mike as they fled the scene. The revelation chilled Mike's blood as they sped towards the safety of Stop Six.
"Man, that don't make no fucking sense." Redd scrunched up his face as his limited thought processes struggled to fit the pieces together.
Redd was an almond-colored brother with a mouth full of bling. He had big lips, a big nose and beady eyes. They all wore their colors proudly, but Redd was the only one who wore red pants all the time. He was short and stocky with a lot of old bruises on his face and arms.
"If it was somebody in that nigga's ride, how come they didn't do nothing?" he asked.
That was the question of the hour. Everyone wanted an explanation for that.
"You didn't see him when you got out the car?" Redd asked Mike.
Mike shook his head. "Naw, I was mostly watching the store. It was this bitch behind the counter, and I was looking for that nigga Will. I was keeping track of where he was."
Mike felt stupid for not being more aware of his surroundings. He had walked right past Will's Cutlass on the way in. If he had taken the time to look, he would have had a clear view of whoever was in the car. The lights from the store were shining right into the vehicle.

If he had looked, Mike would have run back to his getaway car. There was no way he would have continued with his plan, if he knew another crab was sitting there watching him.

"This nigga in the car," Redd said, growing frustrated, "maybe dude didn't have no gat, but he could've blew the horn or something – let that nigga know somebody was creeping on his ass. You had yo pistol out when you got out the car?"

"Yeah." Mike was still embarrassed about that. "I forgot I had that gun in my hand till I was already at the door. I hid it under my shirt then, but I had it out when I went by his car."

"So whoever was in the car knew you was finna go in there and fuck some shit up," Redd deduced. "Maybe he thought it was just gon' be a robbery. You had your colors on?"

"I had on the same shit I got on now."

"That means he knew you was banging Blood. He saw you with a gun in your hand. He had to know you were either gon' rob the store or pop his homeboy." Redd liked his role as detective. Everyone listened to him.

"But if you was gon' rob the store, he should've figured you'd probably shoot Will too, just 'cause he a crab and was in there at the time. You know what I'm saying? Dude in the car had to know you wasn't gon' leave no witnesses, especially not no fucking crab. So whoever was in the car..." Redd's face scrunched up again, "they just *let* that shit go down. Nigga just sat there and watched that shit happen... Was it a bitch?"

"Naw, it was a dude," Spider guessed. He was pretty sure the hairstyle matched a man rather than a woman.

"Even if it was a bitch," Redd continued, "she'd a laid on that horn so hard, that nigga would've knew something was wrong. Ain't no bitch finna watch her nigga get his cap peeled. But if it was a dude..." Redd shook his head. "Ain't no nigga finna let his homeboy get killed either. This shit ain't adding up. I don't think it was nobody in that car."

"It was," Spider insisted. "I saw him."

"Then the motherfucker saw you too," Redd snapped. "Both y'all black asses."

Neither Mike nor Spider could deny that was the case. But that information didn't do anything to help solve the mystery.

CHAPTER EIGHT
THE GATHERING

I hold him as his body shudders
Them fucking dirus killed my brother!
His eyes are transfixed, open wide
I collapse on him and begin to cry
Do they think they'll get away
From all these pistols in their face?
But before I plot my foe's demise
First I'm gon' need an alibi

    Two hours and a full belly later, Tracy proved to be worth the wait. She drove up in a purple Mustang with the top pulled back. She had a purple and black pony tail that bounced in the wind as she pulled behind Chris' bucket. Her system was loud enough to rival some of the pimped-out rides at the Evergreen.
    Before getting out of the car, Tracy turned her stereo down to a tolerable level but didn't shut it off completely. Jason and Chris, alerted by the booming speakers, came to the back porch just as she approached the door. Chris saw that the photos he'd seen of Jason's "homegirl" were 100% accurate. No catfish here.
    The girl was petite, no larger than a size six. She had a small head with a lot of hair glued to it. It was well done, though. The way her hair was pulled back made her forehead look big, but it also made her eyes slant a little, giving her an exotic look. Her nose was small, and her lips were full. Tracy wore bright red lipstick that drew attention to her only obvious flaw; she had large teeth that protruded. It was clear that she had once been a thumb-sucker. Despite this, Chris considered her attractive.
    Tracy wore skin-tight Capri's that turned her barely there booty into a nice bubble butt. She wore a lot of jewelry. If it was

all real, Chris knew that it cost more than his car. He was sure Tracy was out of his league, but he couldn't stop grinning at her like a fat kid at a buffet.

He and Jason stepped outside. Tracy stood a full foot shorter than Chris' six foot frame. She raised a hand to shade the sun as she gazed into his eyes. She then looked him up and down. Her eyes came back to his face and she smiled. Chris was suddenly in love.

"You Chris?" she asked.

"Yeah."

"Jason told me you was a college boy." She gave him another full body scan. "You look like you a Crip or something."

Chris loved her ghetto accent. He watched her lips, her teeth, her tongue formulating each syllable. Jason broke the trance by snickering in the background.

"Told yo ass," he snorted quietly.

"Nah, it's just – my..."

Tracy's smile intensified, which was all the more alluring to Chris, even with that gator mouth.

"It's my brother," he said finally. "I mean, my brother – he's in a gang. He a Crip. I just, I just hang around him a lot. I ain't in no gang. I *do* go to school." Chris felt goose bumps break out on his arms. The same temperature produced beads of sweat on his forehead. "I go to Texas Lutheran. I mean, I will when school starts. I registered yesterday."

He was rambling. He couldn't help it. All outward signs confirmed Tracy was a hood rat, but Chris downplayed them. He liked her face, her body. That little ass. He wanted her. "I registered as a pre-med student."

"*Doctor*," Jason said.

Tracy continued to smile. "You don't look like you finna be no doctor. You look like you finna do a driveby."

This was the third negative response to Chris' attire in less than 24 hours, but it took a female to make the criticism stick. He felt ashamed. He blushed, but with his dark skin, no one noticed.

"This," he said, "I just wear this when I go around my brother and them. Him and his homeboys, they all Crips, and, you know, everybody dresses like this. I try to adapt, to whatever situation I'm in. I'm not in a gang, though. My brother wouldn't let me, even if I wanted to."

COLORED RAGS

"*This nigga...*" Jason said from somewhere behind him.

Thinking he sounded like an idiot, Chris' smile faltered. He eyes fell to the pavement between them. Tracy reached out with one finger and lifted his chin until their eyes met again. Her touch titillated his whole face. There was a nice fragrance on her hand that he couldn't place.

"You know," she said, "you ain't gotta be what everybody else want you to be. You should be yourself. If they don't like you for who you are, you don't need 'em."

The Saturday afternoon cartoon spiel sounded unique coming from Tracy. She withdrew her hand and giggled.

"What?" he said.

"What was that you said? '*Adapt*?' I ain't never been with nobody who use words like that."

"I know a lot of big words," Chris said.

"This nigga," Jason commented again.

Tracy laughed. She backed away from him a bit. "Well, uh, I gotta go. I told Jason I could only stop by for a minute. I just wanted to see what you look like. Did he give you my number? You wanna call me?"

Chris felt elated. She'd seen him, listened to his gibberish, and she still wanted to have something to do with him. It couldn't get any better.

"No, I don't have it. But I want it. I'll give you my number too."

"Okay, I got my phone in the car. Let me put your number in it."

Chris wiped his forehead when she turned away. He couldn't take his eyes off her booty. He wanted to palm it more than he wanted his next breath. Technically Chris wasn't a virgin, but he wasn't in love with either of the two freaks he fornicated with. Since there were no feelings involved, according to *The Color Purple* at least, that meant he was still a virgin.

Tracy sat behind the wheel of her Mustang and fetched her cellphone from her purse. The scent of jasmine wafted from her ride. Chris wanted to ask if the car was hers or someone else's (a dope dealing boyfriend perhaps), but he refrained.

She looked up at him. "You tall."

"I wish I was a little bit taller." He felt like an idiot for saying that, but she laughed.

"What's your number?"

Chris gave it to her, thinking Jason had finally come through for him. Most of the girls in the hood thought Chris was too nerdy. Too soft. They wanted a roughneck who sold drugs, slept with their homegirls, and might call them from jail any given day.

"Give me your number too," he said.

She waited until he was ready to punch it in before she rattled off the digits. She told him, "Well, I guess I'ma go."

"You gon' call me?"

She grinned. "I'll call you," she promised.

"Alright." He backed away, to give her room to close the door. She surprised him by stepping out of the car instead.

"You ain't gon' give me a hug?" she asked.

Chris' heart raced as he moved in. The way things were going, he felt like he could get a kiss too. Even a booty-squeeze didn't seem out of the question, but he buried these thoughts. His mama raised him to be a gentleman. He wrapped his arms around her thin waist and drew her body close to his. His gentlemanly behavior did not stop his erection from rearing up again.

She released him first. They stood before each other, both smiling and wanting.

"I'll call you," she said and got back into the car.

"I hope so," he said as she closed the door.

She drove away, and Chris stood there for a minute, imagining what their future would be like.

"You just gon' stand there?" Jason called out to him.

"Naw." Chris returned to his friend with twinkles in his eyes. Rather than follow him back inside, Chris headed for his car.

"Yo, I'm finna bounce."

"I hope you going home."

Chris didn't bother lying.

Jason shook his head and turned his back on him as Chris started his Plymouth.

● ● ● ● ● ●

Chris stopped by his house to change his shoestrings before he headed to the south. He was glad he did. At four in the afternoon, the parking lot of Evergreen looked like a convention

COLORED RAGS

center. Chris had to creep slowly to avoid running someone over. There was a sea of blue tee shirts and blue flags loitering about. The pistol packing punks didn't care if there was a bumper riding their ass.

Most of these thugs were strangers to Chris. They gave him suspicious, if not intimidating glares as he passed. Some of their expressions were forlorn. Others were anxious. A few were outright enraged; with eyebrows knotted and mouths twisted in hate. They looked impatient and eager.

Chris had never seen anything like it. He knew OG Will was well respected and loved by a good number of people, but he never thought the Crip's death would spark a rally of this proportion. Some tattoos read Polywood, some Bidecker Boys, others were Davis Street and Glen Garden. Chris saw flags that were baby blue, royal blue and navy blue. There were purples, golds and even yellows.

For the first time ever, Chris couldn't find a parking spot in front of his brother's building. He estimated there were twenty or more black faces milling around the stairway that led up to apartment 4F. There were three more men posted on the stairway itself and a dozen more hung out on the breezeway. Chris parked in a handicap spot three buildings down with little fear of being towed. A tow truck driver would face a fate worse than Reginald Denny's if he tried to remove a vehicle from that complex.

With his head held high, Chris exited his vehicle and strode brazenly through the overgrown lawn. The atmosphere was tense, and hesitation would be noticed. No one knew what the bloods were up to. Maybe Will's death was just the beginning. Some men in the crowd had visible bulges under their shirts. Others held their pieces openly, as if the murder of the OG had given them immunity from the ATF. It was as compelling as it was terrorizing.

Most of the Crips let Chris pass with a simple, "What up, cuz," which he returned in kind. A few stuck out a *C* for him to shake, and he did. The real challenge came when a gangsta Chris didn't know took him through a more elaborate handshake involving several different gang signs. Fortunately Chris was able to participate. Trez had practiced the gestures with him many times. A fire lit in his belly when he got through the greeting. He felt like he was a part of something big and important.

By the time he got to the stairway, Chris couldn't wait to get around people he knew. Unfortunately three more hardheads blocked his progress. The first was a large man planted at the foot of the steps. He wore a blue scrub suit, but Chris didn't think he was affiliated with any hospital. When the guy made no effort to move, Chris made the mistake of telling him, "Excuse me."

The man had a lazy left eye that stared off in the direction of Riverside. The other eye focused on Chris with malevolence.

"Yo, who the fuck is you?" he asked.

Two more goons were posted on the stairs above him. They stared down at Chris, hoping he wouldn't have the correct response. Chris felt his heart skip a beat.

"Yo, that's Kody's brother."

The voice came from the breezeway. Chris looked up and was glad to see Dante in the crowd. "Let that nigga up."

Cock-Eye's sneer went away. He focused his good eye a little more clearly and then slid his bulk over enough for Chris to squeeze past.

"Yo, my bad, cuz. Why you didn't say something?"

Chris ignored him and headed up.

The nucleus of the AGG Land set was on the breezeway. Besides Dante, Chris was glad to see Trez, Deuce, Croc and eight other familiar faces. Everyone's mood was downcast. Croc and a couple others were outright crying. They eyed Chris thoughtfully as he approached.

"What's up, Tay," he said.

"Say, nigga, I don't think Kody want you over here tonight," Dante responded. His voice was soft. Red veins discolored the whites of his eyes.

"He in there?" Chris asked. He didn't see Kody's car on the way in, but there were so many people there, he could have missed it.

"Yeah. He in there."

Deuce idled over to him. His hair was uncombed, which wreaked havoc on an afro that big. His wig looked like a deflated basketball that had been kicked in on both sides.

"What's up, cuz."

"What's up." Chris stared down at the kid. Compared to the multitude downstairs, it was clear Deuce was still a child. Chris wondered if it wasn't too late for the pint-sized thug. If he

COLORED RAGS

went home, cut his hair, stopped wearing blue and went back to school, maybe he could make it. All he needed was a role model; a big brother program or something.

"You heard about what happened to Will?" Deuce asked.

"Yeah, I heard," Chris stated.

Trez stood behind Dante. He had a stern look on his face, which was a first for him. Chris didn't think he'd ever seen him in a serious mood. He wondered if his friend had a blunt, but this didn't seem like a good time to ask.

Deuce continued to speak, as if he hadn't heard Chris' response.

"Some slob-ass niggas killed him last night at the Rainbow." He paused for a second to let the intensity of his words sink in. Chris tried to look as remorseful as possible. He shook his head as old folks do when they hear about a driveby taking the life of an innocent.

These kids today. When will they learn?

Deuce sniffled. Chris felt guilty for being in the midst of this sorrow. He didn't love OG Will like the others. He didn't have anything against him – they just weren't that close.

"That nigga's brother was in the car and didn't even do shit," Deuce continued.

Chris' inability to register emotion changed then. "What?"

"His mark-ass brother!" Trez jumped in the conversation. "That ho-ass nigga was sitting in the car when that shit went down."

"They say he was watching," Dante added. "Had my nigga's pistol in his lap and just sat there and *watched*."

"When the laws rolled up," Deuce went on, "he was still sitting in my big homey's car. Looking stupid and shit."

"That nigga was scared," Dante guessed, sneering now. "That's a scary-ass nigga."

Thinking of Dre's inaction angered the whole group. Chris took a moment to put himself in Dre's shoes. If he and Kody were in the same situation, he would shoot, wouldn't he? Of course he would. Fuck jail and fuck college. There was no way he could sit there and watch his brother get aired out. What was Dre thinking? The homies on the breezeway had ways to deal with a coward.

"That nigga is a ho. I bet not *never* see his ass!"

"He gon' get *murked*."

"I'ma kick his ass, but I ain't gon' kill 'em. Shit be disrespecting OG Will to kill that nigga. It's still his brother."

"Fuck that. Will would want us to do 'em."

"No he wouldn't."

"Naw, I don't think so."

"Will don't want his brother dead, cuz. I don't believe that shit..."

As the conversation waned, Chris moved closer to Trez.

Trez smiled at him briefly but caught himself and snapped his mouth closed. A smile on that breezeway at that moment might get you thrown down the stairs.

"What my brother doing in there?" Chris asked.

"It's him and some more OG's. They talking 'bout what's finna go down. We finna go on a *kill a slob a day* campaign."

Chris was pretty sure they weren't going to kill a blood every single day. At least he hoped they wouldn't.

"He told me not to be getting you high all the time," Trez continued.

"When he tell you that?" Chris wasn't surprised that Kody was trying to cut off his weed supply, but it was too much like something a mother would do, rather than a big brother.

"Last night, after you left," Trez said and smiled. He didn't catch himself this time.

Chris shook his head. "So, um, you got some weed?"

Trez's smile broadened. This time he did catch it. He put on his mourning face again and looked around to see if anyone was watching. "Yeah, but we can't smoke here. We can go to this other apartment. Some people moved out a week ago, but they left most of they stuff. Niggas been in there chilling. It's still open."

Things that make you say hmmm...

There was a good chance the police were coming. The complex was full of criminals. Most of them had some type of warrant out for their arrest. And everyone knows there's a loyal police informant at every black gathering. There were so many goons at the apartments, Chris guessed there had to be at least *five* snitches amongst them.

He calculated all of this as he weighed the pros and cons.
Breaking and entering
Trespassing
Possession of narcotics

COLORED RAGS

Public Intoxication
The only pro he could come up with was *Get high*.
"Let's go," he said.

CHAPTER NINE
UP IN SMOKE

I tat my brother's name on my chest
So he'll feel me put those slobs to rest
I'm scheming at my girlfriend's house
She'll lie about my whereabouts
Don't answer the door or pick up the phone
Say Friday night we were here alone
When the detectives say your story's a lie
Be strong and support my alibi

I go to the south to gather my troops
My homeboys loved my brother too
We hunting tonight on Tate Street
I need about five hardcore OG's
We'll divide in groups, catch 'em in the mix
It worked on Kennedy, it'll work in Stop Six
But before we jump into our rides
Y'all better secure your alibis

The front door of apartment 2B was closed. Trez tried the knob. It turned freely but did not open. He tried to shove it in with his shoulder, but it held fast.

Chris stated the obvious. "It's locked."

"Yeah, somebody in there. Crackhead prolly. Watch this. Stand over there."

Trez directed Chris to a spot out of the peephole's view. He then balled a fist and pounded on the door. "OPEN THE DOOR! THIS IS THE POLICE! WE KNOW YOU'RE IN THERE!" Trez's voice was barely recognizable as his own.

COLORED RAGS

"Come on," he said and hurried around the side of the building.

Chris followed cautiously, not sure what to expect. What if a hooker was in there with her trick? Even worse, what if some rowdy niggas were in there cooking crack? Trez expected something comical, but if a couple of thugs flushed their dope because of him, the joke could turn violent.

Chris stood quietly, poised to run, but Trez proved to be the more streetwise of the two. A window popped open, and a distressed face poked out. The head jerked around anxiously, looking in all directions before spotting Trez. The head belonged to a dopefiend named Rufus.

Rufus was 40 years old, but he looked 60. He had one bad eye that was always half closed. Chris wished it was closed all the way. Rufus didn't have an eyeball in that gap, only pink meat. That eye, coupled with his other hobo ailments, made him look spooky and gross.

"It's cops over there?" Rufus asked. His black face, pink lips and raspy voice outdid any minstrel show spectacle. Chris couldn't help but laugh at him.

"What you doing in there?" Trez asked.

"*What?*" Rufus looked around again, growing irritated now. "That was you knocking?"

"Yeah, it was me. Come open the door, nigga!"

"That shit ain't funny," Rufus said, but his expression registered more relief than anger. He stared at Chris. "You Kody's brother, ain't you?"

Chris couldn't take his eyes off the empty eye socket. It was sunken in, and there was crust in the corners. Didn't they still make eye patches, so the public wouldn't have to be exposed to such things?

"Shut up, and go open the door!" Trez demanded.

He and Chris returned to the front of the apartment. By the time they got there, Rufus had the door open. The inside of the unit had the most squalid living conditions Chris had ever seen. The old residents had taken all of the electronics and most of the furniture. Since then someone, probably Rufus, had been refurnishing the place with junk.

Aside from the unsightliness, the apartment smelled like there was raw sewage in one of the back rooms. Chris wrinkled his nose and tried to breathe through his mouth. This was a bad place. Not even worth getting high in. He didn't want to imagine all of the foul things Rufus did there. There was no way an even slightly civilized person would feel comfortable in that apartment.

Trez surprised him by plopping down on the nasty ass couch. "What the hell you doing in here?" he asked Rufus.

"This *my* motherfucking house, nigga," Rufus snapped. "What the fuck *you* doing in here?"

"*Yo* house?" Trez cracked up. "Cuz, you *live* in this motherfucker?"

"Yeah, nigga," Rufus growled. "Say, close my door, motherfucker!" he yelled at Chris.

Chris surprised himself by doing as he was told. Showing respect for his elders didn't exclude crackheads.

"Don't be yelling at my homeboy," Trez warned. "Matter of fact, you need to get the fuck up outta here."

Rufus was indignant. "What you mean? This *my* house!"

"This ain't yo goddamned house, fool! It's a vacant apartment. You got a signed lease?" Trez smirked at him. "Don't make me bring Kody over here. You want me to tell him you in here messing with his little brother?" Trez pulled a bag of weed from his pocket.

"Nope!" Rufus' submission was quick. "Let me," he staggered in one direction and then another. He ended up between Trez's legs. He dropped to his knees and began to pick at the carpet. "Lemme get my shit. I dropped a hit when y'all was playing at the door. I gots me–"

Trez cut him off with a well placed kick to his shoulder. "Man, get yo ass away from me!"

Rufus fell over, more from his own imbalance than Trez's force.

Chris was taken aback. In two years, he never saw Trez get aggressive with anyone. He thought Rufus could whoop Trez if he wanted to, but cocaine had a way of bringing out the punk in people. Trez never took his focus off the weed he was rolling.

"Okay. Alright." Rufus scrambled to his feet. "So, um, y'all wanna kick it in here for a minute?"

Trez ignored him.

"Alright. Shee, that's cool. You know I'm cool with y'all niggas." He looked at Chris and then back to Trez. "So, um." He scratched at his naps. "So, um, you wanna *rent* my house? You got something for me?"

"Get the fuck outta here."

"Naw, I'm just saying. You gots like, a nick or something? Something for me to do while I'm gone? I was, I'm just..."

Trez didn't even look up this time.

Rufus looked back to Chris then lowered his head in defeat. "So, how long y'all gon' be in here?"

Again, no one answered.

"Alright. Um. Okay. So, I can come back, right? I mean, later? I can come back? I don't want nobody else to get my spot."

"Yeah," Trez said. "Bring yo ass back *later*. After we gone. Don't come back while we still here."

Rufus shuffled to the door and stared at Chris on his way out. Chris couldn't stop looking at his bad eye.

When he stepped outside, Rufus asked, "How I know when y'all gone?"

"Close the door, Chris," Trez said.

Chris closed the door.

● ● ● ● ● ●

Chris didn't think he could enjoy a high in the midst of Rufus' filth, but he was wrong. Oh so wrong. He barely noticed the fiery sun give way to stars as they smoked two blunts. While they puff-puff-passed, Trez told him all about the big payback planned for the murderers of OG Will.

The Crips had a considerable amount of information on the assailants. The first clues came from Will's brother Dre. He described the shooter as a young kid with a red tee shirt on. There was another person waiting in their getaway car, but Dre didn't get a good look at him.

The Crips embarked on a campaign to find out which blood set was responsible. Many of the bloods in Stop Six put old grievances aside to help. They didn't do it out of brotherly love. They did it so they wouldn't be targeted during the retaliation.

After barely an afternoon of investigating, a Truman Street blood named Bocco mentioned the name of the Tate Street set. He said they *might* know something and left it at that. After interrogating a dozen more people, mostly dopefiends and hood rats, the Crips had the identity of the shooter. His name was Mike, and he was 16 years old.

Mike had apparently done the deed without the backing of his set, but that didn't matter. The whole Tate Street gang was going to get lit up. The Backhouse bloods were going to get it too because of their lack of cooperation with the Crips. Mike in particular was sure to die.

Chris listened to Trez's story but was barely able to keep up with the information. The weed was so strong, he felt like he would pass out. He didn't think he'd be able to rise from his seat when it was time to go. He thought the high he was experiencing was so complete, anyone who graduated to a more powerful drug had to be out of their minds.

Seriously, what more could they want?

They talked about Kody's leadership role in the gang and how he was taking control of the situation. They talked about Rufus and made fun of his eye, his *home*, and the way he poked his head out of the window looking for the police. They watched cable television and marveled at the fact that Rufus had both a television and cable. The TV was one of the old ones, with a fat back and a turn knob. That was probably the only reason he wasn't able to sell it for crack.

When someone twisted the doorknob, they assumed it was Rufus.

"We ain't through yet!" Trez snapped.

The visitor began to pound the door with his fist. Chris rose to make a quick dash out of the window, like Rufus had, but he heard a familiar voice that stopped him in his tracks.

"Open the door, cuz!" Kody yelled.

Chris was startled, but Trez was downright horrified. The light-skinned gangsta jumped to his feet, knocking the components of what was to be their third blunt from his lap onto the floor. He stared at Chris with his mouth ajar.

"What we gon' do?" he whispered.

"Open the door," Chris said.

"That's yo brother."

Chris couldn't help but laugh. Trez was pathetic, but only because he knew a side of Kody that Chris had never experienced. Kody was an excellent fighter. Everyone on the south side respected his boxing game. Fortunately their mother had a hard

COLORED RAGS

rule against them fighting each other. While growing up, Kody and Chris were taught that hitting each other was the ultimate brotherly sin. To this day, Kody had never laid a hand on his brother in anger.

"Open the fucking door!" the OG barked.

Trez farted loudly.

Chris laughed at him. He walked to the door and swung it open defiantly. He grinned at his brother. The whites of Chris' eyes were bloodshot. It wasn't hard to read his expression: *What the hell do you want? I'm getting high, bro. Aaaaand what?*

Kody's was white hot fury. He stood, fists balled, dressed in all black. The last person who looked upon that particular gaze no doubt received a bullet or a concussion. But Chris was bold enough to maintain his swagger.

"What?" he taunted.

"You smoking again?" It wasn't so much a question, but a demand that Chris acknowledge his delinquency.

Chris couldn't wipe the smile off his face if he wanted to, which, incidentally, wasn't what he wanted. He liked smiling. He felt better than he ever had. He refused to let Kody's nagging take his good times away.

And it wasn't like his big brother was the more innocent of the two. Kody did drugs himself – and not just the light ones either. How long did he expect this, *Do as I say, not as I do*, approach to work? Chris thought Kody was a hypocrite. And besides, what was the worse he could do?

"Yeeeah," Chris mocked. "I'm, uh, yeah. I'm smoking again. You should've seen the size of them blunts." He laughed and turned to get Trez's endorsement. Trez wished he was invisible.

Kody snarled. His nostrils flared. He looked away for a moment. Finally, he nodded and smiled, as if he'd come up with the perfect solution. "I'ma tell Mama."

It took a few moments for the meaning of the words to get through Chris' brain cloud. "You gon', say what?" His smile faded a little. "You gon' what?"

"Fuck it, Chris," Kody said and turned away from him.

He headed back towards the parking lot. Chris followed him.

"You don't wanna listen to me, fuck it," Kody said. "I ain't yo daddy. You wanna get high, go ahead." Kody stopped abruptly and turned to face him. "You can tell Mama why you in a crackhead's house fucking up your life. Did you even look around that apartment? It's shit in there somewhere. The whole place stinks, and you just kicking it, like it's the Ritz or something."

Kody saw Trez following them. "You better get your ass away from me, cuz!"

Trez looked wounded. "I'm going with y'all, ain't I?"

"Hell naw you ain't going!" Kody bellowed. "You can't even do right by my brother. You think I'm finna let yo ass roll with us? Get the fuck outta here!"

Trez headed the other way with his tail tucked between his legs. Chris was pretty sure he wouldn't be able to count on him to get high again.

The brothers stared at each other.

"You gon' tell Mama?" Chris asked.

"Go home, Chris." Kody didn't seem as angry as before.

Chris didn't think he would snitch, but he couldn't be sure unless he heard it. "You gon' tell on me?"

"You don't need to be worried about that right now. What you need to worry about is getting home with all that shit in your system. Catch a DUI if you want to. Bet that'll straighten your ass out. I won't have to tell Mama nothing when you call her from jail."

Kody walked away. Under the bright lights at the apartments, Chris saw that his brother's shoulders were broad and massive. He hoped Kody wouldn't fight Trez for disobeying him. He knew that *someone* was going to feel the OG's wrath tonight.

"Where you going?" Chris asked. He was still very much high but not so happy anymore.

"Don't worry about me," Kody said and rounded the corner towards his destiny.

COLORED RAGS

CHAPTER TEN
REVENGE

Whose car is that on a slow creep?
Y'all know them people in that Jeep?
Be ready to duck, if they throw some heat
Never mind, it's just some bopping-ass freaks

What about this one? Say, nigga, who that is?
I can't see through their window tint
Y'all better be ready, if they start some shit
Wait, that's my nigga Reggie from the pen

I ain't paranoid
'Cause I got my finger on the trigger
I ain't tripping off this weed or liquor
I killed they OG, so I figure
We best be watching for them niggas

    Mike Hammonds thought Shaun's ultimate plan of *business as usual* would be remembered as one of the greatest tactical blunders since a presidential motorcade cruised through a turkey shoot in Dealey Plaza.
    The reasoning behind the decision to keep both dope houses open on this particular night was weak at best: "We ain't finna shut our shit down, like we scared of them niggas," Shaun had said. "That's what everybody think; we gon' close shop and come up missing, go hold up in some damned motel, strapped down, looking out the windows and shit, like some bitches. Everybody think we going out like that.
    "But we don't even know if they know who killed that nigga. If we start hiding, niggas gon' know we had something to

do with it. Naw. We gon' keep it *gangsta*. Business as usual. I mean, we ain't just gon' be sitting up in here like sitting ducks and shit. We ain't stupid. We gon' stay strapped up. We gon' be careful, watching who come by and everything. But we ain't gon' run."

Shaun had looked around the room daring anyone to find flaws in his logic. A few sets of eyes focused on Mike, who would have the most to lose from this *business as usual* shit, but Mike didn't say anything. What was he going to say? *No, Shaun. That's not a good idea. I think we **should** hold up somewhere. I think we **should** lay low until this whole thing blows over. Them niggas is gon' get us!*

Of course not. Mike was the last person in the room who could suggest that. Spider was next to last. No one else argued the point, so it was settled.

Mike and Spider were chosen to run the boy/girl house for the evening. Initially Mike didn't think there was anything wrong with that. He was often paired with Spider to work at one of the dope houses. Mike didn't start to believe something strange was going on until the sun gave way to nightfall, and all of their customers stopped coming. Boy/girl houses do most of their business after dark. But not tonight.

Mike's brain raced as he put the pieces of the puzzle together. He and Spider were best friends. They were the youngest members of the Tate Street set. They were also the one's responsible for the murder of *OG motherfucking Will*. They'd caused a lot of trouble for everyone in the gang, and *they* were the two selected to be left alone at the boy/girl house on this night – this night that was destined to be lit up with murderous revenge.

Mike began to think Shaun had chosen them as sitting ducks after all.

But that could be the weed talking, he reminded himself. Marijuana has a paranoia-inducing effect sometimes.

Shaun gave them more firepower than usual. Mike selected a pistol and a Mossberg pump as his babies that night. He cradled the shotgun with care, carried it to the restroom with him, and checked the chamber ever so often to make sure it was still fully loaded. Spider kept an m&m gun (a 9mm) in his lap. There was a .380 automatic on the coffee table between them.

COLORED RAGS

    Mike favored the shotgun because scattered buckshot pellets covered a lot more space than single rounds. He knew that if he had to use a weapon that night, good aim was not something he could count on. He was lucky to hit OG Will with two of the five shots he let off in the Rainbow, and they were damn near face to face. Luck wasn't going to get him through another shoot out.

    Besides him and Spider, there was a coke head in the living room with them. She sat on the couch with Mike, sniffling and wringing her hands. She was a bopper; she liked to hang around dope boys and ballers, looking for free drugs. Her drug of choice was powder cocaine. Mike didn't remember her name, but he was pretty sure it sounded like stripper or maybe a car. Passion would have been his guess.

    The bitch had come in while the sun was still out. She bought a ten dollar pill and asked them if it was okay for her to snort it there. At the time, Mike was glad for the company. She wasn't bad looking, and he knew her type. Any female who would get high in a dope house was looking for some play.

    After her pill was gone, the bopper eyed Mike as boppers do when they have only one thing left to barter with. It didn't take too much persuasion to get her to snort a small pile of coke off Mike's dick. She didn't mind when Spider started pulling her pants down as she licked the residue from Mike's member.

    Two hours and two pills later, she was still completely naked and fiending badly, but both boys were spent. Her chances of getting more free dope were waning, but Passion was a trooper. She would stay until told to leave, and neither of her providers had grown that weary of her presence. Sooner or later, their perverted eyes would find her again.

    Mike noticed Spider dozing in the loveseat. Jimmy Kimmel was delivering his nightly monologue. That wasn't necessarily edge-of-the-seat entertainment, but Mike couldn't understand how Spider could take a nap at a time like this. In Mike's mind, each tick of the clock brought them closer to their doom. How the hell could he sleep?

    It was Spider, after all, who had talked him into stealing a car last night. The stolen Impala was the only reason they were cutting through the south side. It was Spider who saw Will at the store and told Mike to pull over. Spider was the one who had grabbed the steering wheel and yanked it in Will's direction when

Mike tried to choose a more righteous course of action. Spider was the real murderer.

"Wake yo bitch ass up!" Mike yelled at him.

Passion sat up with a start. Spider slowly raised his head to an upright position. He looked over at Mike and Passion and smiled. She smiled back at him.

"Wake up, nigga," Mike said again.

"What?" Spider's eyes were low.

"How you gon' be sleep at a time like this?" Mike wanted to know.

"What? Why?" Spider tried to fight against his drowsiness. "What's wrong?" He looked around complacently. "Ain't nobody here. What I'm supposed to be doing?"

Mike couldn't believe his friend's naivety. "Why you think ain't nobody here?" he asked. "It's Friday night. Niggas done got paid. They out kicking it. This place ain't never been dead on no Friday night."

Spider focused a little more clearly. "Yeah. It's kinda tripped out," he agreed.

"So what that mean to you?"

Spider thought for a moment. "Niggas prolly scared to come over here. They prolly scared they gon' get caught up, if some shit go down with them crabs."

Passion didn't seem startled or anxious to leave with this revelation.

Mike nodded. "So how the fuck you gon' go to sleep when everybody else is too scared to come here? We ain't had no customer since it got dark."

Spider sat up straighter and lifted the pistol from his lap. He looked around the room as if someone was already there, creeping in the bathroom or kitchen.

"You think they coming tonight?" he asked. He sounded thirteen again, and Mike was glad for that. Thirteen year olds know when to shut up and heed wise counsel.

Mike sucked his teeth and nibbled at his bottom lip. "Yeah. I think they coming. But I been thinking about something else, while you over there *sleeping* and shit."

Spider didn't respond.

"I been thinking maybe Shaun and them changed their mind about handing us over to them rickets. You know, Shaun ain't been here *one* time tonight. Usually he be over here two, damn near three times on a Friday night to pick up the money and drop off, ya know? But that nigga ain't even called or nothing. It's like he *know* we ain't had no business. You feel me?"

Spider didn't like this line of thinking one bit, and neither did the whore. She was sliding into her panties with one hand and pulling her bra from beneath a sofa cushion with the other.

"What? You scared now?" Mike snapped at her.

"Y'all ain't gon' give me no more," she said without looking up.

"Hell, naw! We ain't got shit for you. Get yo ugly ass up outta here!"

"You think they set us up?" Spider asked.

"I don't know."

"Why don't we leave?" Spider wondered.

The question had been on Mike's mind too. Why not just leave – go somewhere safe? Before he could make a decision, a vehicle pulled up to the house so fast the driver had to stomp on the brakes to come to a stop. Bright headlights shined into the dope house's front window. Mike saw that the car wasn't even in the driveway. It had come to a stop in the middle of the front yard.

Passion screamed and dove for the safety of the floor. Mike came up with his Mossberg. Spider leaned back in the loveseat and pointed his piece in the general direction of the front door. He held the gun with both hands, which was good, because he was squinting so hard, Mike knew he wasn't even looking at his target.

The front door was locked.

Mike expected a shoulder or a heavy foot to smash through. Instead he heard voices he recognized. He heard a key scraping around the lock.

"Don't shoot!" Mike yelled to Spider just as the door flew open and crashed hard into the wall behind it.

The whore screamed again.

Spider opened his eyes and saw that it was Shaun in the doorway. Killa Karl was right behind him. Shaun did not look happy at all. His eyes were wild, and his face was stained with what Mike would have guessed were tears if he didn't know his OG better. His chest rose and fell with the intensity of a heart attack.

Killa Karl was angry too, but there was something else in his eyes. Something like *delight*.

Mike checked his weapon, but Spider took too long to do the same. Shaun stepped forward and slapped the gun from the kid's hands.

"Don't point that goddamned shit at me!"

Spider kept his empty hands up to ward off any blows coming his way. He cowered in the chair.

Shaun moved past him and approached Mike. Killa Karl stepped between Spider's legs and sneered at him. Passion tried to blend in to the carpet.

"Put that shit down," Shaun said to Mike.

Mike didn't know what to do. He was short on his money for the night, but that was because it had been so slow. He only tricked off two pills with the bitch. He hesitated in lowering the weapon.

Shaun swung with a left so quick, Mike didn't even see his shoulder move. He had never been struck by his OG. His head whipped to the side from the force of the blow, and the Mossberg fell between his legs. Mike fell sideways on the couch and began to fade out. He could see nothing but gray sprinkled with pink dots. He shook it off quickly enough to block Shaun's next strike with his forearm.

"You got my mama's house shot up!" Shaun yelled.

"Wha-what?" Mike was having a hard time understanding things. His brain was dizzy from the punch in the jaw, but fear pumped enough adrenaline to keep his eyes open.

"What you doing? What's wrong?" he pleaded.

"My *mama*, nigga!" Shaun growled. He enunciated the last word with a solid thump to Mike's skull. "My *mama's* house! Them niggas shot up my mama's house 'cause of yo dumb ass!"

"Wha? *When?*" Mike stalled.

He didn't think Shaun's fit of rage could get any worse, but it did. A new look took over his face. "What, you think it's funny?"

Mike had no idea what he was talking about. He didn't think he was smiling, but he couldn't be sure what expression his face was making. He couldn't feel anything on the right side, where the two blows had landed.

Shaun reached under his Polo and pulled out a .38. He shoved the pistol in Mike's face.

COLORED RAGS

"What he doing?" Spider cried.

Killa Karl cut off his noise with a mean blow to the choppers. "Shut up, nigga."

Karl was twice his size. Spider cowered and began to cry.

Passion took that as her cue to vacate the premises. With nothing on but her panties, she stood and headed for the door. Shaun either didn't notice her or didn't care about her leaving.

Mike pleaded with his mentor, *"Don't do it, Blood! Don't do it!"*

Before the whore could make it out, Mike saw a figure appear in the open doorway and block her path. The new arrival belonged to the blue side. Mike was sure of this, even though the man was wearing all black. He had seven cornrows braided tightly. His skin was dark, his face emotionless. He held a Tec-9 with a banana clip. Mike knew this was the second, and now *only* leader of the fagg land crabs.

"Which one of y'all niggas is Mike?" Kody asked. He didn't raise his voice, but his words were enough to shut. down. everything.

Killa Karl stood over Spider with his back to the crab. If Karl had a weapon, it wasn't in his hand. Shaun had his back to the intruder. Mike had no doubt that, if given time, Shaun would have given him up to the grim reaper. But Kody left no time for a response to his question.

A loud **BOOM!** sent Passion's spleen flying out of her back. She hit the floor promptly. Four more shots went in the direction of Karl and Spider.

BLAK!BLAK!BLAK!BLAK!

With the screams of his comrades in his ears, Shaun began to spin around with the .38. But Kody already had the Tec pointed at him. Mike heard five more shots but only felt one. His shoulder was suddenly on fire, and Shaun was no longer standing before him.

Mike cried out as he fought through the pain. Through bloodshot eyes, he saw that Kody was leaving. He couldn't believe his fortune. The fool didn't even finish the job. Mike didn't have time to assess the damage before the entire house was rocked by the sounds of what had to be a million bullets plowing through the wood, chipping off concrete and shattering windows.

Mike didn't know what was happening, but he knew there were a lot of guns outside, and all of them were pointed at the house. All of the bullets were coming into the house. Debris flew in all directions. Something like a bee stung his left ear. He dove to the floor, towards his shotgun, and landed on a body he knew was Shaun's. The body was wet, but it let out an *"Uhn!"* so Mike knew he was still alive.

Mike didn't try to scramble for his weapon. He knew he wouldn't make it. The noise was enormous. There were loud booms, small cracks and the rapid fire of automatic weaponry. Something heavy fell onto Mike's back, and his shoulder exploded with the worst pain he'd ever felt in his life.

He vaguely heard the gunshots slowing to sporadic pops and then ending altogether as his world faded into a lovely darkness. Mike had never known mercy that was as beautiful as succumbing to sleep.

COLORED RAGS

CHAPTER ELEVEN
BOOTY CALL

Tec-9
You are my Tec-9
You make my foes bleeed
With your quick spraaay
I love to hold yooou
I love to shoot yooou
Don't take my Tec-9 awaaay

    Chris stopped at an intersection less than ten blocks from home and answered his cellphone. "Hello?"
"Hello?" a female voice said.
"Who's this?"
"I can barely hear you."
"Hold on a sec..." Chris turned his radio down. "Can you hear me now?"
"Yeah. Is this Chris?"
"Yeah. Who's this?"
"This Tracy. What other females be calling you?"
Chris figured she was kidding, but he wasn't turned off by the hint of jealousy.
"I'm just playing," she said. "What you doing? You on the road?"
"Just left my brother and them. I'm on my way home."
"Oh. You tired? Finna go to sleep?"
It was only a little after ten. "No. I'm not going to sleep. Why? What's up?"
"You wanna meet me somewhere?"
"Yeah." Chris caught himself, hoping he didn't sound too eager. "I mean, I guess. Where you at?"

"I'm headed towards Miller. You wanna get a room?" She asked as if it was the most casual thing in the world for a first date.

The interior of Chris' Plymouth began to heat up. He didn't want to get ahead of himself, but he was pretty sure she didn't want to meet at a motel so they could play Gin rummy. He couldn't believe his luck. No wining. No dining. He had never even taken her to the movies, but Tracy was ready to get it on.

"Hellooo?" she said.

"Uh, yeah. I'm here."

"I scare you?"

"What?"

"You heard me."

"Naw. I ain't scared," he lied.

In Chris' two previous sexual encounters, both tramps received him easily enough, but they appeared bored with his performance. His ejaculations had come in less than two minutes, which put a smile on his face, but also left him feeling inadequate. The fact that he got drowned in both of those well-used vaginas didn't help any. He was worried that Tracy would decide he wasn't up to par.

"So, you wanna go?" she asked.

"Yes," he said, despite his misgivings. "Yes, I do."

She laughed at his response. Chris thought she had the sweetest giggles. He felt like they had a real connection. His rational side labeled her a ho, but he was reluctant to call her that, just because she wanted to meet at a motel.

"You know where the Sunset is?" she asked.

"No. I don't think so."

"It's on Miller. You know where *Miller* is?"

He felt slighted, like she was checking his hood pedigree. "Yeah I know where Miller is. Everybody knows where Miller is."

"It's right there at Miller and Berry."

Chris thought for a second. He'd been by that intersection many times but never saw a motel. But then again, motels only stand out if you're looking for them.

"I know where that is."

"Well, I'm right over here by it," Tracy said. "I can get the room and wait for you to get here, if you want. I'll pay for it."

Chris didn't think that was very chivalrous, but he wasn't going to haggle over the details. Apparently he was going to *get*

COLORED RAGS

some, and getting some was a necessity. Getting some was more important than food and water.

"Alright."

"Okay," she said. "I'll see you when you get here."

Chris almost hung up before asking, "Wait. You still there?"

"Yeah," Tracy said. "You change your mind?"

"No. How will I know what room you're in?"

"I'll text you the room number. You got some condoms?"

"Huh?"

Tracy hummed, and the connection ended.

Chris placed his phone on the passenger seat with a huge grin on his face. He stopped at 7-11 and picked up a box of Trojans. The cashier smirked at him. He didn't know if she found his booty call amusing or if it was his bloodshot eyes that got her attention. He didn't care one way or another.

By the time he got back to his car, he had a text from Tracy. The message registered only one digit.

8

● ● ● ● ● ●

Though the purple Mustang Tracy drove to Jason's house was parked directly in front of room number eight, Chris still knocked rather than barge in. Tracy opened the door almost immediately. She wore the same outfit she had on earlier that day, except now she had on flats rather than heels. Without the heels, she was shorter than Chris remembered. She looked up and smiled at him with bright eyes that seemed to glisten. Chris was starting to think she was beautiful.

"You coming in?" she asked, "or you wanna stand out there?"

"I'm coming," he said as he crossed the threshold. "I've never been in a motel before," he confessed.

Tracy nodded. "That's good. You don't seem like the kind of guy that would be in a place like this."

The inside of the room was pretty much what Chris had expected. There was only one living area and not much furniture. The only thing that truly mattered was the bed, which was king-size and took up most of the space. There was a closed door in one corner, which he assumed housed the restroom. This wasn't the type of place for someone to live with their family. Even a single, working man wouldn't feel comfortable there for more than a week or two.

The room had a nice television that was turned on. Tracy had set it to a channel that played old school R&B tunes. Chris thought the room's dim lighting would hide his *condition*, but the light proved to be sufficient enough. Tracy pulled him close to her, but it wasn't for the hug or kiss he wanted. A confused expression marred her features. When Chris realized she was looking at his eyes, he knew what the problem was, but he played dumb.

"What?"

Tracy gave him a knowing nod and then said, "You high."

"No, I'm just..." He tried to make light of it by sniffling and rubbing his nose. "It's my allergies," he said and laughed.

Tracy didn't find much humor in that. She backed away and sat on the bed with her arms crossed over her stomach. She looked up at him with clear disappointment.

"Jason didn't tell me you get high."

Chris was surprised by her response. He couldn't tell if she was seriously upset or just giving him a hard time. "I usually don't," he offered.

"What *else* you do?" she asked, as if he might have some cannibalism hidden in his resume.

"Nothing." He gave her a serious look. "I only smoked weed like, three times. I don't get high all the time or nothing. For real. When I go over there sometimes I... Can I sit down?"

"Yeah," Tracy said, "over *there*." She directed him to a spot on the bed that was far away from her.

Chris took a seat and gave her a hound dog expression. "You mad at me for real?"

She didn't respond. In the background the lead singer of Midnight Star asked the DJ to play another slow jam, but this time make it sweet. When that song went off, Rick James and Teena Marie crooned about their fire and desire. Chris wondered if they were going to sit there and listen to music in silence, but Tracy finally turned and looked at him.

"I don't wanna be with no thug."

He stared into her eyes and saw that she was being serious, open and honest.

COLORED RAGS

"I'm not a thug. Anybody at my high school will tell you that."

"If I wanted to be with a thug," she continued, "I could've stayed in Stop Six and got with one of them niggas. I used to hang with them. I used to smoke weed and stay out all night, getting high. I don't wanna do that no more. I stopped doing that."

Chris was taken aback. He hadn't expected any profound revelations from Tracy – especially after she invited him to a motel room. "I'm not a thug," he insisted.

"Yeah, I heard you. You just like to get high sometimes. And you had them shoestrings earlier. And you always hanging on the south side. You gon' end up just like them niggas you hanging around. Watch."

"If you're so against all that stuff, why you ask me to come here?"

Chris regretted the words as soon as they left his mouth. He knew she'd be offended. There was no way she could present herself as changed and sanctified and give him some at the same time. But Tracy surprised him by smiling.

"You ever watch old TV shows on Netflix?"

He frowned. "Old like what, *Happy Days*?"

She laughed. She turned to face him and sat Indian style on the bed. "No, not that old. I've been watching this show called *Dharma and Greg*. Have you ever heard of it?"

"Yeah. I think so. Is that the one with the guy who's all professional, but his girlfriend is weird? She tries to get him to stand on the couch and stuff like that."

"Yeah," Tracy said. Her smile brightened. "That's it. You know what it's about?"

"They have opposite personalities?" Chris guessed.

"It's about this man and woman who meet each other for the first time," Tracy said. "They went on *one* date and then decided to get married." She grinned. "They got married the same day, and they have to spend the rest of their lives getting to know each other. They always find out stuff about each other that's new, and they have a lot of fun. They really love each other."

Chris thought that was a silly premise for a TV show. He wondered why Tracy had brought it up, and then it struck him. She believed in fairy tales. Maybe she thought they were similar to

Dharma and Greg. He liked that idea. He liked how her eyes lit up as she told him about the program.

They talked for more than an hour. Chris told her about his life, his brother, and his aspirations. Tracy told him about her family, her let downs, and her fears. Somewhere in the conversation, Chris told her he wrote poetry and had won a lot of writing awards in high school. Tracy asked him if he could recite a love poem for her – but not one he wrote for another girl. Chris recited a sonnet he'd written for his senior English class. Tracy hung on every word.

When he finished the poem, Teddy Pendergrass was playing on the R&B station. Chris was unsure exactly when they began kissing, but he was delighted with the way their lips and tongues danced. He touched her, but not aggressively. She hummed when his fingers slipped between her legs. He took a deep breath when she enticed his manhood from his pants and applied one of the condoms.

Chris didn't know much about his sexual prowess before that night. His experience with Tracy taught him many things. For one, he did not have a small penis. She was tight around him, and Tracy made it clear that he was pleasing her. He also learned that premature ejaculations did not necessarily spoil the encounter. After he washed up and dove in again, he lasted twenty minutes before he came. The third time he made it thirty minutes before Tracy got on top and did something with her hips that made him lose it again.

Rather than fall asleep, they took a shower together then lay in each other's arms and spooned and talked. Around two in the morning, Chris told her he had to be home before his mother got off work. Tracy was in the same boat. She said her father would be upset if dawn should come without her gracing her own bed. She told Chris he should meet her father. He thought it would be cool if she met his mother.

Although it began to rain, Chris saw nothing but pretty skies during his drive home. He was still smiling when he crawled into bed and drifted off to sleep.

COLORED RAGS

CHAPTER TWELVE
DEAD AND GRINNING

And when my mind is weak, it seems
The dead man lurks within my dreams
He finds my sleep and pulls me out
He smiles with his decaying mouth
He holds me with his cold, dead hands
And pulls me towards the shadowed man
I fight and sweat until I'm soaked
I awake with screams that tear my throat

You know you fucked up, don't you?
You hear me, nigga?
Yeah. You hear me.
Turn yo bitch ass over!
    Mike would not roll over to face the voice that taunted him. Face down in what was left of Shaun's boy/girl house, he tasted the bitter sting of defeat. He tasted filth and carpet, blood and smoke.
    Sick demons knelt beside him and whispered evil things. The beasts were hot and bleeding. Their breath smelled like maggoty road kill. One sounded like he was speaking through a wet hole in his trachea. Mike heard the high-pitched whining of flat lines skating on EKG monitors. All of the sounds were jumbled and overwhelming. He couldn't understand what they were trying to tell him.
    *You gotta get up. Don't you wanna get up? Don't you wanna **be** up?*
Hear it? You finna be it.
Why is it? Why is it now?!
Mister?

Ahh!
Don't you see? Do you feel it?
Now?

Mike buried his face deep in the shag carpet and squeezed his eyes shut. His body trembled uncontrollably. There were creeping things about him. He could feel them touching, scratching him. They breathed on him and tugged with hands that were small, sharp and cold. He tried to force the voices from his mind, and he could, for the most part. But one was persistent. *Familiar*. One required his attention more fiercely than the others.

Get yo bitch ass up, cuz! See this shit, nigga. You gotta see this!

Mike growled at that voice. That was the voice of his enemy. He shook his head, rubbing his face in the floor. He mumbled something like, *Get away from me*, but he didn't think the words made it past his lips.

My niggas took care of this shit. You see this here? My niggas went to work on y'all slob-ass niggas! Look at yo boy over here. Look at him! Y'all supposed to be best friends, right. This yo homeboy, ain't it? Look at 'em, Mikey! Look at yo boy!

Mike fought the compulsion to glance where the demon wanted him to. He squeezed his eye closed even tighter. He knew that if he didn't look, then it didn't have to be. Hot tears forced their way past his eyelids. His breaths on the carpet were hot and moist. His face contorted in a scowl that bled pain.

Look at it! C'mon, Mike. You supposed to be hardcore, right? You trying to get you some rank, ain't ya? Check game: A real motherfucking G ain't finna be lying there crying. A real G will stand tall. You hear me, bitch-nigga? You hear me?!

It was hard not to roll over and face his tormentor, but Mike knew all too well what he would see. OG Will would be hovering over him, dead and grinning. His black face would be knotted in anger, but he'd be smiling. His teeth would be glazed with blood, and some of it would drip on Mike's face.

Rationale told him that OG Will was gone. The most the dead crab could do was taunt him in his dreams. Mike had only to open his eyes to vanquish his demons. *But what if he was wrong?* What if he opened his eyes and Will *was* there; bold and angry and whole? He knew that he would go crazy if he saw that.

COLORED RAGS

When the voice spoke again, it was much closer. It was so close, Mike could feel dead breath on his neck. He felt a hand on his back. He shrank away from it, but it followed. It caressed him. His heart raced.

*Say, I know what you thinking, lil nigga. You think I'm dead, right? That's why you don't wanna see me. You don't wanna see none of this shit. You know Spider dead, and you **definitely** don't wanna see that.*

I can't fault you though, cuz. Shit, if I got my lil homey wet up, I wouldn't want to face up to it either. What about that bitch, though? You shoulda got her outta here a long time ago. You knew what was gon' happen. Wasn't no customers on a Friday night? Come on, Mikey. You knew what that was. Maybe you cool with Karl and Shaun getting it, but them other two, that's gotta be fucking with yo head.

Mike felt tears squirting from his eyes. The gremlin could see into his very soul. The dead hand inched towards his wound, and there was comfort in his touch. Even still, Mike reached to stop him, but he couldn't move his arms. He felt panic rising from deep in his chest.

But you gotta understand something, cuz. You think my niggas blew this motherfucker up and let you live? You think you got a green light to pass through this? Is that what you think? Bad news, bruh. It's only one reason why you can hear me. You can feel me too, right? It's only one reason for that. You know what it is, don't you?

Mike felt spittle sprinkle the back of his neck. Or maybe it was blood. His heart thundered. He had no answers for his tormentor, so the creep provided one.

You can feel me 'cause you with me, nigga. You right here with me. And ain't no pearly gates around this motherfucker. You wanna lay there and act like this ain't happening? You think you ain't gotta see this shit? Fuck that, cuz!

The demon's hand snaked across Mike's back and found his exit wound. A rough finger, calloused from hard living and street fighting, thrust into the bloody hole. The pain was immediate and searing. White hot light flashed in Mike's skull, and he screamed bloody murder. Will laughed. He laughed and laughed. All of the other dead things were excited now. They all laughed with him.

● ● ● ● ● ●

    Mike's eyes flashed open. His chest rose and fell as if he'd been sprinting. Will's laughter faded and was replaced by the sound of his own blood rushing past his ears. He heard thunder and rain, the rhythmic beep of electronic devices.

    Everything was bright now. Too bright. He squinted, wanting to see, but unable to. There was sweat in his eyes. Beyond the natural sounds of the thunderstorm and the beeps that he prayed was hospital equipment, Mike still heard a ghoulish whisper. It was raspy and wet.

    You with me, nigga. You right here with me.

    As his eyes adjusted to the light, Mike reached to wipe his face. But his arm came to a sudden and painful stop before he managed a few inches. He immediately recognized the sting of a handcuff digging into his skin. All of his other limbs were similarly immobilized.

    "Man, what the..."

    By then the brightness had reached a more comfortable level, and he saw the hospital room. He tried to sit up, and an incredible pain exploded from his shoulder. Electric fire shot all the way down his back, all the way to his fingers and toes. From beneath him, a rough, black finger invaded the hole in his back. Mike felt blood rolling down his chest. His stomach was wet. His whole body was.

    Nigga, you know what this is.

    He screamed. He fought to free his arms, knowing the handcuffs wouldn't give. He could see the metal bracelets now. He could see the restraints on his ankles. The only part of his body with any mobility was his hips, so he thrashed about wildly. Each movement made the pain worse, but he fought just the same.

    Another peal of thunder erupted beyond the window. A quick sliver of lightening shrieked by like muted gunfire.

    "*Help! Somebody get me out of here! Get him off me*! Get him off!"

    "What the hell's going on?" A security guard stormed into the room. He fixed a mean glare on Mike, who couldn't believe *he* was the one upset about this predicament.

COLORED RAGS

"What you mean what's going on?" Mike glared at him. "Why you got me handcuffed to this bed? *Get these things off me!*"

"Calm down," the guard said as he approached the bed.

A woman entered the room behind him. She was young, in her early twenties. She wore teal-colored scrubs. She took one look at her patient, and her eyes registered what Mike already knew: He looked like he'd been to hell and back.

Actually, Katie's first thought was *Why do I always get the biggest messes?* You couldn't even trust a shot-up gangbanger to be an easy patient these days. Mike had somehow thrown all of his sheets to the floor. He was sweating and snotting and slobbering all over the place. And from the looks of the blood staining his gown, he had opened his fresh wound.

"Everything's okay, Michael," she told him. "Do you know where you are?"

"Yeah, I know where I'm at!" He felt embarrassed now, in pain and indignant.

"You need to calm down," the guard repeated. He took a step forward, putting himself between the patient and the tech. He hooked this thumbs on his belt, but he didn't have a gun. Mike was cool with the girl, but he didn't like any representation of the law. He and Barney Fife were not going to get along.

"*Quit telling me to calm down!*" he shouted. "How you think I'm supposed to act? I got shot and woke up in this motherfucker, and y'all got me handcuffed to the bed, like *I* did something wrong! What I'm under arrest for? Why y'all got me in cuffs?"

By then a whole group of nurses and techs had crowded his doorway. This was great entertainment for the graveyard shift. Only one of them stepped inside the room. Her scrubs were royal blue. She had dark skin and big lips. She was chubby in all the right places. Mike liked her on sight.

"You're not under arrest," the guard told him. "The police have detained you, until the detective has a chance to talk to you about what happened. They didn't want you to wake up and take off."

"Man, that's some *bullshit!*" Mike sneered at him. "Somebody get shot, you don't put handcuffs on 'em! You can't tell me this is right. You ain't finna have me believing that." At that point, most of his bravado was for the thick nurse. Truth be told, he was glad to be safe in a hospital bed, glad to be out of the darkness, away from the dead things.

"Tell you what," the guard said. "When you decide you want to calm down and act right, I'll call Detective Stevens and let him know you're awake. Till then, you can stay handcuffed to that bed until next week, for all I care."

The man folded his arms and stared down at Mike with an *I dare you* look in his eyes. He had a huge moustache that covered most of his upper lip. He was stocky and not one bit worried about the skinny punk in the bed.

"Nigga—"

"Hush now," Nurse Thickums told Mike as she approached the bed. The guard reached to stop her, but she shooed his hand away. "You know you need to be quiet," she said to Mike. She put her hands on her full hips and stared down at him like his Mama used to do, back when she was still trying to be a Mama.

Mike gave her a condescending look, but he relaxed on the mattress. "Whatever. You know they wrong."

"I don't got nothing to do with that," Thickums said.

Up close, Mike saw that her name was *Anita*, according to her badge. But he preferred to call her Thickums. Nurse Thickums with the DSLs (dick sucking lips).

"All I know is you're my patient," she said. "And me and Katie have a whole lot of work to do to get you cleaned up. Carl's not gonna let us touch you, until you start acting right. So you can lay there all nasty and stay handcuffed to the bed. Or you can act like you got some sense, and everything will go a lot easier for you." She smiled, and all of the fight left him.

"Alright," he told her. He turned and glared at the guard. "Fine. Go call that man and tell him I'm awake. I'ma be good."

"Hmph." Carl grinned. "*Go call that man*? You don't tell me what to do."

Mike's nostril's flared. He locked eyes with Nurse Thickums and sighed. "Could you please tell that detective I'm awake?" he said without looking the guard's way.

"Whatever, punk." Carl turned and strolled out of the room.

"Both of y'all childish," Thickums said with a dismissive shake of her head.

COLORED RAGS

She turned to retrieve a pair of gloves from a box mounted on the wall. Mike's eyes bulged as he watched her.
Damn! That ass!
He tried to sit up and follow it, and his body reminded him that he'd been shot. He grimaced with pain, but it was worth it. He wondered if he should throw up on himself later, so she'd have to fetch more gloves.

CHAPTER THIRTEEN
UNCLE RAY

Andre Broadnax prayed to his gods. He didn't think any god was more special than the other, so he prayed to a lot of them. He even prayed to the Hindu god with four arms.

He tried to convince himself that he could get out of going. If he remained in bed, tuned out the world, allowed his breathing to diminish to a near-hibernation state, and *truly* became one with the sheets, then maybe, *just maybe*, everyone would leave him alone and not make him go.

That was silly though. Quite ridiculous, really. His brother was dead; gunned down at an early age. Will had become another black name to add to the statistics. His *timely* passing was worthy of mourning, but OG Will was not just another dead nigga. He was the most revered gangsta the south side had ever known. He was a martyr.

He was *God* to some of his followers. They stood in awe. They sang his praises and magnified his name.

He was crucified.

Dre knew there was no question of whether he would go to Will's wake or not. If no one else was there, he would be.

● ● ● ● ● ●

A good number of the thugs who got wet up in the war they waged on the streets of Overbrook Meadows left their loved ones in financial despair. Their mothers, the mothers of their children, and their brothers had to scrimp, beg and borrow for cheap caskets to bury the young soldiers. It wasn't at all uncommon for

COLORED RAGS

these boys to spend more than ten days in the funeral home awaiting a proper burial. William Broadnax was not in that category.

OG Will sold a lot of crack. And while that may not guarantee riches, sometimes it's not how much crack you sell, but who you sell it to. Will had a special customer named Otis, who would never show his face in the hood. Will only met him once a month, and he would never discuss the transactions with the homies. Dre only knew about it because Will made him ride shotgun on some of the drop offs.

Otis was a dark-skin gentleman with a large gap between his front teeth. He didn't look special. He didn't look like a crackhead. Dre noticed Otis never seemed to hand Will any money in exchange for the dope he got. Will disclosed that he stopped charging Otis for the dope a long time ago.

"How come?" Dre had asked.

"Don't worry about all that," Will had told him. "Just know that when my number comes up, I'll be good."

It turned out he was right about that. Pinkey's Funeral Home, owned and operated by none other than Otis Pinkey, was prepared to present a wake for OG Will just two days after his passing.

The wake would no doubt be a happening event. Gangstas from all over the metroplex would be there. Dressed in blue, they would sport tee-shirts with the dead man's picture on it. Many of the women loved and scorned by the strapping OG would show up, with their hair and nails done. Their cries of misery would be gut-wrenching.

The homies would file by the casket one by one to pay their respects. They would drape blue handkerchiefs on the coffin. Some would leave bullets, promising Will that someone had paid, and there was still more paying to come.

These gangstas would approach Will's mother and express sympathy for her loss. They would tell her *Will ain't never hurt nobody,* and *He didn't deserve to die like that. If there's anything you need, let me know...*

They would then look at Dre and, what?

Dre wasn't imaginative. He didn't have the creativity it takes to, say, write a decent poem or create something lovely out of clay. But he didn't need much creativity to imagine the drama his presence at the wake would incite.

Those goons would be on edge. They would be fresh from retaliatory driveys on the ones who took the life of their friend, their teacher, their leader. They would be drunk and high.

They would not look upon Dre as the little brother of OG Will, the last of his masculine bloodline. They would see Dre and be reminded of his betrayal. They would think about how he sat in his brother's car and watched the murder without even offering a warning. They would know Dre was a ho, and some would ask if he actually *wanted* his brother dead.

They would fuck him up good.

Funeral parlor or not. Will's mother sitting right there or not. They would twist his motherfucking cap back. Dre knew this definitively, just as he knew his big brother was in hell.

● ● ● ● ● ●

The bedroom door swung open, introducing light, the smell of biscuits, and the faint sound of gospel music into Dre's room. Too late to pull the sheets over his head, he relied on keeping his eyes closed to dispel any interest the visitor may have in him. The guest was no doubt his mother, and she was the last person Dre wanted to talk to.

Since Will's death, Esther had been like half a person. She stopped by Dre's bedroom a few times a day but never pressed him to talk. She didn't urge him to get out of bed to eat or bathe. Sometimes she sat on the corner of the bed and stroked his hair as he feigned sleep. She brought food and retrieved dishes. Mostly she just stood in the doorway swaying slightly; her tears leaking like blood from a wound. She said little, but her silence spoke volumes.

Dre was starting to think his mother was more dead than alive. Her eyes were like a zombie's. She wore the stink of menthol cigarettes and body odor. The part of her that used to laugh and smile died in the same hail of lead that took her first born.

A squeak on the floor was Dre's first indication that the person in his room was not his mother. Esther was a thin woman, even more emaciated than usual as of late. There was only one

COLORED RAGS

person in Dre's family heavy enough to make the floors buckle under his weight.

Uncle Ray was three-hundred and seventy pounds of terror. He was obese, but there were a lot of muscles coiled under that flab. Twenty-five years in the Texas Department of Corrections had taken away anything lovable about the man. He was a lot more of a menace today than he was when a jury gave him a 40 year sentence for murder at the age of nineteen.

In the three years since his release, Dre's uncle had been staying with them. Uncle Ray loved his sister more than anything in the world. Esther was the only person to write and visit him on a regular basis throughout his stretch, and he never forgot that. Next to Esther, everyone knew Ray's next favorite person was her first born son. Will reminded Ray of himself. Ray may have loved Dre too, but if so, Dre imagined it was only because of association.

Dre listened to his uncle's heavy breaths as the big man entered the room. The behemoth remained silent for a full minute before he spoke.

"You just gon', lay there like you, sleep?" Uncle Ray had a deep, grumbling voice, with a slow, southern drawl. He rarely made it through a sentence without needing a couple of inhalations.

Dre remained quiet. Close scrutiny would reveal his eyeballs rolling behind the lids. But he didn't think Uncle Ray would bother him if he didn't respond. Everyone should be allowed to mourn however they choose.

"You, can roll over and eat, and leave all these dishes, for yo mama. But you can't get outta bed long, long enough to see how she doing?"

Uncle Ray's mood was less than comforting. Even still, Dre had no reason to suspect violence. But then again, when it came to his family, there was always a propensity for violence.

"You hear me?"
WHAP!

A large, calloused hand slammed hard into the side of Dre's face with such force blood immediately gushed from his nose and spilled onto his pillow. His whole head was suddenly on fire.

Dre was once struck on the cheek by an errant pitch at a softball game. For ten years that was the marker by which he measured his worse smack to the face. Uncle Ray's blow made that pitch seem like a love tap.

Dre sat up quickly and stared into the eyes of a beast even his nightmares couldn't conjure. Uncle Ray was more than upset. The knot of flesh between his eyebrows pulsated. His nostrils flared. His teeth were gnashed in a fit of emotion Dre would have to describe as *murderous*.

He knew his mother was in the house somewhere. He tried to scream for her, but the large man was quick. He lunged forward and slapped a hand over the boy's mouth and shoved his face back into the pillow. Dre struggled but was not prepared for his uncle's power. Before he could counter, the giant was in bed with him, on top of him, pressing down on his torso with the weight of a Volkswagen.

"Oh, now you got something, to say?" his uncle said.

Dre was a big kid, but the ex-con was huge. Dre quit his struggles and went limp. The weight on his upper body made it nearly impossible to take a breath. His eyes bugged as his lungs burned and begged for oxygen. The hand on his mouth pressed so hard his lips tore against his own teeth. Dre's eyes darted, searching for someone to save him from this beast. But he couldn't see anything past his uncle's bald head.

It didn't appear that Uncle Ray was exerting much effort.

"I, heard what they said, about you, nigga," he told him. He stared into his nephew's terrified eyes.

Dre wondered how his uncle could have so much strength, if his lungs were so messed up. Tears blurred his vision. He fought again, with all his might, but he barely rocked the bigger man.

"You was in that car," Ray said. "You was there, and you didn't, do *nothing*. You *let* them niggas kill yo brother."

Dre tried to tell him that it wasn't true, that he couldn't have done anything to stop it. But the words were mere moans as they escaped his nostrils. Precious oxygen was lost in the attempt, and he wasn't able to take in another breath. His heart kicked like a mule. He barely noticed his bowel movement.

"Yo mama, been in there crying, for *two* days. And you can't get outta bed, to see if she okay? You a *coward*, boy. You laying in here, like it's safe for you. This yo, refuge or something? This ain't shit, boy. Just like you, ain't shit.

COLORED RAGS

"Will, was a *good* boy. He did *good*, by us. You ain't, you ain't never did, nothing. I ain't *never*, liked yo ass. I'd kill you, right now if, it wasn't for yo mama."

Regardless of what the man said, Dre knew that his uncle *was* killing him. He tasted blood. His ears were ringing. The world began to swirl around him, like he just hopped off the merry-go-round.

As his eyes rolled back in his head, the weight lifted from his chest. He opened his mouth, and oxygen flooded his lungs. He coughed it out and managed to keep the next breath down. His uncle's murderous face slowly came back into focus. Ray was saying something, but Dre only caught the end of it.

"... scream, I'ma hurt you bad, right here."

With that, the monster left his bed. Uncle Ray stood and looked down on him with disgust.

"You is gon', get outta this bed, and check on yo mama. And you, you *going* to the wake," Uncle Ray ordered. "You gon', look all them niggas, in the face. You gon', look yo brother, in his face too. And you gon' tell him, you *sorry*. If you don't..."

The big man turned and left the room without saying what Dre's consequence would be.

● ● ● ● ● ●

Dre held his nose closed for three minutes, and it finally stopped bleeding. He remained in bed for another ten minutes after his uncle's departure. The feel and smell of his own cooling feces finally compelled him to get up and bathe for the first time in two days.

CHAPTER FOURTEEN
POLICE ALL IN THE MIX

*Please hold me up, so I can see
This fabled human with black skin
Don't push or shove, for you might fall
Step right up! Come one, come all
To see the last man with black skin*

*Please hold me up so I can see
The fabled man who smoked the crack
Who fiended for the smallest rock
Who murdered for the thrills he got
Sir, would you please remove your hat?*

*Take off your hat, so I can see
The fabled man who shot and killed
Who wrote dead names on vacant walls
Who shot every black man he saw
Gosh, I've never known such thrills!
Please hold me up, so I can see!*

Chris was awakened once again by his mother, but she wasn't in a good mood, like she was when she got home from work yesterday. She looked tired, and disappointed. He wondered if he'd done anything to upset her. Recollections of Kody's ultimate solution to his marijuana problem came to mind.

I'ma tell Mama.

"You didn't hear the phone ringing?" she asked.

Chris wiped his eyes and saw that his mother was wearing a nightgown and slippers, which meant she'd been home for a while. The phone awakened her but not Chris.

COLORED RAGS

"No," he said. "I'm sorry. I was sleep."

"I know you was sleep. Why you sleeping so late? You usually up by now."

"I didn't go to bed till, like three." He caught himself after he said it.

"Why you go to sleep so late? What was you doing last night?"

"I was with Jason." The lie came easily. Chris didn't think his mother would be too upset to learn that he spent the evening with an enchantress, but the subject had never come up. He wasn't sure how she would respond.

"He got this new game, and we was playing," he said, elaborating on his lie. "I didn't know what time it was. When I looked up, it was going on three."

Theresa believed him easily enough. "Your brother's on the phone."

That was odd. Kody knew his cellphone number. "On the house phone?"

"Yeah." His mother turned and walked out of the room. "He in jail again."

Chris' heart sank. Kody had been to jail six times in the last four years. His crimes included assault, possession of a controlled substance and evading arrest. He'd been lucky to avoid prison thus far, but Chris felt uneasy about this one. The last time he saw Kody, he was hell-bent on retaliation. He was usually careful in crime, but revenge made men cocky and reckless.

Chris found the cordless phone and shouted, "I got it!" to his mother. He heard her hang up the other end as he put the receiver to his ear.

"Hello?"

"What you doing? You still sleep?" Kody's voice sounded far away, even though the county jail was no more than twenty miles from their house.

"I was finna get up." Chris checked the clock and saw that it was after noon. "What happened?"

"*Maaan*," Kody said. He always began his spiels about how the system was railroading him with that word. *Maaan*. "These hoes got me jacked up on some *bullshit*." That was another thing Kody was known for; referring to his current charges as "*some bullshit*."

"What happened?" Chris asked again.

"They trying to say I killed somebody."

Chris felt something hard and heavy sink in his stomach. His eyes filled with tears. The worst part about it was this news wasn't even shocking.

"I didn't do nothing, though, cuz," Kody said. "They pulled us over just 'cause we was on that side of town when some shit went down. They ain't got nothing on us, though. They tried to get me to confess. Can you believe that shit?"

Chris' heart shuddered. He knew the calls from jail were recorded, so he played dumb as well. "Why they think it was y'all?"

"They say they saw us throwing guns out the window when they got behind us. But them wasn't our guns, Chris. Ain't no fingerprints on them. Anybody coulda threw 'em."

Chris thought Kody, in all his infinite wisdom, was divulging too much information. If the police did listen to this conversation, they might want to know how Kody knew there were no fingerprints on the weapons.

"So, what you gon' do?" he asked.

"I need you to go to the apartment for me. This is *real important*, Chris. In the closet in my bedroom, I got this jacket. It's a Dockers jacket. You remember that one I use to wear when I was still living with y'all? The gray one?"

Chris remembered the coat. He hadn't seen it in so long, he didn't know it was still around.

"Which bedroom?"

"The one across from the restroom. I need you to get that jacket, bro. I know ain't nobody fucked with it, 'cause it's ugly. Plus it ain't cold. But once they figure I ain't getting out, they'll start going through my shit. I got some money in there. I need it."

"In the jacket?"

"Yeah. It got this inside pocket, but the pocket done wore out. It's a hole in the bottom of it. Everything just falls through to the middle of the coat. I put some money in there. I need it."

Chris' eyes widened. "How much?"

"It's $200. I need that."

Chris knew his brother didn't need $200, which meant there was more than $200 in the coat. Kody was being careful about the call being recorded. Chris wondered how much it really was. $2,000? $20,000?

"Get it for me today, Chris. Niggas know I'm in jail. They gon' start going through my shit."

Chris had several questions about the money, but he didn't want to bring any more attention to it. The cops weren't stupid. They may make it there before he did.

"Alright. I'ma go now." Chris wondered what the apartments would be like today. With OG Will dead and Kody locked up, the gang was without a leader. There might be some infighting before the next OG was chosen.

"I'ma call you later to make sure you got it."

"Alright."

There was a pause, and then Kody asked, "What Mama say about me?"

"She didn't say nothing. She just told me you were on the phone."

"She look mad?"

"No, not really mad. She was..." Chris didn't want to put any additional pressure on his brother. "She looked like, just tired, I guess."

Kody breathed into the phone and then said, "Go do that for me."

"Alright."

Chris hung up and showered. He caught himself pacing the floor as he dressed. He didn't think he would have free range of Kody's bedroom at the Evergreen. He never looked in his brother's closet when Kody was there. The move would definitely rouse suspicion. Even if he was able to find the money, he still had to make it back to his car with it. It was times like this when he wished he had a gun.

● ● ● ● ● ●

Detective Stevens wanted to have an understanding from the beginning: This was not the movies. This was no good cop/bad cop scenario. There was only him, and if Mike jerked him around, he was the bad cop.

He sat across from the juvenile with his legs crossed. He wore a white button-down with slacks. There was a gold badge hooked on his belt and a large pistol holstered on his hip. His eyes were charcoal gray. Mike noticed that his teeth were perfectly aligned.

The detective brought Manning to the hospital with him. He was Mike's mother's boyfriend. Mike's mother wasn't home when the cop stopped by, but Manning represented himself as Mike's guardian and said he'd give consent for their little talk.

Manning sat in the corner and didn't speak. Mike didn't know why his mom was going with the guy. Manning was ignorant and scummy and didn't even clean himself up for the trip. He had the unmistakable air of a dopefiend. Mike's mom abused as many drugs as her boyfriend, but that didn't matter. Mike loved his mom. He couldn't stand Manning.

"He can't sign nothing for me," Mike balked. "He ain't my daddy."

Manning sighed. "I told you he was gon' say that."

The detective was unmoved. "This man has been living at your house for more than a year, Mike. That qualifies him as your guardian. I tried to bring your mother. We've been looking for her all morning..."

Mike didn't like how he said that. He felt like the cop was putting his mom down. "Where my mama at?" he asked Manning.

"Man, your guess is as good as mine," the addict said. *Man, you know your mama's a ho*, his tone said. *I can't keep tabs on that bitch.*

Mike seethed. Even if his mother was unpredictable, that didn't give the police the right to bring her boyfriend. They were trying to railroad him. Manning didn't have sense enough to know he was being used.

"Ain't I supposed to have a lawyer?" Mike asked defiantly. He tried not to move too much, despite his anxiety. The doctors told him he was lucky that his gunshot had gone completely through, but the pain didn't make him feel lucky.

To his chagrin, the detective smiled. "You want a lawyer? I got no problem with that. Who do you want me to call? I'll get him down here."

"You said one could be provided for me, if I couldn't afford one."

COLORED RAGS

"Yes, that's the law. But that's only *after* you've been charged with a crime. We haven't charged you with anything, Mike."

"Yeah, that's why I got handcuffs on."

"You're being detained. That's not the same as under arrest." The detective was patient with him. Patient like a funnel-web spider. Mike didn't trust any cops, but he knew to be particularly wary of this one.

"If I talk to you, I can leave? You'll take these cuffs off?"

"When you leave the hospital is up to your doctors," the cop said. "But I won't detain you any longer after we're done talking."

Mike thought the cop was lying about letting him go, so he didn't have anything to lose. Maybe he could find out if they were on to him for the OG Will murder. He knew he was smart enough to avoid saying anything that would be incriminating.

"Okay. What you wanna know?"

Stevens produced a recording device and placed it on Mike's mattress. He read him his rights again and asked Manning if he consented to the questioning. Manning said he did. With that done, they got down to business.

"Do you know a man named Shaun Simmons?"

A curveball right off the bat. "Yeah," Mike said. Cops love it when you elaborate, so he didn't.

"Who is he to you?"

"He my homey."

"Is he the leader of a gang?"

"I don't know."

"Are you in a gang?"

Mike had the name of his set tattooed on his arm. Plus Overbrook Meadows' gang unit had a file on him since he was thirteen.

"Yeah."

"What's the name of your gang?"

"The Tate Street Bloods."

"And what do the Tate Street Bloods do?" the officer asked.

"I don't know. What do any gangs do?"

"Do you sell drugs?"

"What? You mean *me*?" This was one of the traps Mike was waiting for.

118

"No, not necessarily *you*. I mean you as a gang. Does your gang sell drugs?"

"Some of 'em prolly do. I don't know."

Detective Stevens nodded. "Does your gang sell drugs on the corner, or do you have a crack house?"

"I don't know."

"A boy/girl house?"

"I don't know."

"Who's the leader of your gang, Mike?"

The boy didn't answer. Snitching on himself was one thing, but he'd be damned if he'd rat out his OG.

"Is Shaun the leader of your gang?"

"I don't know," Mike said. "It's a lot of them higher up than me."

"Is Shaun *higher up* than you?"

"I don't know."

The detective smiled. "Look Mike, you don't have to protect Shaun anymore. He's dead."

A hard knot formed in Mike's throat. The air grew denser. He didn't know whether to believe the man or not. He saw Shaun get shot, but shot and dead are two different things. Cops will lie about anything to get you to talk.

The detective reached between his legs and came up with a manila folder. He didn't have to fish through it for too long before finding what he wanted. He produced a color photograph and held it up for Mike to see. What Mike saw made his hospital lunch rumble all the way up to his throat. He swallowed it back down.

Shaun lie on his back on a metal table. He was completely nude. There was a large hole on the right side of his chest. There was a lot of dried blood on his body that had not been wiped away. Shaun's eyes were wide open, his mouth slack. The last time they saw each other, this man stuck a gun in Mike's face. But that was all forgiven now. Mike loved his OG and couldn't stop the tears from welling.

"I know Shaun was the leader of your gang," Detective Stevens said. "I know a lot about you and your gang. You wanna tell me who shot Shaun?"

Mike shook his head. He thought about Spider and wondered if the cop had more pictures from the morgue. The folder was filled with papers.

"You're going to have to speak, Mike. The recorder doesn't know if you're shaking your head or nodding. Do you know who killed Shaun?"

Mike's voice quavered. "No."

"You were there, weren't you?"

"Yeah."

"But you don't know who shot him?"

"No."

"Was it the same guy who shot you?"

"I don't know."

The detective nodded and returned his folder to the floor.

"What about Spider," Mike asked quietly.

"I can barely hear you, Mike."

"What about Spider?" he asked again.

"Who's Spider?"

"His name Derrick." Mike sniffled. "Derrick, uh, Lane."

"Derrick Lane," the detective mulled over the name. "Is he a member of your gang?"

"Yeah," Mike said without thinking.

"Was he with you on the south side two nights ago?"

Two nights ago? Mike knew this was another trap. He felt sweat forming on his neck and face. He was in over his head, but he didn't want to end the interview abruptly.

"He with me a lot of times," he said. "What you talking about?"

The cop stared at him for a long time without emotion. Mike was eager to break the silence, but it wasn't his turn to speak. When Stevens resumed the interview, his approach was different.

"You think you're smarter than me?"

"What, what you mean?"

"Mike, I don't know how many people *you've* killed, but I've been catching killers for a long time. Everything you've said to me so far is bullshit. Do you think I believe any of it? Do I look like an idiot to you?"

Mike looked to Manning to intervene, but the junkie sat quietly.

"I didn't kill nobody."

"Yeah, and your word means a whole lot to me. You tell me you don't know who the leader of your own gang is. That's a lie. That's a dumb lie. You don't know about any drugs. That's a lie."

Mike thought he was starting to sound like Maury Povich giving polygraph results.

"Man, you can't tell me what I know–"

"Don't get smart with me. That's your problem right there. You think you're smart enough to know what you're doing. You still think this is some kind of game. These bodies dropping, you think it's a cartoon. You know what you did, and I know what you did. And it was real stupid, Mike. *Real fucking stupid.*"

"I didn't do nothing!"

"You and Spider killed OG Will!"

"No we didn't!"

The cop didn't respond right away. He waited a few beats, while Mike's chest rose and fell with his hurried breaths.

"I know more about this than you think I do," the detective said. "I know you're a blood, and the man you shot was a crip. Everything should have been fine and dandy, as far as that goes, but you fucked up big time. Your homeboys didn't back your move. And you got your OG and a couple more homies killed.

"The rest of your gang wants you dead – I know this, 'cause the streets are talking. And all the crips want you dead too. You're currently shot-up at the hospital. The only thing keeping you alive is the guard I posted outside your door. The minute you hit the street, you'll have bullets flying at you from every direction. Any of that sound right to you?"

Mike's expression of shock was frozen in place. "No."

"No?"

"They lying, whoever said I did that."

"No, Mike. *You're lying.* How am I supposed to help you, if you won't tell me the truth? I know Will was no choir boy. Did he hit you first? You should tell me, if you felt threatened."

"You ain't trying to help me. You trying to lock me up for something I didn't do."

"Look, kid, either you're going to accept my offer to help and work with me, or you're going to take on all of those bad asses by yourself. This is the only window of opportunity you have, and it's closing, real quick."

"I didn't do it."

"Okay," the detective said with a shrug of his shoulders. "I'm not gonna dick around with you all morning. Because of you, I have two more cases to work. What's it going to take for you to

COLORED RAGS

see that I'm your safest bet right now? You wanna go at it alone? Is that what you want?"

Anxiety ate away at Mike and dumped adrenaline into his veins. The police knew everything, but there was something missing. If it was so open and shut, why did they need a confession?

"Where's Spider?" he asked, his voice quavering.

The detective shot to his feet. "Spider's *dead*, Mike! Don't you hear what I'm saying? You got *nothing*! No *homies*! Nowhere to run! I'm the only person who can help you. You won't last *one night* outside of this hospital."

"Spider ain't dead." But Mike knew the truth. His face contorted in grief. What had he done to his best friend? He knew the cop had more photos in his folder. He didn't want to see them.

The detective softened. "He is dead, Mike. I'm sorry. But if you don't talk to me, you're gonna end up just like him."

He produced a card from his breast pocket and tossed it onto the bed. He picked up his recording device and bent to retrieve his file folder.

"When you change your mind, you got my number." He shook his head. "Don't take too long." Before he exited the room, Stevens told him, "I'm taking my officer with me. If the hospital wants to post security outside your door, that's up to them. You want a ride back, or you staying with this guy?" he asked Manning.

"I'ma, I'm going with you." Manning got up quickly and followed the detective out of the room.

"You gon' unlock these cuffs?" Mike called after them. Tears streamed down his face. There was no response. He thought he'd been tricked. He really was under arrest. But a uniformed officer sauntered into the room a moment later and removed all of his restraints.

Mike waited twenty minutes before he left the hospital against medical advice. He did not take Detective Stevens' card with him.

KEITH THOMAS WALKER

CHAPTER FIFTEEN
KODY'S GRAY COAT

Unlike the previous evening, Chris found ample parking at Evergreen Terrace. There were thugs about, but the air of excitement was gone. Chris was glad to see no one was openly packing a weapon.

A few blue tee shirts loitered on Kody's breezeway. Chris hoped one of them was Deuce or Trez, but with tensions so high, even they might not have the clout to get him in the apartment. He didn't know who was in charge of the gang now. Dante would have been the next in line, but he was in jail with Kody.

As he exited his vehicle, a familiar face stepped down and met him at the foot of the stairs.

"The fuck you doing over here?"

Croc smiled, but that didn't mean he was joking. The Crip had a medium build that was not physically imposing. What he lacked in size, he made up for with sheer desperation. He was always hungry; his face and hands were covered with war wounds. You could tell he didn't mind taking a few punches, as long as he was the one standing when the fight was over.

Croc wore khakis and an oversized blue tee shirt that was brand new. In the center of the shirt was a decent Rest in Peace picture of OG Will.

"I came to see what's up," Chris told him.

"You know yo brother locked up?"

Chris thought it was wrong for Croc to say that while smiling. "Yeah, I know."

"So, what you doing here, cuz? You ain't no loc, 'less, you want us to put you down..."

Chris couldn't believe he brought that up again. Kody had only been in jail for one day. Didn't Croc remember what happened last time?

"You wanna put me down?" Chris said.

Croc looked around. "It ain't gon' take too much. Just me and a couple more locs. Won't last too long. You ain't even gotta be standing when it's over. You still be in."

Chris' body wanted to take a couple of steps back, but he stood his ground.

"Trez here?"

Croc hmphed and shook his head in dismissal. "Yeah, he up there. I'll get him, though. You stay down here. Some shit going on; some *real loc* shit. And you ain't no loc." With that he turned and headed back up the stairs.

Chris went to wait in his car. After a few minutes, he wondered if Croc was sending anyone down. He was about to come up with a Plan B when a thin figure appeared on the breezeway and hopped down the stairs two at a time. Chris was never so happy to see Trez.

"What up, Chris!"

Chris got out of his car and they embraced briefly. Trez wore the same tee-shirt Croc had on. Chris wondered where he could get his own OG Will shirt.

"What you up to?" Trez asked.

"Shee, nothing."

"You just sitting in your car, listening to the radio?"

"I came to see what y'all was doing."

Trez followed him back to the car, and they both got in.

"You know yo brother in jail?"

"Yeah. He called me this morning."

"That's fucked up," Trez mused. "My nigga Will got murked, and now Kody gone too. I already miss that nigga. Everybody love yo brother, cuz."

"Yeah," Chris said.

"They think it was a set up, 'cause they got them niggas so quick. After they did that shit, they only hit, like two corners, and the laws was all over 'em. You know they got Tay too. And Bunchi. Deuce..."

"They got Deuce? Kody didn't tell me that."

"Yeah," Trez said reflectively. "That nigga ain't nothing but thirteen. His mama came by here tripping."

"What she do?"

"She ran up on some locs talking shit, asking where Kody at, 'cause that's the only name she know. She say her boy been hanging out with somebody named Kody, so she wanna tell him off, I guess. I don't know what the fuck she was on."

"What they tell her?"

"They told her Kody was in jail too. She started tripping even more, talking about how they fucked up her son's life. She said they had to pay for his bail and his lawyer. I wish I would've seen that shit."

Chris thought the lady had a point. "So, what happened?"

"She didn't get no money. That's for sure. She wasn't even talking to nobody from the set. They blew that bitch off, and she drove around looking ugly for a while. She left after that."

"What they charge Deuce with?"

"*Murder*, like everybody else. Everybody in the car got charged with murder."

"Who they kill?"

"Three or four people got killed last night. I don't know which one they charged Kody and them for. I know them slobs' OG got killed."

Chris felt sick to his stomach.

"But I don't know why they saying it was a set up," Trez continued. "Them laws ain't stupid, Chris. They knew what was going down, just like everybody else. They was all over Stop Six; posted up, waiting for some Crips to show up. We shot up one of them niggas' mama's house. We shot up that gambling shack on Ramey. It was all going down at the same time. They was bound to catch some of us."

"Why y'all do it then?" Chris asked.

"Fool, we had to do *something*. We can't let no slobs roll on our OG. That ain't finna happen. That's just how it go." Trez produced an ounce of marijuana from his front pocket.

"You wanna smoke?"

Chris had no intention of getting high, but the sight and smell of weed ignited a powerful urge. "Yeah," he said. "I mean, *no*. Not right now. That ain't why I came over here. I gotta do something for Kody."

COLORED RAGS

"What's that?" Trez asked, fiddling with the baggie.

Chris debated telling him but knew he needed an ally. "Alright. I gotta tell you something. But you can't tell *nobody*."

Intrigued, Trez's smile faltered. "What, cuz?"

They were in the car alone, but Chris still looked around to make sure no one was ear hustling. "Kody wants me to get something out of the apartment."

Trez shook his head. "Man, you ain't gon' be able to get shit outta that apartment. That nigga Croc up there tripping. He trying to lock everything down, like *he* running things."

"I know. He was fucking with me when I first got here." Chris told him what happened.

"That nigga don't give a fuck about you being down," Trez informed him. "He just don't like you. Remember when Kody had to whoop his ass?"

Chris nodded. "I remember. That's why I can't believe he tried it again."

"You want me to tell the locs what happened? They'll kick that nigga's ass for fucking with you. He can't be disrespecting the OG's little brother."

Chris considered how enjoyable it would be to watch that beat-down, but he'd make himself a real-live enemy for sure. He never had one of those before.

"Nah. Don't worry about it. I just need you to help me with this thing for Kody."

"You still haven't said what it is."

"It's a coat."

"What the fuck? How a coat gon' help that nigga? It's cold in jail?"

"It's some money in the coat. It's in the closet where Kody sleeps. It's a gray Dockers jacket."

Trez thought for a moment. "How much money?"

Chris felt a double-cross coming. "I'm not sure. And it don't matter, Trez. Just get it for me. Get it for *Kody*," he said, making it a matter of loyalty.

"Man..." Trez shook his head. "I don't think they gon' let me walk out of there with a stack of money."

"You ain't gotta walk out with it in your hands, Trez. Bring the whole coat."

"That ain't gon' work. It ain't cold."

"I know," Chris said. "I was thinking about it while I was waiting for you. I got an idea. There's a window up there." He pointed. "I think that's the one to Kody's bedroom."

"Yeah, I think so," Trez agreed.

"Go in there, like you gotta use the bathroom," Chris suggested. "Drop the coat out the window, and I'll catch it."

Trez shook his head. "I don't think that's gon' work. That window, I think it's nailed shut. I ain't never seen nobody use it. What if it make a lot of noise, and they hear me?"

"They won't hear you. Music always blasting in there."

Trez stuffed the weed back into his pocket. "Alright. I'll give it a try. You gon' be down here?"

"Yeah. Of course. I came over here for the money. I'm not leaving without it."

"You gon' tell Kody *I* got it for him?"

"Trez, I'll tell him you whooped a bunch of niggas asses to get it, if you want me to."

He chuckled. "You ain't gotta say all that. But I'ma do it for Kody."

"Alright," Chris said. "Do it for Kody."

Trez got out of the car and headed up the stairs with less enthusiasm than he had coming down. After sixty seconds, Chris got out and made his way to the spot beneath his brother's window. If it didn't open soon, he decided he would march up there and get the money himself.

COLORED RAGS

CHAPTER SIXTEEN
MIKE'S BUS RIDE &
CHRIS' NEW FRIEND

I've forgotten all my high school days
Like so many unattended graves
My outer being won't fill a page
But underneath I writhe with rage
My father never sees the stars
Or moonlight from his prison bars
My friends die slowly on dead streets
Obituaries don't make me weep
Another homey lost his brains
But it's not me. I don't complain

  The paramedics had ripped off Mike's shirt when they found him on the floor of Shaun's boy/girl house. They'd cut off his pants as well. His untimely departure from the caring hands at Jackson Memorial allowed no time for a friend to visit with a fresh set of clothing, so Mike stepped out of the main entrance wearing the same faded scrubs the surgical staff wore.
  The rain was now gone, leaving the hospital's lawn damp. The prevailing sun had already dried the sidewalks. The smell of dew and ozone comforted Mike. It reminded him of waking up in a cabin during a weeklong stint at the Outdoor Learning Center in the fifth grade. Mike loved that field trip. He got to pet cows and goats and ride horses. That was one of few childhood memories he would consider "normal."
  Mike's left arm was secured in a sling. The pain felt like a grub worm was constantly burrowing in the wound, but it wasn't intolerable. The bullet that passed through him didn't hit any

bones or major arteries. The doctor said the wound would heal, but Mike may need another surgery to fully regain mobility of his arm. And if he didn't remain under the care of a physician, an infection was almost guaranteed.

Mike's lovely nurse implored him to stay for at least one more week.

Mike told her, "I can get some Neosporin, if I run out of this stuff," in regards to one of the ointments she gave him.

Nurse Thickums' eyes widened. "Now I know you know better than that. You have a serious wound, Mike. Thinking you can take care of it yourself is like trying to cure cancer with a grade school chemistry set. If you leave, you'll be back with a temperature over 105, and you'll probably have gangrene."

Mike left anyway.

He didn't stay long enough for his doctor to prescribe heavy-duty pain killers, so all he had were the non-prescription pills Nurse Thickums found on the unit. She gave him enough gauze and bandages to change his dressings a few times. Mike carried these items in a clear plastic bag labeled PERSONAL BELONGINGS. Before he left, a security guard gave him the $84 he had in his pocket at the time of the shooting. This was technically Shaun's money, but Shaun had no need for finances anymore.

Mike thought about calling a cab when he left the hospital, but he had no idea how much they cost. He still didn't know what his SOLUTION was going to be, but he knew he needed one. He was pretty sure whatever plan he came up with would require more than eighty-four dollars.

So he crossed the street and posted up at the nearest bus stop. There was a middle-aged woman waiting there. She looked like the pictures of Harriet Tubman that popped up around Mike's old school every February. She said something, but when Mike turned to respond, he saw she was only talking to herself. She was toothless, and she worked her jaw like she had chewing gum.

Mike knew that all of the city busses either came from downtown or were headed there. Once he made it downtown, he could catch a second bus to his destination. There was no schedule posted at his stop, but three different routes passed the bench, so he knew it wouldn't take long. He wanted to sit down,

COLORED RAGS

but it would be hell trying to get back up. So he leaned and waited and watched the old lady chew her cud.

● ● ● ● ● ●

Six minutes later, the number two rolled to a squeaky stop in front of them. Mike tried to jump right on, but the driver made him wait for a few passengers to unload. He assumed he'd be greeted with uncomfortable stares, but the strangers were not taken aback by his disheveled appearance. Mike felt wonderfully anonymous. No one, not even his closest friends, would expect to see him on a city bus.

After the last passenger exited, Mike used the handrail and grimaced as he pulled himself up the stairs. The driver gave him a concerned look.

"You headed downtown?" Mike asked him, breathing harder than he should after only three steps.

"Yes, sir." The driver had fair skin and freckles. His afro had a natural red tint.

"What bus do I catch to get to Meadowbrook?" Mike asked him. "It's some apartments off Meadowbrook and Handley I'm trying to get to."

"You gonna want the, uh, number seven. It goes to Meadowbrook and Handley."

Mike fished out his wad of cash. "How much it cost to ride?"

"A dollar fifty."

"You got change for a dollar?"

"We don't have change."

Mike slid two dollars into the slot. The machine rattled and, despite what the driver just told him, he was surprised when his two quarters didn't come out somewhere. How the hell could they ask for a fare that included change without providing change?

"You gon' need a transfer," the driver told him.

The same machine that stole his fifty cents spit out a paper slip. Mike took it, and the driver closed the door behind him. Mike looked back to the mumbling woman and saw her walking away. He wondered why she was hanging around the bus stop, if she didn't need a ride. He didn't think he would live to be as old as her, but if he did, he hoped he wouldn't get all mushy in the head.

He lowered himself in one of the seats behind the driver. The pain in his back had dulled, but when he rested his weight on the wound, it began to throb again. He inhaled sharply and had to squeeze his lips closed to keep from crying out. He had a bottle of ibuprofens, but he didn't have any water to take them with.

The ride to the city's center took only ten minutes. This wasn't enough time for Mike to work on his SOLUTION, but it was more than enough time for the comforting caress of nostalgia to visit him. Mike watched the city pass by through the large windows and smiled, despite his circumstances.

The last time he rode a bus, he and Spider were headed downtown to generate revenues for their increasingly persistent marijuana cravings. Mike was fourteen. Spider was only eleven. Their hustling back then was weak. There was a comic book store on Main Street that sold as well as purchased the collectibles. The scam was simple: Spider went in and stole as many comics as possible. Mike waited around the corner to retrieve and sell the books back to the same store. They would only get about twenty dollars, but that was enough.

They also hustled in parking lots. If money can be folded and pushed into a slot, Murphy's Law says it can come right back out of that same slot. No one could wiggle a coat hanger better than Spider. Whatever the scheme, the boys always split their earnings fifty-fifty. Sometimes, despite how corny it sounded, they would get ice cream on the way home. Thinking about Spider made tears twinkle in Mike's eyes. He wiped them away before they could fall.

The driver announced *"Downtown transfer center,"* over an intercom.

The passengers gathered their belongings and rushed to the exits. Mike tried to lift himself from his seat, but the pain in his chest boomed like 20 inch speakers. He had to sit back down and take a breather. He wished he had stolen his morphine drip from the hospital. He prayed he'd have enough strength for one more bus ride.

When the last passenger made it off, Mike tried to stand again. The throbbing was so intense, tears sprang to his eyes. But at least he made it up. When he staggered past the driver, the man stared at his face and then his injury.

"You alright?"

COLORED RAGS

"Yeah. I'm just trying to get home."
"You sweating bad, son. And you *bleeding*."
Mike looked down and saw a dark stain blossoming on his shirt. He wondered what authority the driver might have over the situation. Was he required to call 911? Could he detain him or call the police?
"I'm alright," Mike said and stepped quickly down the steps.
He found the stop for his next bus and waited with five other commuters. A few gave him concerned looks, but no one questioned him. Texans are generally friendly folk, but minding your own business is a poor people's trait worldwide.
The bus pulled up in less than two minutes. Mike couldn't wait to sit down. He felt like he was about to pass out. By then sweat poured down his face. The new driver was olive-skinned and overweight. She wore a ring on every finger. Mike was the first passenger on this time. The driver looked down at him over her thick bifocals.
"You going over by Meadowbrook and Handley?" he asked.
"Yeah, baby. But you prolly want the number *two*. Look like you need to go to the hospital."
"Naw. I just left there," Mike said. He wiped some of the sweat. "I'm alright. It's just hot. It's a hundred degrees out here."
The driver was about to say something else, but he stepped past her without looking back. *Motherfuckers is nosey*, he thought.
The handicapped seats were all taken by individuals hardly in need, so Mike made his way to the back of the bus. He threw his leg up on the spot next to him – as if anyone wanted to sit next to a half-dead punk. He looked around and didn't recognize any of the passengers, which was perfect. There would be gang members in Meadowbrook, but no one from a set Mike knew.
The bus idled at the stop for ten minutes before taking off.

● ● ● ● ● ●

An unintentionally rough shove against his wounded shoulder startled Mike almost to the point of screaming. He woke angrily from a slumber he didn't know he'd slipped in to. The bus was at a complete stop. Mike stared dreamily out of the windows and realized he wasn't downtown anymore. The nudge had come from an awfully dressed gentleman with the round face of Down syndrome.

"She say you supposed to get off here," the man said. His lower lip hung and collected saliva.

It took Mike a few moments to realize he'd made it to Meadowbrook. The bus sat in front of a Conoco gas station. The apartment complex he planned to visit was only three blocks away.

"You said you wanna get off here, didn't you?" the driver shouted from her seat up front. She stared at him in the rearview mirror. Mike saw that all of the passengers were looking at him.

"Sorry," he said as he pulled himself to his feet. He didn't have any discomfort while asleep, but the pain woke up with him. Big time. He gritted his teeth and tried to look normal. The wound reignited a sense of urgency; reminding him of evil acts committed and the greater need for a SOLUTION.

"Baby, you can't be falling asleep on no bus," the driver chastised him. "You'll end up somewhere you don't wanna be."

"My bad," he said, heading for the back door.

"You *bleeding*," the man who woke him said.

Mike saw that the stain on his shirt had spread to the size of a cantaloupe. He couldn't believe he made it halfway across the city looking like that. He exited the bus and was immediately warmed by the afternoon sun. Ten seconds later, it was too damned hot.

The bus pulled away, and Mike crossed the street, heading for the Handley Oaks Apartments. He was halfway there when he realized he'd lost his bag of medical supplies somewhere between routes.

● ● ● ● ● ●

Chris knew something would go wrong. How could it not? The idea of a fuck up like Trez getting everything perfectly right was absurd. But he stood under Kody's bedroom window for two minutes, and the impossible happened. The window slid open smoothly, and Trez's anxious mug appeared in the gap.

"*Chris*," he whispered. He looked towards the car, where he last saw his friend.

COLORED RAGS

"I'm down here, fool!" Chris announced with a slightly louder whisper.

Trez looked down at him and then looked back over his shoulder. Chris saw that he was spooked.

"I got it," Trez hissed. "It's heavy. Something's in here."

"I told you it was something in there." Chris spoke patiently, though his heart was pounding out Morse code. He knew Croc was somewhere around. The fact that he might catch them smuggling Kody's money out of the apartment was more worrying than it should have been. Who was this creep, that he should warrant such fear?

"Throw it down," Chris said.

Trez looked away again, and his head disappeared back through the window. Chris' eyes widened. *Shit*! They were so close, but Trez got caught.

Thankfully he was wrong about that. Trez tossed the coat a second later and slammed the window down without checking to see if Chris caught it. He didn't. The coat thudded to the ground a few feet in front of his groping hands. He scooped it up and was aware of two things: There were plenty of bulges in the jacket that could be attributed to money, but Trez was right; there was something else in there. Something hard and heavy.

Chris looked up at the window and saw the shades were already drawn. He hurried to his car and stabbed his key in the ignition. Only then did he feel comfortable enough to inspect his booty.

He slid his hand into the pocket Kody mentioned and came in contact with the wonderful feel of money. But there was more. He reached deeper, pushing the bills out of the way until he had it. The feel of his discovery made his heart skip a beat. He knew what it was before he pulled it free.

His eyes gleamed at a pistol, a .380 automatic. It looked brand new. It was shiny chrome with a black, cross-stitch pattern on the handle. Chris found himself captivated. The gun was small but just as deadly as one twice its size. It felt *right* in his hand, although he never owned one.

You own one now, said a voice in his head. *Where Croc at?*

Chris looked up and saw a blue tee shirt skating down the stairs. He hurriedly reached between his legs and deposited the

134

pistol under his seat. He was glad to see it was only Trez approaching.

"What you doing? You finna bail?" his friend asked when he made it to the passenger window.

"Naw, I just... I didn't know if you got caught or something."

"Didn't nobody see me," Trez said. He got back in and stared at the coat in Chris' lap. "How much money's in there?"

"I don't know. I haven't looked yet. Over the phone he said it was two hundred, but I knew it was more than that. It feels like twenty *thousand*."

Trez's eyes bugged. "*Twenty thousand?*" He looked silly enough to be in a cartoon. "Damn, cuz! I knew my nigga was stacking, but *damn*! Them niggas would've had a field day if they found that."

"I know," Chris said. "That's why Kody sent me over here. He know what's up."

"What else in there?" Trez asked. "It's something hard, like a brick of dope or something. You looked in it yet?"

"No," Chris lied. "I think it's just money, though."

"You gon' look?" Trez asked anxiously.

Chris debated flashing such a large amount of money, but he knew Trez wouldn't be satisfied there were no drugs inside unless he saw for himself. Besides, Chris figured he could take Trez in a fist fight, if it came down to it. Even better, he had a brand new pistol under his seat. That put a little more favor on his side.

With Trez watching, he began to pull the money from his brother's coat. After awhile, he felt like a clown pulling handkerchiefs from his pocket. There seemed to be no end in sight. They didn't count, but by the time he was finished there was a sizeable amount of twenties, fifties and hundred dollar bills. Stacked bill on bill, the money would have measured at least a foot, from top to bottom.

Trez watched the happenings with unblinking eyes. He couldn't have been more impressed if Chris turned water into wine.

"That's a lotta money."
"It's all Kody's."
"What else in there?"

"Nothing."

"Man, that coat was heavy, cuz. It's something else in there."

"That's it," Chris said and tossed the empty jacket to him. "Go ahead and look. If you find anything else, you can have it."

Trez squeezed the coat anxiously and shoved his arm in the inner pocket, all the way up to his elbow. After a few moments of digging, he drew back an empty palm. He shook his head and handed the garment back to Chris.

"I could've swore it was something else in there."

Chris shrugged. "I don't know what to tell you."

"I guess." Trez still looked confused. "So what you gon' do with all that?"

Chris shoved the money back into the coat. "I'ma give it to Kody or do whatever he want me to do with it. Why? What you think I'ma do with it?"

Trez looked away awkwardly. "You think he gon' miss, like, a C note? I mean, he got all that..."

Chris smacked his lips and sneered at him. "Nigga, I outta tell Kody you said that."

"Naw, cuz, I was just–"

"Man, fuck that. I heard you. You really tripping. You wanna steal from my brother?"

"Naw. Man, forget it." Trez grinned. "I was just kidding, fool. You thought I was serious? I just wanted to see what *you* was gon' say. I wouldn't never steal from my OG."

Chris grinned. "I know cuz. You did good, though. I'ma tell him you got it for me."

Trez smiled. "So, you wanna hit this blunt now?"

"Alright. Let me put this in the trunk." Chris folded the coat into a tight wad and got out of his car. Standing out in the open with so much money felt weird, and he was glad to get it stored away. He shoved the jacket under his spare tire and looked around to make sure no one was watching. By the time he got back behind the wheel, Trez had a sickly-looking blunt in hand.

"You rolled it that quick?"

"I already had it. You wanna light it?"

Chris took the cigar, and Trez gave him a red lighter. Chris pondered the irony of a Crip with a red lighter but only for a moment. As the smoke filled his car and the sound of a stray seed popping filled his ears, his thoughts kept returning to the firearm under his seat.

He had a gun now; a real live *Stop-or-I'll-shoot!* gun. It may have been his brother's before, but Kody was locked up. It was Chris' now, and no one would ever take it from him.

COLORED RAGS

CHAPTER SEVENTEEN
THE WAKE

Choir, please don't sing that sad, sad song
I don't want my baby to be gone
Lord, I can't make it through this day
I never thought I'd see him this way
Can't walk. Can't talk. I crawl on my knees
He wasn't supposed to die before me
I can't eat, and my blood pressure's bad
How you gon' leave your mama like that?
I lost your daddy, and now I lost you
Sometimes I wish God would take me too
Preacher man, don't make this sermon too long
And choir, please don't sing that sad, sad song

    Andre Broadnax dressed for the wake without turning his back on the bedroom door. He did everything requested of him, including getting out of bed and tracking down his mother in an attempt to console her. But he felt his uncle would return anyway to continue the measured assault he started. In his nineteen years on earth, Dre had never experienced such bold ferocity.
    He'd had it out with Will a few times, sure, but that was different. Will would strike out in a fit of rage and calm down just as quickly. He even apologized most of the time. Uncle Ray's attack had lasting effects. Dre was convinced he was the boogeyman himself.
    He had trouble deciding what to wear to the funeral home. Dre's family was not the church-going type, so his supply of slacks was slim. The only ones he had were high-water and too small for his current waistline. He folded them neatly and put them back in

the closet, unsure why he was keeping them, but not wanting to throw them away.

Dre sorted through the rest of his clothes for a while before accepting that he had nothing to wear. He dreaded leaving his bedroom to deliver the news to his mother. The last time he spoke to her, it was at Uncle Ray's request, and it didn't go well.

His mom had sat in the living room cradling a cup of cold coffee. Her hair hung over her face like seaweed as a cigarette smoked itself in her hand. Her breath reeked of alcohol. Her eyes stared off into space, thinking of better times perhaps. So caught up in her own despair, Esther didn't notice Dre's swollen lip or his wide-eyed terror.

Dre knew he'd have to come up with a solution to his fashion crisis all by himself, so he entered the closet again, this time rummaging through Will's old clothes. It turned out to be a good move. The dead OG left three pairs of Dickeys in there. Two were blue and one pair was black. Dre was shorter and wider than his brother, but the black pants were an okay fit. The Dickeys were pressed and clean, so he didn't have to look for the iron.

Dre found a white button-down to top off the outfit. He had to wear tennis shoes, but that was okay. Fully dressed, he stared at himself in the mirror, and his eyes unexpectedly filled with tears. The tears weren't for Will, rather his own pitiful predicament. The injury his uncle inflicted stood out like an albino on a slave ship. The left side of his bottom lip was twice as big as the right. How could his mom allow this to happen?

He decided the tears would work to his advantage, and he let them flow. He stepped out into the hallway and was greeted at once by his uncle. He froze in fright and lowered his eyes. To his surprise, Uncle Ray grunted a *hmph* that sounded complimentary.

"You, ready to go?" he asked, as if they were enemies no longer. The attack earlier that day was an accident, is all.

"Yeah, yes. Yes sir."

"Good. We gon' be leaving, here pretty soon. We gon' get there, early."

Dre felt sweat leak from his armpit and snake down his side. He was unable to meet the big man's eyes. He was vaguely aware that this was the type of encounter Will used to lecture him about. If Will was here, he would advise Dre to wait until the behemoth turned his back, and then attack him with something

COLORED RAGS

big and heavy. He'd tell him to keep delivering blows to the head, until he was certain his opponent wasn't getting up. But Will was dead, so his lessons no longer mattered.

"Okay," Dre said and returned to his room. He sat on his hands and listened to his own breathing for ten minutes before Uncle Ray stopped in the doorway again to tell him it was time to go.

● ● ● ● ● ●

Pinkey's Funeral Home had the air and appearance of a church, an expensive one. The foyer was immaculate with hardwood flooring, brass end tables with glass tops, and two leather sofas for visitors weary from their journey from the parking lot. The chapel doors were dark and solid, made from cherry wood. The brass door handles had intricate designs worthy of a cathedral.

The beauty of the vestibule belied the fact that dead men and women were wheeled in through the back. Lately, a lot of the young corpses had bloody holes in them. Most people would never see that side of their loved one. Once Pinkey got through with them, they'd have a fresh haircut, perm, makeup, manicure and a nice outfit they most likely never would have worn while breathing.

Dre knew it was just one big magic trick. The deceased weren't really smiling; their mouths were molded in that position. Beneath the thick coat of foundation, their cheeks weren't really rosy. And everyone knew the bodies would stink to the high heavens, if they weren't pumped full of embalming fluid. The whole thing was a farce. The deception began the moment you walked in and commented on how beautiful everything was.

Pinkey's Funeral Home had been in the business of deceiving for many years. There were four photos on the main wall. They were all enclosed in elaborate frames. The first was a passionate painting of the Lord carrying an exhausted sinner in his arms. Christ stood stoically, bleeding from holes in his hands and feet. The sinner wore jeans and a tee-shirt, limply holding a hammer in one of his hands. The painting was so detailed, you could almost feel the savior's pain. Dre stared at it for a few minutes.

The other portraits depicted three generations of the Pinkey bloodline. Emmanuel Pinkey founded their first funeral home in 1933. When most Texas Negroes were content cleaning floors and hauling garbage, this man was a visionary. According to a plaque, he left the business to his son, Otis Sr. in 1974. Otis Jr. inherited the legacy 35 years later. He was now one of only six black millionaires in Overbrook Meadows.

The millionaire talked to Esther Broadnax for a few minutes before Dre stepped closer to hear what he was saying.

"...and, as you know, that was kinda hard to do with your son. He had that issue with his neck, and we had to work around it." Otis Pinkey referred to Wills' fatal gunshot wound the same way others might refer to a birthmark. Dre found that amusing.

"But I know you wanted an open casket," Pinkey said. "We had to get a little creative, but I think you're gonna like it."

Otis wore a silver, three-piece suit with his trademark horn-rimmed spectacles. His eyes were warm, and his mouth was big. Dre couldn't tell if he had too many teeth or if his teeth stuck out too much. He couldn't get over the fact that this was the same man who used to make midnight crack buys from his dead brother.

"Would you like to see your son?" Otis asked. He held Esther gently with one arm around her back. He was smooth and professional.

Esther sighed audibly. She straightened her shoulders and sniffed back one last tear before nodding. Uncle Ray put a large hand on her shoulder. It was the same hand he'd used to stifle the screams of her only living son, but now it comforted her. Mr. Pinkey pulled open one of the large doors that led to the chapel, and the trio stepped inside; each man holding Esther with a tenderness you'd have to lose a son to warrant.

Dre hoped they would ignore him, allow him to find deeper meaning in the Jesus painting perhaps, but Ray looked back over his shoulder and gave him a glare that probably had inmates giving up their stamps without a fight when he was locked up.

"You coming, Dre?"

Dre swallowed roughly, lowered his head, and followed the group inside.

● ● ● ● ● ●

COLORED RAGS

    The chapel was as regal as the foyer. A large aisle separated a hundred seats that had plush, red cushions. There were more paintings on the walls, but Dre didn't take in too much of his surroundings. Thirty paces ahead of his mother, there was a coffin. Dre's breath caught in his throat. The casket was black and shiny, lined with brass handles on either side.
    He didn't know how much dope Will gave Pinkey for the arrangements, but from the looks of it, quite a debt had been paid. It all seemed a little extravagant for a manipulator of men and peddler of drugs.
    "Now, I know you gon' be happy with what we did here," Pinkey went on.
    Dre didn't realize how slowly he was moving, until the trio had a good lead on him. The closer he got to the coffin, the more reluctant he became. Finally he stopped moving altogether. Under no circumstances did he want to see his brother's corpse. Dolled up or not, Will was dead. No perm or new suit was going to take away from the ugliness of his passing.
    "I know you wanted to see him before everyone else arrived," Otis was saying. He lifted the lid of the coffin with one hand and braced the bereaved mother with the other. Dre looked over the undertaker's shoulder and saw that the coffin's inner lining was white and silky. He couldn't see his brother's body through the group of people, which was fine by him.
    Esther did not disappoint. Her body went limp, and she let loose a mighty wail that reverberated off the walls of the chapel. It was a profound scream; a gut wrenching cry that rose from a deep well of pain no mother wanted to experience.
    Mr. Pinkey grabbed her with both arms and allowed her to lean into him. "It's okay, Miss Broadnax. It's *alright*, there. It's okay to feel pain when we lose someone we love. You just go right on and get it out."
    Uncle Ray looked back at Dre angrily. Dre didn't know if the look was for not rushing to his mother's side or for allowing Will to die in the first place. Either way, there was nothing he could do about it. He watched quietly as the preacher man comforted Esther.

"Everything happens according to God's divine will," Pinkey told her. "Will's in a better place now. There's no more hurting. No more pain."

None of his words seemed to ease her misery. It became apparent that Esther would stand there wailing until forced to move on, so Uncle Ray helped the mortician escort her away from the source of despair. As they passed Dre, Ray's eyes became stone cold. But Dre knew he was safe for now. Ray would get sent back to prison for sure, if he assaulted him in front of witnesses.

● ● ● ● ● ●

Left alone with the coffin, Dre's first thought was to follow them out, but he still couldn't get his legs to move. He thought about what the preacher said about divine will. That wasn't a concept he believed in, but he felt there was *something* going on at that moment that he couldn't control. He felt hypnotized. Perhaps there was a task he needed to perform, and his body wouldn't let him leave until it was done.

The last time Dre was alone with his brother, Will had him hold a capsule of heroin as he snorted the powder. Minutes later Will stood helpless in a convenience store while a young thug opted to skyrocket his status the old-fashioned way.

And everything they said was true; Dre watched it go down. He had Will's gun but was afraid to use it. Will was gone now, and Dre was actually a little happy about that, but fate brought them together again, and Dre couldn't move.

But why?

Repentance? Dre scoffed at the idea of apologizing to a dead man. *Why should I feel guilty?* he asked himself. Was it his fault Will led a lifestyle that doomed him to an early grave? Should Dre have risked his own life to save him? What good would that have done? If Will didn't get shot that night, he would have got shot sooner or later. If not, he would have gone to prison and wasted his livelihood there. The Overbrook Meadows PD had probably chalked OG Will's death up to *good riddance.* Was it wrong for Will's little brother to feel the same way?

Whatever revelation he was meant to have was lost on Dre. Rather than sympathy, he felt annoyed for having the weight of the world on his shoulders. He turned his back on his brother's coffin

COLORED RAGS

and headed out of the chapel. He could move his legs after all, which was proof that his thoughts were valid. Maybe God wanted him to accept that Will got what he deserved.
You a ho ass nigga.
The words were slow, quiet, and deliberate. Dre's eyes widened as he came to an abrupt stop. The temperature in the sanctuary dropped twenty degrees, and the hairs stood up on the back of his neck. A small whimper escaped his lips.
The voice he heard had spoken the truth, but that wasn't why Dre was poised to soil his pants for the second time that day. Not only did Will use that phrase to insult him time and time again, but the words Dre heard were spoken in Will's voice.
Even worse, it was obvious the voice had come from Will's casket.
Don't be stupid, he told himself. There was no way he would entertain that. It wasn't even worth thinking about. There was no reason to turn around and look back at the coffin. Doing so would speak volumes about his gullibility. No, the only sensible thing to do was to get the hell out of there.
But despite knowing it was a prank, Dre's heart rumbled like an outboard motor. He quickened his escape, heading in the direction his mother and uncle had gone. But what seemed like twenty steps a moment ago now looked like a hundred.
I swear to God, you's a ho ass nigga, cuz.
Dre stopped again, just a few feet from the exit. He realized running was what they expected him to do. There was no mistaking what was going on here: The voice came from the casket behind him, and it was Will's voice. It was gravely, and a bit raspy, but there was no doubt it was his brother.
Even still, there was a rational explanation. Someone recorded it before his death. Uncle Ray or maybe Otis Pinkey knew Dre would be alone with the coffin at some point. They were waiting in the foyer to laugh at him when Dre ran from the room, screaming for his life.
They knew Dre wouldn't take the time to inspect the coffin and uncover the ruse. Once a coward, always a coward – but that's where they were wrong. Although he was terrified, Dre forced himself to make the move no one expected. He turned to confront the gimmick.
What he saw forced a girlish whimper up his throat.

OG *motherfucking* Will, leader of thugs, dealer of drugs, and tormentor of his little brother, sat up in his coffin and opened his dead eyes. His cornrows were plaited thick and neat, just how he liked them. His goatee; professionally trimmed. He wore a dark blue suit with a blue bandana neatly folded in the breast pocket. Otis Pinkey's solution to the hole in his throat was another bandana tied around his neck, like the cowboys did in the days of Wyatt Earp. Will's skin was only slightly ashen.

You let them niggas do this shit, cuz. You had that big ass pistol in yo hands, and you let 'em do it!

Watching his dead brother's lips form the same words Dre was hearing was more than his fragile mind could bear. The sanctuary spun about him. He stumbled backwards, almost tripped over a bench, and his butt came in contact with the door. He reached behind himself numbly for a handle or push bar but could find none. His throat squeezed closed, and he couldn't even cry out for help. What he saw was not possible, but it was as real as the nose on his face.

Will struggled to lift himself from the casket. He looked at his brother and snarled.

You don't want me to get out this motherfucker. I'ma get yo ass, Dre...

Will flashed a queer smile, and the blood drained from Dre's face. As he watched, his dead brother gripped both sides of the casket and pushed himself up, until his upper body was free. He began to kick with his legs. Soon his hips rose above the plush, silky lining.

Uh oh...

Dre did not stick around to see what *Uh oh* meant. He turned and slammed into the chapel doors with the force of a linebacker. He expected a little resistance, but the doors flew open effortlessly, sending him sprawling to the floor at the foot of his broken family. Uncle Ray registered surprise as he stepped back to avoid being bowled over by his portly nephew.

"What the–," Mr. Pinkey exclaimed.

Esther reached for her son for the first time in two days. "*Dre!*"

She screamed something else, but Dre couldn't hear it over the freight train sound of his heartbeats. He was large, but he

COLORED RAGS

managed to roll out of his tumble and regain his feet. His legs never stopped pedaling.

Shrieking like a banshee, he ran full speed, with both arms swinging. He blasted through the foyer, shoved the glass doors open, and bolted from the funeral home.

The warmth of the waning sun was comforting, but not nearly enough. Nothing was right. His world didn't make sense, but Dre knew it would be alright if he kept running. Nothing could harm him if he ran. No way was a zombie going to catch him.

KEITH THOMAS WALKER

CHAPTER EIGHTEEN
FAMILY TIES

*I think I got hit in the chest
But I'm not totally sure
My whole body wants to rest
From the pain it has endured
I think I felt two bullets drill me
But I don't know who to blame
Why would my people want to kill me?
I'm not even in a gang
Maybe it's 'cause of what I wore
Tonight I think I had on red
Is that what he shot me for?
That's why he tried to split my head?
And these doctors need to quit
Asking if I can feel my toes
I told them fools I can't feel shit!
And why am I so goddamned cold?
Are you people gonna save me?
Y'all gon' put me back in place?
And what about the fool that sprayed me?
I guess he just gon' get away
And tell me why I feel so cold
How come it's so hard to breathe?
Doctor, please don't let me go
I don't want my mom to grieve
Did he think I was a Blood
Or now is wearing colors enough?
When that fool said, "What up, cuz?"
I told him, "I ain't in that stuff"
Then my body had new holes
And I was staring at the sky*

COLORED RAGS

> *Please tell me why I feel so cold*
> *Doctor, please don't let me die*

Ernest Gooden was not in the mood for surprises. The ride home from work was normally his favorite part of the day, but today it was a festering knot of stress. The thought of the stunt he pulled at work bounced around in his head like a small caliber bullet in a rib cage, giving the normally pleasant commuter a nice fit of road rage. Ernest hammered the steering wheel. He sped and shouted (mostly to himself). He fixed hostile glares at any drivers focusing concerned looks in his direction.

At thirty-nine years of age, he should have known better. He didn't have the best job in the world, but it was worth keeping. Victorious Graphics and Awnings was a small but thriving business. Ernest had punched the clock there for the last six years. When he first started, they only had one truck and had to outsource most of their welding and fabric work. Now they had their very own metal shop and sewing department. They had five crews trekking across the metroplex six days a week to provide decorative shade structures and covered walkways to homes and businesses. Ernest was proud to have been there from the ground up.

The owner of the company was a shrewd asshole, sure, but Lathan Beck trusted Ernest with the number two position on their best truck. He did this despite the fact that Ernest readily admitted to having three felony convictions on his long rap sheet. He wasn't always an honest man. He hadn't been a good father, a good son, or even a good person for most of his life. But Beck saw promise in Ernest's broad shoulders and coarse hands. He gave the ex-con his first drill set, and on his first day of work Ernest displayed a characteristic that didn't show up in his background check: He was a damn fine worker.

Rain or shine, blistering August heat or numbing January freezes, Ernest outworked every employee in the building. He studied his co-workers and inherited a motto: *If you wanna be the man, you gotta beat the man.*

Five years after hiring the ex-con, Beck began to call on Ernest to hang awnings for his most prized clients. Any difficult metal work also went to Ernest, but over the years the hardest worker in the building was forced to accept his limitations. He was only the number *two* man on his crew. Jimmy Beck, Lathan's favorite nephew, was the lead man.

The fact that he was better than the guy who gave him orders did not offend Ernest, because he was grateful for the opportunity. His starting salary was eight dollars an hour. He'd worked himself up to fifteen and was comfortable with that. He was not, however, comfortable with a young white boy nearly half his age pointing a finger in his face and yelling at him in public. The finger was aggravating enough. Having the finger in his face while in the right proved too much for poor Ernest to bear.

Today's job was simple: A physician's office under construction called for a ten foot awning over the main entrance. Jimmy unloaded a twelve foot ladder from the truck and stood it in the doorway of the building while Ernest unbolted the awning from their trailer. With the parking lot still unpaved, the ladder's footing proved to be lacking. It began to rock in the wind as Jimmy headed back to the truck.

"Yo ladder finna fall," Ernest called over his shoulder.

"Well get it," Jimmy said as he fished through his tool bag.

"I'm getting the awning. You get it," Ernest told him. "You the one set it up."

A nice gush of wind stormed in from the south. Ernest looked back in time to watch the ladder fall; crashing through one of four mounted windows. The sound of glass breaking brought electricians, painters, and construction workers from all over the site to gawk at the damage. Jimmy was embarrassed, but he didn't act like a prick until the contractor stormed out and glared first at the ladder then at Ernest and Jimmy.

"I told you to get that fucking ladder!" Jimmy yelled.

Ernest ignored him. He knew white people had to yell at somebody when they fucked up. But Jimmy wouldn't leave it at that. He kept ranting and raving. Ernest let it roll off his shoulder until the kid stuck a finger in his face and demanded he pick up that damned ladder and clean up that fucking glass. Before Ernest could think better of it, he shoved the scarecrow hard in the chest with both hands, sending the CEO's favorite nephew flying into the side of the truck. His head bounced hard off the fender.

COLORED RAGS

The sound of skull hitting steel was loud enough, but Jimmy let out a startled howl that brought more spectators than the ladder falling.

"You pick it up!" Ernest told him and then returned to his task of unloading the awning. The matter settled, Jimmy picked himself up and then the ladder, and he cleaned up the glass. He apologized to the contractor and sat in the truck pouting while Ernest hung the awning by himself. Back at the shop, Jimmy went straight to the boss' office, and Ernest headed straight to his car.

He argued with himself the whole ride home; debating the rights and wrongs of a nigga's life in general. He wondered if he should call his boss or just show up for work tomorrow. He didn't know if he even had a job to go to anymore. He wondered if the shove qualified as an *assault*, and if so whether Jimmy would send him back to the pen.

Ernest's disposition was as unstable as a possum in the pantry when he turned into his apartment complex. He wanted a beer. He wanted to take his boots off, lie on his couch and smoke a joint. What he saw waiting for him on his porch rattled him more than anything that happened at work.

He parked his truck and stared at the boy for a full minute before getting out. Ernest had seen his son less than a dozen times since birth, but a father always knows his seed, no matter how sweaty, shot up or tattered they might be. The kid was so out of it, he barely noticed him approaching.

"I don't know what the hell you done got yourself into, boy. But you can't stay here," Ernest said matter-of-factly.

"I don't got nowhere else to go," Mike said.

"How the hell you get over here?"

Mike thought his biological father should ask about his injuries first, but he was in no position to debate father/son etiquette.

"I rode the bus." His father's huge presence hovered over him. Mike wasn't sure how long he'd be able to maintain clarity. *Why the fuck can't you just open the door and let me in*, he wondered. *You ain't done shit for me my whole life.*

"You come over here from the hospital?" Ernest inquired.
"Yeah."
"Where yo mama at?"
"I don't know. She at home, I guess."

"She know you over here?"

"Naw," Mike said weakly. "Don't nobody know I'm over here."

"So why you didn't go home? Why you come here?"

"I can't go home. Peoples looking for me. That's why I left the hospital. They looking for me there too. I'm in trouble, man. I ain't got nowhere to go."

"Look like you need a doctor," Ernest noted. "I don't know what you expect from me. I ain't got no money. And I ain't no doctor."

Mike grinned slightly. Ernest Gooden wore tan Husky boots with the soles worn down to less than a quarter-inch. His jeans were well past their prime, and his shirt was in similar disrepair. He had large hands that were dirty and calloused. You might confuse him for a janitor or mechanic, but no one would ever think Ernest was a doctor.

"I just need to lay down for a while. Catch my breath. I'll leave as soon as I wake up. I promise." Mike knew his word wasn't worth a damn, but he had the luxury of history on his side. He didn't know his father and therefore had never promised or broken any promises made to him.

"*I promise*," he said again.

Ernest had a wide nose with equally large nostrils. They flared and a sneer rose in the corner of his mouth. He squinted and studied his son closely.

"You been shot?"

"Yeah."

"In the chest? It get yo lung?"

"Naw," Mike said. "They took some X-Rays. They said it didn't hit nothing. Just went straight through."

"Didn't hit no bones?" Ernest asked skeptically.

"Naw. It barely missed the ribs. Just hit muscle and tissue. In and out."

The sun beat down on them like a furnace. Mike knew he was either going to get invited inside, while he still had the strength to walk by himself, or Ernest was going to have to carry his limp body.

"Why you bleeding so bad?" his father asked.

The blood stain on Mike's shirt went all the way down to his waistline. The boy's skin was ashen. He had crust in the

COLORED RAGS

corners of his mouth and blood on his hospital sandals. Beads of sweat stood out on his forehead.

"'Cause I been moving," Mike whispered hoarsely. "I wasn't supposed to get out of bed for, like a week. But I came all the way over here."

"They didn't give you no medicine or nothing?"

Mike closed his eyes and shook his head. "I lost it."

Ernest sighed. He shook his head, and the taut muscles in his face relaxed. "You can't stay overnight, or nothing like that."

Mike nodded.

"I go to work tomorrow morning. I ain't leaving you here when I go."

Mike nodded again.

"Them niggas who shot you know you over here? I swear if them niggas come over here starting some shit..."

"Man, they don't know where I'm at. Mama don't even know where I'm at. Peoples is getting *killed* over there. I got away. Shaun dead. Spider..."

Ernest had no idea who those people were. But he felt the waves of pain emanating from his son. He stepped over the bloody body to unlock the door and then helped the boy to a standing position. Mike didn't offer much assistance, but Ernest managed to get him all the way to the couch before he fell out. There was a lot of dried blood on the back of Mike's shirt. Ernest wanted to put towels down but didn't have time.

Mike slumped on the cushions and mumbled something that might have been *Thanks* before closing his eyes. A moment later he snored lightly, either asleep or passed out, Ernest couldn't tell.

He stood over his son for a moment, marveling at the frailty of the boy, the uncertainty of life and all its empty promises. He retrieved a handkerchief from his back pocket and wiped Mike's brow with it.

Ten minutes ago he wanted nothing more than to slouch on this very couch with a cold beer and his joint, but life has a way of throwing curve balls. Sometimes you go to work just fine and dandy, and by the end of the day you don't know if you have a job to go to tomorrow. Sometimes you come home and find a child you barely know dying on your doorstep.

Ernest held Mike gently and straightened his upper body on the couch. The sofa wasn't long enough for him to stretch out his son's legs, but he got most of him on the cushions. He took off Mike's sandals before heading for the door. He knew nothing about caring for bullet wounds but figured the hardest part was already done by the doctors. All he had to do was maintain what they started. Mike would need painkillers, gauze and some kind of antibiotic cream. There was a drug store right up the street.

COLORED RAGS

CHAPTER NINETEEN
THE LOVE BUG

Drivebys
Children die

AIDS disease
Brothers bleed

Everybody
Smoking weed

Prostitutes
Children shoot

Crack cocaine
Countless gangs

Drug deals
Brothers killed

Carjacks
Can't have it back

Gangstas bleed
Mothers grieve

Michael Jackson I agree
They don't really care about us

Chris declined Trez's offer to hang out with the locs for a while and go to OG Will's wake with them. Even in his inebriated state, he knew he needed to drop Kody's money off before anything else. Driving high amidst daytime traffic was something he decided he would not purposefully do again. He waited at a green light at Berry and Riverside in a pleasant daze until horns started blaring at him. He stopped again at an intersection a couple of blocks from home and didn't understand why his turn to go was taking so long. He finally realized he wasn't at a four-way stop.

By the time he made it home, it was nearly five pm. His mother was gone to work, which was a blessing. He didn't have to worry about sneaking the money in or her noticing he was high.

He brought the jacket inside and removed all of the money again. Without counting, he knew he was right about it being close to twenty grand. He walked around the house, looking for a good place to hide it. The attic was his first choice, but he wouldn't be able to retrieve it without his mom noticing, if she was home at the time. He could dig a hole in the backyard, but that would leave way too much evidence.

Chris finally stuffed the cash under his mattress. He flattened it out as best he could. His mother might still find it, if she did some snooping, but that was beyond his control. Besides, Kody never said specifically not to tell her about it.

Back in the kitchen, he found a fried chicken dinner his mother left for him. It looked okay, but chicken was one of those meals that was best served fresh out of the fryer. He figured his friend Jason would have something more appetizing.

On the way out, Chris hesitated in the doorway, wondering if he shouldn't find a better hiding spot for the money. Trez might get a wild hair up his ass and decide to break in. *That's just the weed talking,* he told himself. Trez wouldn't burglarize his OG's house. No way.

When Chris got back in his car, he reached under the seat to make sure the gun was still there. He held it in his lap and studied it for the first time, marveling at its weight and potential. He flipped it over and found a release for the clip. There were two bullets visible. He wanted to pop them out to see if the clip was full but figured it was probably not a good idea to have your fingerprints on a shell. Coincidentally, it might not be a good idea to have your fingerprints on a clip either, so he wiped it off with his shirt before pushing it back into the handle of the weapon.

COLORED RAGS

Should I have my fingerprints on the gun at all? he wondered and decided he shouldn't.

He started wiping the .380 off before realizing he would need a pair of rubber gloves to do it right. Chris laughed at himself and abandoned his efforts. He figured it was the weed that was making him paranoid again. He gazed at the weapon lovingly before returning it to the floorboard.

●●●●●●

Jason lounged in front of his big screen TV with another full plate on his lap. At this hour, he was enjoying a meal he referred to as *supper*. Supper came between lunch and dinner. Today's supper consisted of sliced brisket, macaroni and cheese (with extra cheddar melted on top), and a couple of slices of white bread. Staring at the food made Chris salivate. He hadn't eaten anything all day.

"You hungry boy?" Jason asked around a mouthful.

"Yeah," Chris readily admitted. "I'm starving."

"That's 'cause of that weed," Jason said. He sat his plate aside and got up to fix a serving for his friend.

Chris followed him to the kitchen. "What you mean?"

"You high. I knew it as soon as you walked in. Keep fucking around with that weed. That's why you skinny now."

"I thought the munchies make you eat a lot," Chris commented. "Why would it keep me skinny?"

"Because when you high, you don't take the time to eat right," Jason said as he heaped a pile of deliciousness onto Chris' plate. "You'll just grab a bag of chips or something and keep it moving. That's another thing about weed; it makes you lazy."

Jason put the plate in the microwave and turned to stare at him. "But that ain't gon' happen to you, is it?"

"Hell naw."

"You too smart for that, huh?"

"Yeah," Chris said.

"We'll see when you get to college and that homework starts to pile up on your ass. What you gon' pick up first, a book or a blunt?"

Before Chris could answer, his cellphone went off. He pulled it from his pocket and smiled when he saw the number. He headed to the den before he answered.

"Hello?"

"What's up, Chris," Tracy said. "So, you can't call nobody?"

"I was gon' call you," he said.

"You wanted me to call you first?"

"No, it's not that. I didn't want you to think I was too eager." Chris wasn't sure why he was being so honest with her.

"Who told you girls think like that?"

"I don't know. I heard it somewhere."

"You know what a *woman* thinks when you get some and don't call her back?"

Chris' face grew warm. He didn't think a woman would like that very much. "I don't know."

"She think you *got some* and don't want nothing else to do with her."

"That's not it," he said, feeling flustered. "I had to do something this morning. I *do* want something to do with you."

"Something like what? You wanna get you some more?"

"Naw. I mean yeah I do, but that's not all I want from you."

Tracy giggled. "What you want from me, Chris?"

"I, uh, I don't know." He looked over his shoulder, glad to see Jason was still in the kitchen. "Why you asking me that? No matter what I say, you gon' think I'm stupid."

"Why would I think that?"

"'Cause if I say I wanna *get some*, then I'm a dog. But if I say I wanna be with you, you gon' think I'm sprung."

"Is that what you want?" she asked.

"Yeah," Chris admitted.

"Which one? To get some or to be with me?"

"You know what I mean. You just wanna hear me say it?"

"Yeah," Tracy said, and Chris would swear he heard the faintest sigh.

He inhaled nervously. "I wanna be with you."

There was a long pause, during which his heart did not beat, and then Tracy said, "I wanna be with you too. What you doing?" she asked.

"I'm over at Jason's house. We finna eat."

COLORED RAGS

As he spoke, his friend appeared in the doorway with his plate. Jason eyed him queerly and then sat down. He focused his attention on the television, but Chris knew he was ear hustling.

"What you gon' do when you get through?" Tracy asked.

"I don't know. Nothing."

"You wanna see me today?"

"Yeah," Chris said without pause. "You gonna come over here?"

"Over to Jason's? Naw. I don't wanna see him."

Chris thought that was odd but didn't question it. "You want me to go over there? Where you live?"

"Naw. My brothers are over here. What about your house? Can I come over there?"

"Yeah, nobody's home."

"Where you live?"

"I stay right around the corner from Jason; on Forbes." Chris had never been alone at home with a girl, or *woman* for that matter, but he could think of no reason why it wouldn't be a good idea. "My mama gone to work. She won't be back till tomorrow morning."

Jason hummed.

"When you want me to come?" Tracy asked.

"I'll be through in about thirty minutes."

"Okay. Call me when you get home."

"Alright," Chris said and disconnected.

He looked up to find Jason staring at him with a smile that was something like pride. Chris couldn't stop grinning himself as he dove into the brisket.

"That was Tracy?" Jason asked.

"Yeah. She finna come over my house."

"And your mama's at work?"

"Yeah."

"That's what I'm talking about, nigga." Jason leaned back with his hands on his belly. "You know, we was starting to worry about your ass."

"What you mean?"

"You was always hitting the books and everything, which is cool. I mean, look how far you done made it. But you wasn't never hitting no *broads*, man. We was starting to think you wasn't never gon' get none."

"Whatever. You know I ain't no virgin."

Jason gave him a sarcastic look. "I hope you ain't talking about that bitch we ran a train on at Daryl's house."

Chris didn't answer because that was one of the girls he was talking about.

"That shit don't count, Chris. Everybody hit that. And you didn't even get none."

"Yeah I did."

" No you didn't, fool. I remember."

"I didn't have no condom," Chris noted, his mouth full. "She gave me some head, though."

"First of all, you nasty for letting that bitch suck you off raw. You lucky you didn't catch nothing. Second, that still don't count. But anyway, you about to get your first *real* nut now – from somebody who actually likes you. I'm proud of you."

"I got my first *real* nut last night, Jaybird. Couple of 'em."

Jason smacked his lips. "Nigga, I don't wanna hear about you jacking off."

"Naw, fool. It wasn't no *jacking off*. I was with Tracy."

"Where?"

"A motel," Chris said nonchalantly. "Some place called the Sunset. I hadn't been before, but it's a nice place. *Real nice*." He smiled around his food and Jason laughed.

"Hell yeah, nigga! That's what I'm talking about. I knew you was gon' hit that, but *damn*, the same day? It took Demarcus damned near a week, and he had to get the bitch drunk first."

That comment took all of the excitement out of the conversation and all of the taste from Chris' meal. He suddenly had to go. He had to get up and walk out of the house without hearing anymore. There was a tight pressure in his chest that he couldn't blame on heartburn. It was a stinking, sinking feeling.

"What? What's wrong?" Jason asked.

"Nothing," Chris said. His fork wavered in the air with a heap of macaroni on it, but he couldn't eat anymore. He lowered the fork and braced himself for the news.

"You ain't catching no feelings for the bitch, is you?" Jason asked.

"Naw. I mean, she cool." Chris leaned back and wondered why he hadn't expected this. Nothing was perfect. Never pure.

COLORED RAGS

Always tainted. Everything in the hood was foul. He should have known better.

"Say, don't be falling in love with Tracy, homey. She a ho, Chris. Done fucked every nigga in Stop Six. She just a little *something something* we pass around." Jason gave him a look. "I mean, what kinda broad gon' fuck the first day she meet you?"

Chris thought about *Dharma and Greg*.

"You ain't falling in love, is you?" Jason asked. "Don't start acting like a mark. She'll run all over you."

"Naw. She cool," Chris said. The food in his belly stirred uneasily. "Why you didn't tell me?" he asked.

"Tell you what? She a ho? Nigga, I'm telling you *now*. You ain't bought the bitch nothing. You ain't took her out or spent no money on her. What, you paid for the room? That's just thirty dollars. She worth it for that. Just don't have that broad taking you to the jewelry store or nothing stupid. You can still hit it. *Hit it all you want.* I'm just saying don't be falling in love with her, that's all."

Chris stood with his plate. "I gotta go."

"I thought she wasn't coming for thirty minutes."

"You shouldn't be listening while I'm on the phone. Anyway, I gotta take a bath. Change clothes. Plus the house ain't clean."

"Man, you ain't gotta clean up for that ho."

Chris wanted nothing more than for Jason to stop referring to Tracy as a ho or a bitch. He took his plate to the kitchen and then headed for the back door.

"You ain't gon' finish eating?"

"Sorry. I thought I had time, but I don't."

"Nigga, don't' be coming over here wasting no food!"

Chris stepped outside and Jason's mutts started barking at him. He got in his car thinking about the gun under the seat. The .380 couldn't help with this particular problem, but he was sure it would be useful at some point.

CHAPTER TWENTY
THE RUNNING MAN &
THE TRACY SITUATION

Dre ran like a drunken monkey. Fast and furious. His sneakers clomped the pavement. He did not look over his shoulder. No way. In all the horror movies he'd seen, that was the *soon-to-be-murdered's* downfall. If he looked back, his feet would get tangled beneath him. Or worse, with his luck a stop sign would appear where there was none before. His face would impact the pole with the finesse of Daffy Duck stepping on a rake.

The last time Dre ran this hard, it was Field Day at Wedgewood Elementary. He didn't want to run then, but participation was mandatory, so he took the second string in a 400 meter relay. By the time he rounded the corner to pass off to the third leg, their lead was lost. Regaining it was a task better suited for Carl Lewis than the eleven-year-olds who cursed their teacher for putting Dre on their team.

Will wasn't at the race, but in the back of his mind, Dre remembered hearing his voice. His brother's role of antagonist had always been solid.

You messed up the whole race! You had the lead and you messed it up! They shoulda never let you run with them. You sorry, Dre. You can't do nothing right!

Dre heard his brother's voice now. There was no way any of what happened was real. Will did not get out of his casket. Dre forced himself to believe that. Will *did not* get out of his casket. He *did not* speak. Even if he did, he couldn't have made it all the

COLORED RAGS

way out of the funeral home without someone else seeing him. But the voice wouldn't go away.

You's a ho ass nigga, Dre!
I swear to God.

Dre scurried into a busy intersection without the slightest regard for right of way. Fortunately people in his predicament did not get mowed down by SUVs. Maybe if he had a winning lottery ticket, he could rely on fate to sarcastically remove him from this world. But there was no accidental death for people fleeing from phantoms. They had to stay alive until the phantom got them.

Tires screeched and horns blared as motorists acted quickly to avoid plowing into the pudgy sprinter. Shouts of anger filled the intersection.

"Get yo fat ass out the street!"
"What the fuck wrong with you?"

A prostituted posted on the corner gave the best advice.
"Run, nigga! Run!"

Dre didn't know who she thought he was running from, but it didn't matter. She was right. He scampered like an antelope, dodging lampposts and hobos. His dress shirt caught a bubble of air and fluttered behind him like a parachute.

Dre did not divert from the main street. He didn't think ducking in alleyways would offer him any advantage. On the contrary, finding himself in an isolated area was the last thing he wanted. Will would get him for sure. But if Will was a ghost, wouldn't he find Dre no matter where he ran? This realization caused his heart to shudder. A deep grimace marred his features.

Dre's shoulders slumped, and his speed gradually slowed. He came to a teetering stop and immediately began to wheeze. His burning feet and sore ankles begged for mercy. He bent over gagging, with his hands on his knees. He couldn't get enough oxygen. His throat began to contract, attempting to bring up a meal that wasn't there.

As the world twisted around him, Dre found himself at Field Day again. Nappy-headed kids screamed for him to *run faster*, but he had nothing left. The third runner from his relay team snatched the baton from his sweaty hand and gave him an ugly sneer before turning quickly; valiantly trying to catch up with the other racers.

He closed his eyes and begged God for mercy. And he got it. Gradually the deep gulps of air stayed down, and he didn't cough so much. Once he caught his breath, Dre looked up weakly and saw he was in an area he recognized. He was still on Miller Avenue, as was Pinkey's Funeral Home. Having made no turns in his escape, he could see the full distance he'd traveled. Dre whimpered in dismay. He hadn't gone very far at all; probably less than half a mile. If he squinted, he could make out Pinkey's parking lot in the distance.

Sweat dripped off his chin and blotted the sidewalk. As the sun beat down on him, he revoked his prayer for mercy and wished instead for death. Knowing he wouldn't be delivered, he had to figure out what his next move would be.

He looked around and saw that he had stopped at a large brick building he wasn't familiar with. It had the looks of a church but sported no crosses or message board warning passerby's that STOP DROP AND ROLL DOESN'T WORK IN HELL!

The building had windows close to the ground that were darkly tinted. Dre approached one of them and was not surprised by the dilapidated reflection that stared back at him. To describe himself as a *hot mess* would be generous. The bruises from his uncle's assault looked terrible. He was sweating so hard, it looked like it was raining outside, but only on him.

Dre had little time to marvel at the disaster that was himself before a tall figure approached from behind. The tint on the window did not offer a great reflection, but Dre saw that the man had dark skin and wore a dark blue suit. Dre's heart was stressed from the running, but it found enough juice to kick into overdrive again.

He knew he couldn't get away from Will. There was nowhere to run. Nowhere to hide.

"You here for the meeting?"

Dre jumped and cowered from the voice, but he recognized right away that it wasn't his dead brother. He turned slowly, and a cool wave of relief washed over him. The man had dark skin, but his similarities to Will ended there. His hair was short. He had a large nose and thin lips. Instead of a blue bandana around his neck, he wore a neat bowtie. And his suit was actually black, not blue.

COLORED RAGS

    His eyes widened for a moment as he took in Dre's appearance, but his next emotion was a look of concern that was real and inviting.
    "You in trouble, brother?" the stranger asked.
    Dre shook his head but his mouth said, "Yes, sir."
    The man nodded as if he'd seen it all and dealt with the worse. "We can help you," he offered.
    Despite the ongoing terror that was his life, Dre chuckled. "God can't even help me."
    The man smiled. "Maybe you been asking for help from a god who sent his blonde-haired, blue-eyed son down here to save the world. Maybe the god you praying to is the wrong god."

• • • • • •

    Chris brought the .380 inside when he got home. He knew no one would steal his car. The piece of shit only cost him $500. The first time it broke down was on the way home after he purchased it. The gun, however, was precious. If someone stole that, it would hurt Chris in a deep and personal way.
    He straightened up the kitchen and living room a bit, but he'd lied to Jason. The front room was rarely used and always presentable. He turned on the stereo, which was tuned in to an R&B station. The music brought back memories from last night. He switched it to hip hop instead.
    He went to the kitchen to heat up the chicken his mother left him. He wasn't hungry, but he'd be damned if he'd give Jason the satisfaction of watching him lose weight while smoking weed. He ate quickly, knowing he'd lose his appetite a second time after Tracy arrived. There was still some food left when he finished, so he fixed another helping for her.
    His cellphone rang while he washed the dishes. Tracy was on the road this time.
    "What's up?"
    "What's your house number?"
    He told her.
    "I'm on your street."
    By the time he got outside, she was pulling into the driveway. She hopped out of her car wearing a short skirt with a skin-tight halter top. She didn't really have the body for the outfit,

but she managed to pull it off with a high degree of sexuality. She wore her hair in a pony tail. Her lips glistened with bright red lipstick. Chris thought she looked great, but he saw her in a different light now. He was guarded rather than excited by her arrival.

They embraced in the driveway.

"I missed you," she whispered against his neck. Her breath was warm and sweet.

"I missed you too," he said. "I made you dinner."

Tracy broke from the embrace and stared up at him. There was a twinkle in her eyes.

"You did?"

"Yeah. It ain't much. Some chicken, beans. It's good, though. I had some already."

Tracy smiled. "Nobody ever made me dinner before, except my mom."

They didn't have to make you dinner to get what they wanted, Chris thought but said nothing. He turned and led her into his home.

He sat with her at the dining table while she ate. Tracy didn't want to eat alone, so Chris found some lettuce and made himself a basic salad.

Tracy told him more about herself during the meal. To Chris' surprise, she aspired to be a physical therapist. Her lack of a high school diploma was a definite hindrance. If she couldn't make it to college, Tracy had entertained going to cosmetology school. Chris told her that was a good job too, but he suggested she follow her dreams and become a therapist.

After dinner, they moved to the living room and sat together on the couch. Tracy seemed content with the quiet evening, but Chris found it hard to keep his peace. Awful thoughts flooded his mind when she kissed him. He wondered how often kissing was on the agenda for a girl like her. How many times had her lips been wrapped around someone's penis? Even her sensual caresses made him uneasy. Tracy finally backed away and asked what was wrong.

Chris had been wondering how he would bring up the questions raging through his mind. He still didn't know where to begin.

"You know somebody named Demarcus?" he asked.

Tracy stared back without answering. She pursed her lips and lowered her head slowly. When she looked up again, Chris was shocked to see tears in her eyes.

"What he tell you?" she asked.

"Who, Demarcus?" Chris tried to maintain his callousness, but his stomach churned with compassion.

"No. Jason. What Jason tell you?" she asked.

Chris shrugged. "He told me a lot of stuff."

"Like what?" Tracy managed to maintain eye contact.

Chris shook his head. "He told me some things about you. I don't wanna say."

"He told you I been with Demarcus?"

"Yeah."

"Who else he say I been with?"

"He didn't say nobody else's name."

"He told you I was a ho?" Tracy asked, and the first tear fell.

Chris felt like shit. The girl had done nothing more than make him happy, and he repaid her by making her cry. But there was too much at stake for him to be weak. He could console her later, maybe. For now he had to know the truth.

"He said they pass you around," Chris said without batting an eye.

Tracy looked away, but only for a moment. Both eyes leaked now. "You believe him?"

"I don't know. I don't really know you."

"Why you make me dinner?" she asked.

"What you mean? What's wrong with that?"

"You got a good heart," Tracy said. She reached to touch him but drew back at the last moment.

"You do too," Chris said.

"I been through a lot," she admitted. "I used to do a lot of fucked up shit. I used to get high and drunk. I was, I was hanging around a lot of bad people, Chris. I was young. A lot of people took advantage of me when I was in school. I knew better, but I didn't believe in myself."

She sniffled and wiped her eyes with the back of her hand. "I don't wanna be like that no more. I wish I could move far away, where nobody knows me. I think about it all the time. I wanna go somewhere where I don't have no past. I wanna meet somebody,

somebody like you, and start all over, have a regular life. You know? A relationship like they do on TV." She frowned. "I know it can't happen though. I know that. I don't know why I thought it was gon' be different with you."

She stood to leave, but Chris grabbed her wrist and gently pulled her back to the couch. She cried and chuckled nervously.

"You a good person, Chris. I don't wanna fuck up your life."

"How you gon' fuck up my life?" he wondered.

"They not gon' let you alone about this. They gon' tell you, '*You messing with a ho. Tracy ain't shit. Everybody fucked her.*' They won't never let it go," she cried. "You don't deserve all that."

Chris gave it some thought. He figured she was probably right, but he wasn't one to judge people for their past. It seemed like a cold-hearted thing to do. He didn't consider every aspect of his decision, but there was something in his heart that wanted to give her a chance. He reached to wipe her tears.

"How long ago was all this happening?" he asked.

"It's been, like a year, but don't nobody wanna forget it."

"Did you have sex with Jason?" If she did, he knew he'd have to rethink his position on second chances. Jason wasn't a bad person, but that was a little too close for comfort.

"Hell naw!" Tracy said. *"Never!"*

That was good enough for Chris.

COLORED RAGS

CHAPTER TWENTY-ONE
NATION OF ISLAM

> *I travel through disgruntled hoods*
> *Through cemeteries, long since full*
> *Through hospitals on countless nights*
> *Where black men cling to fleeting life*
> *I travel through disgruntled streets*
> *Where my kind bring their own defeat*
> *Past bodies tossed amongst the shrubs*
> *Past gutters that await fresh blood*
> *Past toe tags with my brothers' names*
> *But still my people don't complain*

Dre was nearly an hour late to his first Nation of Islam meeting but found that he hadn't missed much. The stranger who invited him inside introduced himself as Brother Alfeni. He led Dre to a spacious room with fifty folding chairs facing the front. Less than half the chairs were filled, but that was probably a good crowd for a Wednesday night.

The lighting in the room was dim. All eyes were focused on a television stand parked front and center. A lot of the men wore suits similar to Alfeni's, but the rest were regular people from the neighborhood.

Dre sat on the back row, hoping he wouldn't draw attention to himself. Brother Alfeni sat next to him. Dre figured the Muslim stuck with him either to explain what was going on or to escort him out quickly if he started to act up. Either way, Dre was glad for the company. He couldn't stop from looking over his shoulder, expecting the next suited figure coming down the aisle to be his dead brother. Brother Alfeni placed a large, comforting hand on his shoulder.

"You're alright here, son," he whispered.

Dre hoped he was right about that.

On the television, a clean cut gentleman with fair skin spoke clearly and efficiently about the plight of the black man in America. The speaker explained that gangs, drugs, and prisons overcrowded with people of color could all be attributed to one central evil; *the white man.*

The speaker, who Dre later learned was the Honorable Louis Farrakhan, said black fathers were not good providers for their families, but this wasn't because they chose to get high and gangbang. It was because the concept of a black family was obliterated by the white man during the days of slavery.

The black man stole because he could not afford to buy the things he needed in the lop-sided economic system the white man created. The black man killed other black men because he was taught to hate himself by the white man. Dre knew he was being condescending and oversimplifying the speaker's message, but it seemed the black man had no problems that couldn't be attributed to the white man.

When the DVD ended, a short gentleman, who introduced himself as Brother Usama, stepped forward. He turned off the television and greeted the crowd. He asked for any new visitors to introduce themselves. A few people volunteered.

They greeted the crowd with a Muslim greeting Dre had only heard on television before. They all expressed frustration for the black man's plight and indicated they were on board for the resolution phase. Brother Alfeni asked Dre to introduce himself, but he didn't pressure him when Dre remained seated.

Brother Usama talked for another thirty minutes, mostly about the same things the man on the video said, but he made the conflict relatable to things that were happening in Overbrook Meadows. Towards the end of his speech, he brought up the recent gang killings. Usama didn't mention any names or locations, but Dre knew he was talking about his brother and the retaliation against the bloods. Usama did not blame these deaths on the white man. He said the Muslims in the city could prevent tragedies like this from being such a daily occurrence, if they had more support.

The meeting concluded with Brother Usama passing around the latest edition of *The Final Call.* He brought out a

COLORED RAGS

display with books, tapes, fruit baskets, and even natural hair tonics that were available for purchase from the Nation of Islam. There wasn't much money exchanged, but every dollar was received graciously.

● ● ● ● ● ●

Dre exited the building amidst a group of talkative men. He loitered in the parking lot, while the others headed for their vehicles. The sun was gone by then. A full moon beamed down on them, providing adequate lighting where the street lamps failed. Dre knew where he was and how to get home, but it would be a three mile walk. He didn't want to call his mother, because he knew she'd want answers. He didn't have an explanation for what happened at the funeral home.

He was grateful to find that the Muslims possessed a great deal of compassion.

"You don't talk much, do you?"

He turned and saw Brother Alfeni standing a few yards away.

"I don't know," he said. "I didn't know what to say in there. I ain't never been to a meeting like that."

"What'd you think about the message," the man asked.

"I don't know. I liked it," Dre lied.

"How'd you get here?"

"I walked."

"From where?"

"I live on the south side."

"You need a ride home, brother?"

Dre smiled.

● ● ● ● ● ●

They didn't talk much during the ride. Brother Alfeni did not turn on the radio. The silence was only broken by Dre's instructions to "Turn here," or "Make a left at that light." When they pulled to a stop in front of his house, Dre was surprised to see the residence was completely dark. The porch light wasn't even on. It was only nine o'clock, and Uncle Ray's car was in the driveway. A sliver of dread rolled down his spine.

Dre turned to thank the Muslim for the ride. He was alarmed to see Brother Alfeni staring at him with dark, unblinking eyes. In the darkness, the man was starting to look like Will again. There was so much going wrong in Dre's life, he wouldn't have been surprised if the Muslim attacked him.

But Brother Alfeni simply asked, "Who's hurting you, son?"

Dre shook his head and reached for the door handle. "I don't know. Prolly nobody."

"You were running like someone was after you. If you need help, maybe I can do something for you."

"Like what?" Dre asked, surprised by his own cockiness. He suspected many things that occurred in the days to come would be uncharacteristic of him. "My brother got killed a couple days ago," he told him. "He was one of the gangbangers that man was talking about."

"Is that who's after you?" Brother Alfeni asked, "the people who killed your brother?"

Dre wished it was that simple. "They think I could've did something; my brother's friends do. They think I could've stopped Will from getting killed, 'cause I was there. *But I couldn't.*" He looked to his dark house again. "It's not them, though. It's... I don't know what it was."

"Sometimes..." Brother Alfeni thought for a second. "Sometimes the pressures of this world can be too much for us to bear. Sometimes incidents like what's been happening in your neighborhood can unleash demons that torment the living. They torment the survivors. But you gotta be strong, Dre. Do you pray?"

He shook his head.

"Do you believe in God?"

Dre was hesitant but felt he had nothing to lose. "I do, but I guess not the same one y'all believe in."

"I'm not trying to convert you, young brother. Not right now, anyway. I just want you to be okay. As long as you believe in some greater being that has the power to loosen the devil's grip on you, that's fine.

"Listen, you know where our building is. If you ever want to come by and talk, you're always welcome there. If you decide that Jesus isn't the answer, I can certainly help you build a relationship with Allah. There is only one true God, but I

COLORED RAGS

understand if you're not ready to receive that knowledge. I'm here for you either way."

The man stuck out a large hand for him to shake. Dre feared that if he took it, the Muslim would pull him close and strangle the life out of him. Knowing that was silly, he shook the man's hand.

"Thanks for the ride."

"You be careful, brother. I'm gonna pray for you."

● ● ● ● ● ●

Inside the house, Dre found that all of the lights weren't off. One of the bedrooms offered enough illumination for him to make it to his room without bumping in to anything. As he drew nearer, he saw that the light was coming from his mother's room. Dre wanted to apologize for his antics at the wake, but he heard her snoring lightly as he passed. He reached in and turned her light off without waking her.

When he turned the light on in his bedroom, Dre got such a shock, he stumbled backwards in fear. He fell into the hallway wall, which was the only thing that stopped him from landing on his butt. Uncle Ray sat on his bed. Apparently he'd been sitting in the dark. Even more surprising, Ray wore nothing but his boxer shorts. Because of his many folds, his body appeared more massive than usual. The big man was staring at the floor. He didn't seem to notice the light or his nephew.

Dre prayed his uncle wouldn't start more trouble, but he had already decided not to fight back. He'd go limp and allow the beast to toss him around freely. Surely he would eventually get bored and leave him alone.

Dre waited in silence until his uncle looked up at him with weary eyes. Dre did not enter his room. They stared at each other for a few moments, and then the larger man took a deep breath.

"You, *you ran*. You running like that. What that supposed, to mean? I was, thinking you, that you just didn't want, to go to the wake. I was gon' wait for you. For you to get home. I was gon', hurt you, Dre. Hurt you *bad*, for leaving yo mama, like that. You know what she, told me? She said, you having a hard time, dealing with what, happened. She say you can't, stand to look, at yo brother. That's why, you ran."

Dre's heart thundered. He shifted his weight from one foot to another.

"This one on me," Ray went on. "I'ma let you, let you make it, this time. But don't think, you ain't going to that, that boy's funeral. You gon' face him, Dre. You going."

Uncle Ray stood, and Dre retreated into the darkness, even though the behemoth just promised to let him make it. The ex-con left his room without another word. He flipped the light off on his way out. The house was completely dark then. Dre let out a stale, pent up breath as he crept into his room. He lay on his bed fully clothed with no intention of getting up until sunrise.

After a while his heartbeats slowed, and he could think about his dreadful day with a little clarity.

Brother Alfeni said the devil was attacking him. It was easy for Satan to get a foothold, because Dre's life was in such disarray. He never thought about it like that, but it made sense in a way. Only a demon could rise from the dead, and the way Uncle Ray was preying on his own flesh and blood was certainly demonic.

Dre wondered if he had to become a Muslim to vanquish the evil spirits that had targeted him. He had never been too gung-ho for Jesus either, so maybe it was his overall lack of faith that led to this quandary. He knew there was a bible in the house somewhere. Maybe there was a passage he could read for ghosts and goblins.

Dre closed his eyes and felt sleep rushing over him like many powerful waves. He didn't realize how exhausted he was. He felt like his body and mind had been overstressed for the past two days. Unfortunately sleep would remain elusive tonight.

A rustling sound coming from the closet made Dre's eyelids pop open. He experienced mice before – no ghetto dwelling was free of the vermin for very long – but the sound he heard had not come from a rodent. In his closet, he distinctly heard a coat hanger slide across the rail.

Dre squeezed his eyes shut and fought off the new wave of terror that was trying to take hold. There were no ghosts. There was nothing in his closet. Whatever he heard was in his mind, because even if there were demons lurking about, they did not have the ability to move objects in the world of the living.

Demons do not have the power to open doors either, but Dre heard the hinges of his closet door squeaking, and he knew it

COLORED RAGS

was not in his mind. He heard labored breathing also, which was as real as the sound of Dre's teeth gnashing together behind his closed lips.
    Why you run, Dre? You think them Muslims can help you? Will chuckled. It was a wet, bloody snicker, void of humor. *Nigga, you really is stupid.*

CHAPTER TWENTY-TWO
PAPA ERNEST &
DRE'S BEDMATE

And when the night finds me alone
His ghastly figure prowls my home
My mirrors reflect only his face
He's in the shadows when I awake
His grisly visage haunts me so
My life's an anchor for his soul

And when I drive by where he died
Where sirens wailed and mourners cried
I hear screams come from everywhere
I see a body that's no longer there
I have fulfilled the devil's plan
I now know fear. I killed a man

    Michael Hammonds attempted to open his eyes. He felt his body being jostled by unseen hands; fingers that were rough and cold.
    Stop! he shouted but was dimly aware that no words left his mouth.
    What? What's wrong? a voice asked him. The voice was familiar but sounded muffled and far away. It sounded like someone was speaking to him from a well.
    What you doing? Mike asked.
    I'm hooking you up, nigga! You know what a fucking mess you are? Blood and pus everywhere. Check this out.

COLORED RAGS

Mike heard a rough, ripping sound. A moment later he felt excruciating pain as his shirt was torn away from his wound, taking skin, hair and a hardening scab with it.

Mike cried out in agony. He tried to reach up to block his tormentor, but his arms were too heavy. There were fifty pound barbells affixed to both wrists.

You see this? the voice asked, and there was another

WRIIIP!

Blood and pus everywhere! Fresh blood! You bleeding like a stuck pig.

Bloody red red rum rum rum rum rum rum

Stop! Mike screamed.

Oh, no. Can't stop. Gotta get you ready, cuz. Gotta get you ready for The Murder Show.

Killa, Mike spat defiantly.

What?

Killa, nigga. Ain't no cuz here, dog. This Blood!

Blood, huh? Oh, yeah. That's right. Y'all go hard. You and Spider and them. Y'all some hardcore gangstas, ain't cha? I better watch my back.

You already dead, Mike reminded the phantom.

See, now that's just wrong, cuz. Nigga ain't do nothing but try to help you; make sure you look decent for the party. And you wanna throw that shit in a nigga's face.

Leave me alone!

The creep chuckled. There was a wet, whistling quality to his laughter.

*You know what, cuz? You sound like a ho-ass nigga right about now with that 'leave me alone,' shit. Mikey, you know I ain't going nowhere. We're like soul mates, ya dig? You and me, we got what they call **destiny**.*

Leave me alone, Mike said again, pleading this time.

Alright, cuz. Alright. I just got this one last...

● ● ● ● ● ●

WRIIIP!

This time the pain was fiery and most definitely real. Mike sat up with a start and lashed out at his caretaker. His father backed away quickly, catching only a glancing blow on his massive chest.

Mike's breaths came quick and haggard. The two men stared at each other for a couple of seconds; the elder serious and concerned, while the youngster was confused, sweaty and bloody.

"What the fuck you doing?!" Mike bellowed.

The lights were on, but the apartment had a dull luminescence. It was as if Ernest only used 40 watt bulbs. The smell of boiling bologna filled Mike's nostrils and brought him to the verge of vomiting.

Ernest sighed and shook his head dispassionately. "You do know how fucked up your shit is, don't you?" he asked finally.

Mike looked down at himself. His shirt was gone, and he could see his wound clearly. His father was not exaggerating. The hole in his chest was ragged and clotted with gooey globs of coagulated blood that ranged in color from bright pink to impenetrable black in some spots. The outer edges of his wound were swollen, and they protruded a bit. Even with stitches closing the hole, Mike thought it looked like a vagina; a hairless, swollen, pus-filled vagina. He thought it smelled like a funky vagina too.

He wondered what the exit wound on his back looked like and figured it had to be worse. The pain he felt was something out of a hellish nightmare. It was unadulterated and un-medicated. Someone could have shoved a glowing fireplace poker in the wound and produced no further agony.

Ernest watched him closely. Mike sweated like he was in a sauna. His hair was rough and nappy. His lips were chapped, and his complexion had taken on an ashen shade.

"You ain't gon' make it, boy," he said matter-of-factly. "Uh-uhn. Not like this. Not the way you looking." He reached to the floor and brought up the torn top of Mike's blue scrub suit. It was filthy, caked with dried blood.

"I had to tear it to get it off you. That hole in your chest was starting to heal around it."

Mike squinted at the rags. He couldn't believe it was the same thing he wore from the hospital.

Ernest dropped the shirt and gestured to a plastic bag on the coffee table. "I went to the drug store to try to get you something. I got some stuff to clean you up with, some medicine and ibuprofens. I thought I could help you, but *shit boy*, this ain't gon' do it. You been sleep since you got here. Never seen nobody sleep that hard. I tried to wake you up, to get you in the shower. But you was dead to the world. It's four in the morning, and you just now opening your eyes."

Mike looked around but couldn't find a clock in the room.

"You didn't come around till I started pulling that shirt off," Ernest said. "You got a fever too. I don't know how bad it is, but you hot as hell. You sweating so bad, you got the whole couch wet. Feel it."

Mike didn't need to run his hand across the cushions to know how sick he was. Ernest wrinkled his brow, looked away and spat. He spat on his own floor in his own house. Mike was more awed by that sight than anything the man had said.

"I said you had to be outta here before I left for work today," Ernest reminded him. "I was trying to help you, you know, let you make it for a while till you got shit settled about where you was gon' go. But hell, boy, it ain't nothing for you to get settled. You either going to the doctor or to the morgue. I'm scared to go to sleep, 'cause I don't wanna wake up and find you dead on my couch. How the hell am I supposed to explain that?"

Mike felt his resentment for the man rising. He swallowed it down like vomit in the back of his throat. "I'm alright," he said hoarsely.

"Naw, *you ain't*! You been shot, boy! You needs a doctor. I can't put no Band-Aid on that. You gotta go back to the hospital, let them people finish fixing you up, before you decide to run off again."

Mike's eyes filled with tears, and the man softened.

"I ain't never did nothing for you," Ernest acknowledged. "I know you want me to do something to make this right, but I can't do nothing for you now, even if I wanted to. You been here damned near twelve hours, and you ain't ate nothing. When was the last time you had something to eat?"

Mike couldn't remember. His stay at the hospital felt like years ago.

"That's what I thought," Ernest grunted. "You want me to let you die in here, but I can't do it. I figure, the best thing I can do for you is to get you back to the hospital. You may not wanna go now, but later on, once you heal up, you'll thank me for it."

Mike's face contorted with anguish. *"They gon' kill me, man! Don't you get it? I'm gon' die if I go back there!"*

Ernest shook his head. "That don't make no sense, Mike. Even if it did, what you want me to do?"

"Let me stay here," he whined.

"*Why?* Why you wanna die here? What's the difference? At least over there you got a fighting chance. Over here you just—"

"*I'm not gon' die!*" Mike shouted with as much resilience as he could muster. "I can eat. I can take a shower, if you want me to."

Ernest sneered. "You ain't been off this couch—"

"I can get up," Mike assured him. He threw his legs to the floor and gathered enough strength to sit up. It was hard. His arms shook like he had Parkinson's.

His father sat on the coffee table and watched him without expression. After another strong push, Mike managed to rise to his feet. But he knew his father was right. His head hurt, and the world swam in gray and black dots. He looked past them and focused on his provider.

"I'm alright," he said. "I'm not dying."

Ernest watched him with more pity in his eyes than love. "Sit down," he said.

"*I'm alright.*"

"Boy, sit down," his father urged.

Mike eased his body down carefully. He felt the dampness of the sofa cushions. They really were soaked.

"You think you gon' get better?" his father asked. Mike opened his mouth to respond but was cut off. "I know for a fact you ain't gon' make it without going back to the doctor." Ernest sighed. "Look, I'm not gon' argue with you. I gotta go to work in a couple of hours." He gave Mike a hard look. "I know I'ma regret this, but I'ma let you stay here till I get back."

Mike's elation was so great, he almost leaned in for a hug.

"We gon' get you cleaned up before I go. And I'ma fix you something to eat."

Mike hoped it wasn't boiled bologna.

"Take some of them pills too," Ernest went on.

Mike nodded.

COLORED RAGS

"When I get back from work, if you don't look no better, if you still sweating and you ain't stopped bleeding, you going back to the hospital." He waited for his son to argue the point.

Mike didn't say anything.

"I mean it, boy. If you don't say you cool with that, you gotta go right now."

"I'm okay," Mike repeated.

"I'm talking about when I get home from work."

"I'll be okay then too. If I ain't better when you get back, you can take me. I won't argue or nothing."

Ernest nodded as if he'd won a battle.

Mike grinned inwardly because he felt the same way. Whatever was to happen, he knew he could do it while the man was at work. Eight hours was plenty of time.

The matter settled, Ernest stood. "I'ma run you some water for your bath, unless you wanna take a shower.

Mike knew the gig would be up if he fell in the shower. "I'll take a bath."

"I want you to take you some of them ibuprofens," Ernest called over his shoulder as he left the room. "I'ma fix you something to eat too. I ain't leaving till you eat."

Mike fought the pain as he rifled through the bag on the coffee table. His father had spent no more than twenty dollars on him, but that was more than Mike could remember him spending his entire life. According to the bottle of ibuprofens, they would help with his pain as well as the fever. The antibiotic ointments probably wouldn't do much, but he would spread the cream on his wound if it pleased Ernest. The best thing in the bag was the gauze and medical tape. It was similar to the supplies he left on the bus yesterday.

Mike did not feel love or compassion for his father in the traditional sense. But he had to admit Ernest came through for him at a time when he had no one else to turn to. On a gangster level, he developed a new respect for the man. He only felt marginally bad about his intentions to burn him. It had to be done. Burning his father was not only an option, it was part of the SOLUTION all along.

● ● ● ● ● ●

Dre lay on his side as far on *his* side of the bed as he could get. His eyes were wide and bloodshot. He gripped the mattress tightly with fingertips that were white and cold. He held on to the mattress for dear life because Will was in bed with him, and *dead* Will was heavy. The mattress sank under dead Will's weight. If Dre let go, he would roll into his brother's body.

The clock on the nightstand registered 4:23 am. Dre stared at the bright, red digits, waiting for the three to become a four. When he was a child, he remembered playing this clock game; watching without blinking to try to catch the numbers change. The game wasn't as fun now. When a minute passed, it would be the 429th time in a row he saw the time change since Will got in bed with him at 9:14 pm.

In the past seven hours, Dre had a lot of time to think about things. His mother raised him to look for a bright side, so he considered how his predicament could be any worse. He figured he *could be* buried up to his neck on the beach with no options but to wait for the rising tide to drown him. He saw that in a movie once and had nightmares about it for months. A few other worst case scenarios came to mind, but Dre knew his current dilemma was as close to hell as he was likely to get above ground.

In the 429 minutes since Will got in bed with him, Dre had time to evaluate his sanity. He was fairly certain he'd gone insane, but it wasn't that cut and dry. As bizarre as it sounded, a lot of evidence pointed to the possibility that Will really was there. How else could he interact with all five of Dre's senses?

Not only could Dre see his dead brother, but he could hear him clearly as Will coughed, breathed and snored. And how could a ghost cause a mattress to sink, like it did when Will got into bed? Dre was not imagining the depression behind him. The only thing keeping him away from his dead brother was his grip on the mattress. His mind couldn't fake all of that. His mind couldn't fake the moist breaths he felt on the back of his neck. It was all very real.

As Dre watched the clock, 4:23 became 4:24. Behind him his dead brother breathed roughly and feigned sleep. Dre knew Will was faking because dead people had no need for slumber. Will repositioned himself on the mattress ever so often. He coughed and wheezed but didn't talk. He only said one thing when

COLORED RAGS

he got into bed. Those words played over and over in Dre's frazzled mind.
We'll talk about this tomorrow.
This shit'll all be over tomorrow.
In a couple of hours the sun would rise.

Dre couldn't wait for the new day. He desperately wanted to get out of bed. He would've done so by now, but he knew Will didn't want him to. He wasn't sure what would happen if he tried. Even if Will only reached and pulled him back down, Dre knew it would be more than he could bear.

The slightest caress from that cold, dead hand would send him spiraling into an abyss of frantic screams. Once they began, the shrieks would never stop. Dre imagined himself in a white room with padded walls. Straight-jacketed and chained to the floor, he would still be screaming. He would have grown a beard and a full afro, and he would still be screaming.

So Dre remained as motionless as possible. His breaths were shallow. His pulse knocked like tap shoes. He listened to the dead sounds behind him as Thursday gradually gave way to Friday. He was surprised that he made it this long.

But that was before Will started stinking.

It was a dreadful odor. Dre gagged and sneered at the stink. He closed his mouth to avoid getting it on his tongue but found that inhaling through his nose was much worse. It occurred to him that he had encountered this stench before.

When they were 10 and 8 respectively, Will and Dre went to Sycamore Park, after their mother demanded they get some fresh air. It was too early and too hot for basketball, so the brothers explored the grounds, finding adventures in the shadowy creek that ran through it. The brook was congested with litter, dragonflies, clouds of gnats and the occasional bullfrog that always managed to elude the boys in the high grass along the bank.

Midway through their expedition, the brothers made a discovery that was grotesque and gruesome but also morbidly fascinating. A full grown pit bull dog floated, bloated in a deeper section of the creek. Deep scars and gouges around the beast's muzzle and forearms led Will to conclude the animal was a fighting dog, a loser most likely. Floating in the water, the pit had not been afforded the opportunity to decompose properly. Maggots swarmed on every mound of flesh above water.

The skin around the dog's face was stretched taut, revealing a death mask that frightened Dre. As filthy as the creature was, its teeth were very white and very sharp.

Dre wanted to move on, but this was too great a find for Will to walk away from. He got a long, skinny branch and commenced to poke and prod the corpse. He found a spool of fishing line and tried to lasso one of the dog's legs, so he could pull it ashore. When the carcass drifted too far to be prodded, the boys settled on throwing rocks at it.

The stench of the pit bull ten years ago was the same odor Will had now. In his delusion, Dre began to believe the body in bed with him was not Will at all. It was the dog carcass. Maggots dripped from its muzzle and squirmed on Dre's pillow. Bloated, with eyes foggy like cataracts, the monster filled the bedroom with an odor so foul Dre couldn't understand why his mother or uncle hadn't come to investigate.

At 6:23 the first twinkles of sunrise invaded his room. A new day had come. Dre had no doubt a new batch of horrors had come with it, but he was grateful for the sun. He knew that if he made it through this Friday, his brother would torment him no longer.

Will may have been dead, but he was still an OG, and his word was his bond. He told his little brother, *This shit'll all be over with tomorrow.* For better or worse, Dre looked forward to a resolution.

CHAPTER TWENTY-THREE
KODY'S STASH

Man, I done been through a lot of shit
I guess the gang life made me hard
I'm the type of nigga that most white people
Try to avoid or disregard
Man, I done had some fine ass women
A fat bankroll and some fancy cars
But I ain't never gon' get used to this
I can't stand these goddamn bars!

I told the judge I was an innocent nigga
"Your Honor, I never touched a dime"
I told him the cops must've planted that dope
'Cause it sure as hell wasn't mine
That fat-ass fool just smiled at me
He said, "Boy, I know who you are"
Then that ham hock eating sonofabitch
Put my ass behind these goddamn bars!

I ain't never regretted nothing I did
Not even smoking that nigga Shaun
Everybody know I'm quick to slap a bitch
That type of shit don't bother me none
But I'd give up every cent I made
If I could jump in one of my cars
And floor it until the engine screams
To get away from these goddamn bars!

Chris was awake when his brother called.
"Did you get the money?"

"Damn, bro. *I'm doing alright.* How are you?"

"What?" Kody didn't appreciate the sarcasm. "What you talking about, fool?"

"I said I'm doing alright – even though you didn't ask."

"You full of shit, nigga."

Chris knew he was being a dick, but he didn't like how Kody always bossed him around. No *Hi* or *Hello*, just *Where's my money*? Now that Kody was in jail, his control over his little brother had greatly diminished.

"I got the money," Chris said. "But it was messed up trying to get that coat outta there. Croc over there tripping. He wouldn't even let me in."

"What you mean he wouldn't let you in? He tripping how?"

"Trez said he's trying to lock shit down, like he's running things."

"That nigga a goddamn fool. How you get my coat, if they wouldn't let you in?"

"I had to get Trez to go in there and get it for me," Chris said, thinking he'd be applauded for his ingenuity.

"*Man*! Why you do that?" Kody scowled.

"What was I supposed to do?"

"You can't trust that nigga! You can't trust *none of them niggas*. They all looking for a come-up, cuz. What you think we do at that apartment?"

Chris didn't want to say. He knew the calls were being recorded, and Kody knew it too.

"All they think about is money," Kody said. "Day in and day out. They don't do nothing that ain't finna put some paper in they pocket."

"I know that," Chris told him.

"Then how you know Trez didn't dip in it?"

"Because I could tell how surprised he was when I showed him what was in–"

"*You showed him*? Damn, nigga! Why you do that?"

"'Cause he kept asking what it was. Plus he went and got it for me. He got it for *you*. He told me to tell you that. You didn't tell me not to show nobody."

COLORED RAGS

"Damn, Chris. You shouldn't have did that. You can't trust them niggas. They my homeboys, but still. Even I don't trust 'em like that."

"My bad," was all Chris could say.

"Did you count it?" Kody asked. "Is all 200 there?"

Chris knew he was still using 200 to represent the $20,000 he actually had. "Yeah, I counted it yesterday. It's all there."

"All two hundred?"

"Yes. All of it."

Chris could hear his brother smiling over the phone.

"That's good, Chris. Man, I love you, cuz. Take a hundred out and get one of those things you always getting from your homeboy over there, so you don't have to go to them apartments no more. If you gon' do what you do, you might as well have your own shit."

He was using more detailed code words now, but Chris knew what he was saying. Kody just rewarded him with a hundred dollars to buy his own weed from Trez, in an effort to keep him away from the Evergreen. Chris didn't have a job. His mother rarely gave him that much money outside of school shopping. He was ecstatic.

"Thanks."

"You put my ends up somewhere safe?" Kody asked.

"Yeah. I guess so."

"You ain't gotta say where it's at," Kody said. "Just don't leave it nowhere stupid, like under your mattress."

Chris was sitting on his bed at the moment. His ears burned with embarrassment. "Okay."

"What about the other thing in the coat?"

Chris knew he was talking about the gun. His whole body froze. "What other thing?"

"Quit playing. I know it was in there."

"There wasn't anything else, just the two hundred," Chris lied effortlessly.

"Don't worry about it," Kody said.

Chris didn't know if he was dropping the subject because of the recording or if he didn't remember if he'd left the gun in the coat or not. Either way, he felt a rush of exhilaration. He just stole a gun – from his big brother, no less.

"Are you gonna get a lawyer?" he asked.

"Maybe. I don't know. They supposed to get me a court-appointed. If he know what he's doing, I might let him work the case. If I can beat this without spending my money, that would be good. I guess I'm just gon' cool out for now, wait to hear what the punk ass prosecutor got to say."

"How you holding up."

"This ain't shit," Kody said. He was all bravado. "You know I been through this before. Everybody in here know me. They looking at me like I'm the black Charles Manson or some shit. I'm getting much respect. *Mad love.* You ain't even gotta put no money on my books. These niggas give me anything I want."

From a lesser man, Chris would have doubted what he just heard, but he knew his brother was telling the truth.

"Did they set a bail for you yet?"

"Hmph. Yeah, but not really. They still bullshitting. They want a quarter-million. You believe that? *A quarter-million dollar bail.*" Kody laughed. Chris could tell it was forced. "I don't know who the hell they think I am."

The black Charles Manson? Chris thought.

"They gon' reduce it, though," Kody said. "They just want me to sit in here till I get antsy enough to take a plea. This ain't nothing new."

Kody sounded confident, but Chris felt chills roll down his body. Would they put his brother away for real this time? For decades? He was afraid to consider it. He was glad when Kody changed the subject.

"Anyway, how Mama doing...?"

● ● ● ● ● ●

When he got off the phone, Chris took his money from his brother's stash. He knew the cash was dirty, but short of giving it to one of the crackheads Kody victimized, there was nothing he could do to make it clean.

He showered and dressed quickly. He checked on his mother and found her fast asleep. It was eleven am, so she'd be asleep for several more hours. Today was the last day of her work week. He looked forward to spending time with her over the weekend.

COLORED RAGS

    The .380 was the last thing he picked up before leaving. It was in his underwear drawer; shiny and inviting. He stuffed it in his front pocket and pulled it out again the second he made it to his car. Chris sat in his hooptie and popped the clip out again. He cocked the weapon, to make sure the chamber was empty. It felt good to manipulate the gun. He figured he should be comfortable with it, since it was his property now.

    He was so captivated by the pistol, he barely had time to stash it under his seat when a car pulled in the driveway behind him. A thin figure jumped out of the passenger seat. It was Trez. Chris watched him warily through the rear-view mirror.

    Without his trademark giddiness, Chris expected his friend to have more sour news from the south side of town. But why would Trez come to him with the news? As Croc so eloquently pointed out, Chris wasn't a loc.

    Instead of something asinine, Trez jogged up to his car, poked his head in the open passenger window, and delivered information so ominous, it made all the hairs stand on Chris' arms.

    Trez's eyes were wide and very concerned.

    "Hey, you still got that money, cuz? Croc say that's *his* money."

KEITH THOMAS WALKER

CHAPTER TWENTY-FOUR
GANGSTA GHOUL

We congregate in the parking lot
Though slow, dark cars are creeping near
If I die crumpled on this block
Then I'm immortal, so there's no fear
Sneaky Crown Vic's are slow and mean
When their windows spit, our bodies are lifted
Sometimes slugs go through smooth and clean
We still throw up signs with missing digits
Sometimes I think about myself
Bullets that miss stay on my mind
Fuck all the fame, I just want wealth
But fame and wealth are intertwined
My enemies shoot every time we meet
Shotgun blasts start to sound like bombs
Every slow car might bring defeat
Daily it feels like Vietnam
Sometimes I contemplate my race
I've developed a theory a million strong
Even if we don't say, it's blacks that blacks hate
A million blasting pistols can't be wrong

Dre's eyes flashed open, and he sat up in bed with a jolt. The digital clock on his dresser read 11:02 am. He didn't remember falling asleep – didn't think it was possible under the circumstances – but somehow he must have succumbed to slumber. He turned quickly, relieved to see he was the only one in the bed. There was an indention in the sheets where someone had slept next to him, but it wasn't concrete evidence. He wouldn't be

COLORED RAGS

able to show it to his mother as proof that Will had spent the night in there.

Dre scanned the room, not sure what he was looking for. There was no ectoplasmic ooze on the wall from a ghost portal. He couldn't find any other evidence that Will had been in his room. No footprints. No burial garments discarded. No blood. Dre noticed the closet door was closed, but he was sure Will had left it open. The smell of a long dead canine was faint but still present.

It was a new day, but that didn't mean it was a better day. Dre knew his brother would pop up at some point. But he was starting to wonder if it might be possible to thwart Will's plans. Will could do a lot of things, for a ghost, but the one thing he hadn't done yet could work to Dre's advantage: So far, Will had not manifested a visible presence before anyone but his little brother.

Dre smiled a little as the smell of dog carcass titillated his nasal passage. He had a plan, and it was simple. All he had to do was make sure he stayed around other people. Today was Will's last chance to accomplish whatever his mission was. If Dre wasn't available for haunting, he would have to find another unlucky soul to manipulate.

Dre threw his legs over the bed but he caught himself. He snatched his feet from the floor and let out a dry chuckle.

That's what you want me to do, he thought.

"You almost got me," he whispered.

Instead of getting up, Dre lay flat on his stomach and pushed his body forward, until his head hung over the bed. He inched his face down until he could see the creep hiding on the floor. There he was. Will lay flat on his stomach. He smiled. His arms were cocked back, and his hands were bent like hooks; ready to snatch unsuspecting ankles and pull frightened little boys into the darkness with him.

Will's eyes caught a glint of morning sunlight, and they flared with all the intensity of a demon scheming. His lips were pulled back over massive teeth. His canines glistened like fangs. His fingernails had continued to grow after death. They were now fierce talons, ready to rip skin from flesh, muscles from tendons and meat from bones.

But – there was no one under the bed.

Dre blinked a few times to make sure. Blood rushed to his head and made his face tingle.

"You ain't under there?" he asked an old sock and combat boot. "That's alright. I know you in the closet."

Dre got out of bed and stood on wet noodle legs that protested his lack of sleep. He boldly approached the closet. It would only take a moment to open it and put an end to all of the fear, misconceptions, and impractical nonsense.

There would be clothes in there. There would be shoes on the floor, along with a couple of shirts that had fallen off the hangers. There would be comic books and a few nudie magazines on the top shelf. There would be shadows and maybe a roach or two, but there would be no corpse. Dre was *almost* sure of this. But…

"Naw," he said with a knowing grin. "That's what you want me to do."

Dre left his room without changing clothes and sought the refuge only an eyewitness could offer.

● ● ● ● ● ●

He found his mother in the kitchen, making a feeble attempt to straighten up. She looked up and smiled at her son as he rounded the corner. Dre felt like she was looking at him without really seeing him. She sported dark, raccoon eyes that reminded him of blows she used to take from her last boyfriend.

It was Will who got rid of Johnny Lee. Dre had sat in the blacked-out Cutlass and watched him and three of his homeboys beat the man viciously for nearly five minutes. Will accented each of his blows with a warning to stay away from his mother. Johnny spent two nights in the hospital, and they never saw him again.

Seeing his mother in the kitchen, Dre felt a mixture of pity and admiration. Will had been her sun, her moon and all of the stars that twinkled at night. There was no problem she couldn't go to him with, and the same went for Will. He shared his deepest secrets with her. Esther never officially condoned his lifestyle, but she respected him and prayed for all of the bad decisions he made.

That morning she wore a purple nightgown with a thin robe that dragged on the floor. Esther was very thin, with features that were borderline skeletal. Dre knew she hadn't eaten much

COLORED RAGS

since Will's death, but she looked a lot worse than he expected. She reminded him of Diana Ross towards the end of *Lady Sings the Blues*.

    Esther wiped the counter with a soiled washcloth and sent a coffee cup careening to the floor without noticing. Dre moved quickly but was not able to catch it in time. Luckily, the cup was sturdy. It only lost the handle upon impact. Dre reached between his mother's legs to retrieve the broken pieces. She stepped back but didn't comment on what he was doing.

    He opened the pantry to discard the mug and found the small waste basket so full it was regurgitating trash.

    "You want me to wash the dishes?" he asked.

    "Naw," Esther said. She returned to the sink and turned the water on. "I don't have nothing else to do." She was so detached, Dre feared she might slit her wrist on a stray knife while reaching into the sink.

    "I'ma take this trash out. Then I'll help you," he told her. She didn't respond, but Dre knew his company would be welcome.

    When he was younger, he and his mother often washed dishes together. He would usually dry and put them away while she washed. He didn't think it would be the same today as it was back when they were cheerful and more naive. But he looked forward to standing shoulder to shoulder with her again.

    Maybe she would touch him, hold him and possibly kiss him. If nothing else, he hoped they could talk and cry together, instead of crying in separate rooms, battling separate demons.

● ● ● ● ● ●

    It was not a scheduled pick up day for Overbrook Meadows' garbage collectors, so Dre had to take his trash bag around the side of the house, where they kept two large bins.

    The sun was sweltering. It was unusually hot and humid for eleven o'clock in the morning. Dre found himself sweating as he held the bag with one hand and opened the trash can with the other. The waste bin was half-full. Maggots were everywhere – not just on the trash, but also on the underside of the lid. An odor Dre would describe as *dead rat* wafted from the garbage, but there was another smell. It was the stench of Sycamore Creek and bullfrogs and a bloated pit bull dog.

Dre dropped the bag and looked around warily. He was not terribly surprised to see his dead brother creep from around the back of the house. He was, however, surprised by the goon's appearance. Will looked like he woke up early and decided to make a clubhouse in the bushes. His suit was grubby, past the point of anything a drycleaner could do to restore it. There were deep, ground-in stains on his knees and shoulders. His jacket was open, revealing clumps of dried blood on his shirt. One of his shoes was completely caked in dried mud. The other was missing altogether, probably sucked off in the same puddle that mucked up the other.

Will's face reminded Dre of their mother. His eyes were sunken deep in the sockets, with whites so deeply crimson, it was hard to tell where the pupil ended. His cheekbones were sharp and pronounced. Will's teeth, pointy and glistening, were bared in an interminable grimace as he struggled to shorten the distance between himself and his brother. He marched with obvious pain on legs that were stiff and jerky. A noticeable flash of distress shone on his face with each step he managed. Despite all of this, Will moved quickly. His dexterity was surreal.

Dre stood frozen in place. He wondered how Will was able to get around, with all of the pain he seemed to be experiencing. Will looked like he would fall flat on his face with each step, but he didn't. When he reached his little brother, he steadied himself by placing the crooked claw his hand had become on the rim of the trash bin. Dre still held the lid open. He saw that Will's hand landed in a swarming pile of maggots. They wiggled between his fingers in a continuous death dance.

Dre frowned as he studied his brother's gruesome face. He fought the urge to pick blades of yellowed grass from Will's goatee.

You ready? Will asked. His voice was deep and gravely. He lowered his head and panted, his bony shoulders rising and falling.

"Ready for what?" Dre asked.

Will looked up at him with an almost pleading expression, but his death mask gave Dre the impression of a smile. Will had a sinister visage that would put cracks in the faith of even the staunchest believer in Christ. He spat out a huge wad of burgundy mucus before speaking.

It's time, Dre. You said you was gon' help me today.

COLORED RAGS

"What's *wrong* with you?" Dre asked. His face wrinkled in disgust rather than fear of his dead, ailing sibling.

I got shot, nigga, Will said, his notorious temper rising. *But you know that, don't you? You was there. Remember?*

"But you dead," Dre reasoned. "Why you looking like that?"

Man... Will gave him a sarcastic look. *It's a lot you don't know about this here, cuz. But we gotta go. We gotta talk.*

Dre shook his head. "I don't wanna go. You *dead*, Will. You not even really here."

Will emitted a dark, creepy chuckle that sent waves of horror down Dre's spine.

Oh, you going, Dre. You ain't got no choice.

Dre knew there had to be some mystical logic to what his brother said, but had to hear it for himself.

"What if I don't go?"

Will stared deeply into his eyes. *If you don't go, then I ain't going either. You wanna help Mama with the dishes? Shee, we can both help. I don't think she wanna see me like this, though. She'll prolly go crazy, cuz. You know how she is. I don't think her little heart can take no more.*

"But she can't see you," Dre told him. "I'm the only one who can see you."

Will's head cocked slowly to the side. *Who told you that shit, Dre? You been reading books about this or what? You wanna find out if she can see me, nigga? If you wanna put that on her, we can. It's up to you.*

Dre considered calling his bluff, but he couldn't risk sending his mother to an asylum. He wanted to slam the trash can lid down on his brother's hand. While caught up in the agony of his maggoty fingers being crushed, Dre could shove him hard in the chest. He was never able to over-power his big brother in life, but he felt he had an advantage over Will in death. He could follow up the shove with a clever kick to the nuts. But what then? There was no winning this fight. There was no end.

Oh, there is an end to this, Dre, Will informed him. *I told you, this will all be over with today. But we gotta start right now.*

Dre looked around and was not surprised to find no one around to witness this conversation. He picked up the bag and dropped it in the trash can. He let the lid fall, but Will moved his hand away in time to avoid injury. Dre brought a hand to his mouth subconsciously and began to nibble his thumbnail.

"You got a maggot on your hand," he told his brother.

Will looked and then used his free hand to thump it off. *I been having problems with them motherfuckers*, he admitted.

Will lifted his shirt. Dre wished he hadn't. The gunshot wound to his belly was like a deep bedsore. A whole tennis ball could fit in the hole. Fat maggots squirmed around in a frothy mixture of blood and pus. A couple of them rolled out and wiggled down Will's pants leg.

He lowered his shirt and smiled. *C'mon, Dre. Let's do this.*

"Where we going?"

To Sycamore Park, Will said and began to stagger down the street. *We going to the park like we used to, when we was little.*

COLORED RAGS

CHAPTER TWENTY-FIVE
THE MISSION

You got hit
Do you remember?
You were at the spot
Kicking it with your boys
Snorting that powder
Don't you remember?
Didn't you try to run when someone started shooting?
And then you felt something like a sledgehammer
Hit you in the chest
And then your legs stopped working
Do you remember when you fell in slow motion
And hit the ground
And felt your blood leaking from you?
Drip drop

    Mike waited until after eleven before embarking on his mission. Ernest said he was going to work and would assess his condition when he got home. But only a fool would believe that based on his word alone.
    Ernest may not have gone to work at all. Maybe he was planning to double-back and catch his son in some mischief. He might call Mike's mother and tell her what was going on. Even worse, Ernest might call the police to see if there was a reward for his shot-up son. So Mike waited until 11 o'clock before he felt confident that his father had done none of the above.
    Not knowing where to look for the things he needed, Mike had to search his father's apartment thoroughly. If Ernest worked the same shift as yesterday, he wouldn't be home until after six, which gave him plenty of time. He started in the kitchen. Using

only his good arm to move things around made things slow and tedious. Ernest was right about one thing: It wouldn't be long before the wound on Mike's chest left him bedridden.

He ate a nice helping of grits with sausage and toast before his father left. He took four ibuprofens, even though the bottle suggested no more than two. He bathed, cleaned his wound, and applied the ointments and gauze Ernest bought him. What he needed now was rest. But that was the problem. Mike didn't have time to lay up. There was much to do. So much to do.

The original plan was to leave no evidence of his search, but he abandoned it almost immediately. The first drawer he opened was packed with silverware, ketchup packets and other unsorted items. Mike fished through it for a second and then dumped the whole drawer on the floor. The utensils crashed to like cymbals in an empty auditorium. A few roaches emerged from the debris and sought refuge, but what Mike needed was not there.

He did the same with the next drawer and followed suit with most of the boxes of dried food in the cabinets. Mike was in the process of liberating a box of Raisin Bran from its contents when he realized there were a dozen other boxes of taco shells, Hamburger Helper's and Little Debbie's that would all have to be checked. Tearing open all of those boxes would require two hands.

Mike closed the cabinet, hoping his father wasn't smart enough to hide anything in a box of cereal. He checked a few obvious places in the fridge before backing out of the kitchen. Surprisingly, he felt no shame for the mess Ernest would discover upon returning home to check on his ailing son.

Mike returned to the living room and threw all of the sofa cushions on the floor. There was nothing there. Already sweating, he sat on his father's coffee table and closed his eyes. His breaths were quick. The fresh gauze on his chest had a new red stain the size of a quarter.

Work smarter, not harder, he told himself. This was one of many encouraging phrases his 8th grade pre-algebra teacher had instilled in him. Mr. Murphy taught him very little math, but Mike remembered a few of his mottos, like *There's no I in TEAM, Failing to plan is a plan to fail* and *Work smarter, not harder.*

Mike gave it some thought and decided what he was looking for wouldn't be in the kitchen, living room or bathroom.

COLORED RAGS

What he wanted was important to his father. And where would Ernest keep something that was important to him?

Close to him.

Mike went to the bedroom and found the first item he needed almost immediately. In a small dresser next to the bed was a .38 special. The pistol was old and a little weathered, but a quick examination revealed a fresh bullet in each of the six chambers. Even better, there was a box of shells in the same drawer. Mike went to the closet and came out with a small duffle bag. He dumped the contents and placed the pistol and shells inside.

He didn't let himself get too excited. The other item he sought might be more elusive. It was, but he found it in less than thirty minutes. There were five pairs of shoes scattered about the floor in Ernest's closet. Two were sneakers, one was work boots, and the other two were dress shoes. Tucked in the toe of one of the loafers was a small wad of cash.

Initially Mike was disappointed by the size of the stash, but his father's savings account proved to be sufficient. All of the bills had Benjamin Franklin's picture on them, and there were twelve bills in all.

Tell me about my daddy.

Mike's own childish voice rang in his ears as he sweated and grinned at the loot. At the tender age of eight he had asked his mother about the man who got on top of her and deposited his seed. Immediately bitter, his mother had only bad things to say about Ernest. She told Mike his father was selfish. He was an addict. Crack had consumed him and destroyed every relationship he ever had.

Ironically, Ernest managed to kick his habit after they split up, while Mike's mother continued to spiral out of control. She didn't have a dime to her name, let alone twelve hundred dollars.

Mike counted the cash three times before stuffing it into his pocket. He thought there might be more money in the apartment but didn't look for it. He wasn't trying to break the old man. Besides, twelve hundred was more than enough to accomplish his goals. As far as stealing from a man who took him in and cared for him in his time of need, *Fuck him.* Ernest had been ducking child support for years. As far as Mike was concerned, this was his reckoning.

Back in the living room, Mike saw that it was almost noon. He didn't know where his father worked and wasn't sure if he ate at the job or came home for lunch. The notion that he might want to check on his wounded son didn't sound too farfetched.

There was a phone book in the living room. Mike located the listings for taxi cabs and called the first one. He gave his father's address as the pickup point. When asked about his destination, he offered a vague intersection on the west side of town. The man said a driver would be at his location in fifteen minutes.

While he waited, Mike changed the dressing on his wound. He found a pair of jeans in his father's closet that fit him fairly well. There were no red tee shirts, but that was cool. He selected a dark blue shirt, thinking it would help him remain incognito. Putting on the shirt was so painful, Mike screamed behind his clenched teeth. By the time he was done, he was sweating profusely. He took three more ibuprofens, but the pharmaceuticals he wanted couldn't be found at Walgreen's.

He returned to the bedroom and stuffed another pair of pants and a few shirts in the duffle bag to fill it out. He checked the clock and saw that he had five minutes before the cab would be there. Back in the front room, he sat down and stared at his father's telephone. He knew he shouldn't use it again. He was sure to be a wanted man by now.

But Mike needed answers. He nibbled on his bottom lip as he weighed his options. Everyone had Caller ID, but the person he needed to speak to *might not* give his number to the police. Assuming they did snitch, Mike guessed it would take fifteen minutes before a black and white showed up at Ernest's apartment. He would be long gone by then.

He picked up the phone and dialed the numbers. Derrick's sister picked up after two rings.

"Hello?"

"Hey," Mike said.

"Hello?"

"Yo, this Mike."

After a long pause, she spoke a little softer.

"Where you at?"

"Is Spider okay?" he asked her.

COLORED RAGS

The cops told him his friend was dead, but Mike had been hoping it was an interrogation tactic. The detective never pulled Spider's morgue pictures from his folder.

There was another long pause on the line. Instinct told him to hang up, but Mike was in too deep. Whatever was happening on the other end was going to happen regardless of what he did. He could hear Spider's sister breathing deeply.

"Why you playing?"

Mike's throat caught. "I'm not playing. I don't know what happened after I got shot. I, I ain't talked to nobody." He listened to the girl breathe for a moment. "Is he dead?" Mike finally asked.

"Yeah," she said. "He dead, Mike."

Mike's whole world fell from beneath him. He felt as if his body was floating upwards, into a parallel universe of beer bottles, weed smoke and gunshots. His eyes tried to well up with tears, but he blinked hard and wiped them away angrily. There was no time to mourn. Self-preservation came first. Retaliation would come later. Most assuredly retaliation would come swift, calculated and brutal.

"Where you at?" the girl asked.

"I gotta go," he said and hung up.

He went to the bathroom to check his appearance one more time before he left the apartment. His eyes were red, his hair unkempt, and his features were drawn, but he didn't think he'd draw a lot of attention. The phone in the living room started to ring. Mike headed in that direction, but he didn't answer it. He snatched the duffle bag from the couch and exited the apartment.

Outside, an orange taxi cab waited for him. Mike tried to look normal as he approached it.

"You Lewis?" the driver asked.

"Yeah, that's me," Mike said as he climbed in the passenger side.

"Where we going exactly?" the driver asked. He eyed the boy suspiciously.

"I gotta make a few stops," Mike told him. "You charge by the mile or the hour? I ain't never been in no cab before."

"You wanna drive around, make a few stops? The meter keeps running the whole time," the driver informed him. He was a Hispanic man; middle-aged and handsome.

"That's cool," Mike said. He got comfortable in his seat, but the driver didn't back out of the parking spot. "What?" Mike asked after a few seconds.

The man rolled his eyes and sighed loudly. "Look kid, I been around for a while. You wanna go *here*, you wanna go *there*, and somewhere on one of these stops you decide not to come back out and pay me. You don't look like you can run too fast, but it ain't that hard to ditch a fare. I'm trying to make a living. I don't have time for this."

Mike reached into his pocket and produced two of the bills he'd pilfered. He handed the money to the driver.

"I got a couple of places to go," he said, "but I ain't trying to skip out on no fare. You can hold this till we get done. If I owe you more, I'll give it to you. I got some more money."

The driver took the $200 and examined it before stuffing it into his breast pocket. He put the car in gear and they got moving.

"Where to first?"

"I need to go to Walmart."

The driver was surprised to hear that. His passenger looked like he might want some dope, a prostitute maybe. But Walmart?

"The meter runs the whole time you're in there, if you want me to wait on you."

"Yeah, I want you to wait," Mike said.

"You're the boss," the driver said as they rolled out of the apartment complex.

COLORED RAGS

CHAPTER TWENTY-SIX
DIRTY MONEY

I'm tired of
Gangbanging
Dope slanging
On the corner hanging
It's a money thanging
Fuck with me and it's BANG!BANG!
Ass niggas

I'm tired of
Car stealing
Donut peeling
Black man killing
Rainbow Gas & Grocery chilling
Ass niggas

I'm tired of
I killed yo kid? So?
What you looking at me fo'?
Beat yo ass down to the flo'
Don't come 'round this street no mo'
Say, help me rob this corner sto'
Ass niggas

  Chris stared into Trez's beady eyes as if he was trying to sell him a bridge in Brooklyn.
  "Man, what the fuck you do?"
  "What?" Trez said. "I'm trying to help you, nigga."
  "*Help me?*" Chris was nearly belligerent. "How the hell you trying to help me?"

Trez looked back to the car he arrived in. "I came over here to let you know what's up. I tried to get here before Croc came."

"What? I know that nigga ain't coming over here."

"Yeah, he is. He coming to get his money, Chris."

"*That's not his money, Trez!* That's Kody's money."

Trez looked confused. "Croc said it was his."

Chris couldn't believe what he was hearing. He rubbed his face while shaking his head. He spoke calmly, though the world was moving 80 miles per hour. "Trez, what the hell you do?"

"It ain't me!"

"Why you tell Croc about the money, man? I told you not to tell *nobody*."

Trez looked down, for the first time embarrassed about his part in this.

"Man, Chris. Cuz, I didn't mean to. We was just kicking it, you know, smoking weed and shit. And it came out. I wasn't trying to get nobody in trouble. We was talking about Kody and them, and everybody was saying how he was fucked. And, man, I just said something like how he was gon' be alright. You know I just be talking."

Chris was still shaking his head. "When you tell him this?"

"Just now. Like thirty minutes ago."

"And what he say?"

"He said that's *his* money. He say Kody trying to get over 'cause he know he gon' need a lawyer."

"That fool can't be serious."

"He is, cuz. I mean, I don't know what's really going on. I just know that nigga mad than a motherfucker."

Chris gritted his teeth. "He know you over here?"

"Yeah. He was finna come hisself, but he didn't want to start no trouble with y'all moms or nothing. I told him I would go, 'cause you and him don't really get along. He figured you'd give it to me before you'd give it to him."

Chris watched him talk; studied his face and gestures and found no reason to believe Trez was scheming, which meant Kody was right. Chris couldn't trust any of them.

"So, you think I'm gon' give that man my brother's money?"

"What if he telling the truth?"

COLORED RAGS

"Trez, I know you not that stupid." Chris realized he might be wrong about that. "That's not Croc's money," he said plainly. "He didn't even know about it until you told him."

Trez stared without blinking.

"You really think Croc got twenty thousand dollars?" Chris asked. "That fool be copping bags from my brother. He ain't even got a car. He stay in *my brother's* dope house, and he sleep on the floor most of the time. You in there running your mouth, and now this nigga think he finna come up."

"But what if—"

"Trez, Kody wouldn't send me to those apartments to steal from somebody. You know how he is. He don't even want me to smoke weed. Why would he get me caught up in some shit that could get me killed?"

Trez was quiet as he mulled things over. But there was no doubt in Chris' mind that the money belonged to his brother. He was surprised Croc would pull this. The loss of both of the gang's OGs had apparently left them in a free fall.

"Damn, cuz. You right," Trez decided. "So what you gon' do?"

"I'm not giving him the money. That's for damn sure," Chris replied boldly. He had no crew and only one pistol, but he would face anything short of death to protect his brother's savings.

"I feel you," Trez said. "But what you gon' do? He gon' come over here looking for you."

"I don't know, man. I'm finna go, though. I ain't gon' be home when he get here, and he bet not fuck with my mama about that shit."

"Where you finna go?"

Chris couldn't believe he asked. He wrinkled his face in disgust. "Nigga, you think I'm finna tell you?"

He banged his fist on the steering wheel, his mind racing. Jason was the only person who would take him in with no questions asked, but he lived right around the corner. Chris wondered if he should stay home and guard the money. If Croc came starting trouble while his mom was there, she might tell him to give up the loot, just to avoid the drama. But if Croc didn't see Chris' car there, it was unlikely he'd knock on the door.

Chris wondered how far the goon was willing to go with this. Twenty thousand was enough to get your door kicked in and your family duct-taped. He needed to talk to Kody. But his brother wouldn't call again until tomorrow morning. Chris considered paying him a visit at the jail.

"What you want me to tell him?" Trez asked.

"Tell him it's Kody's money, and he ain't getting it," Chris spat defiantly.

Trez backed away from the gloom cloud hovering over Chris' car.

"He ain't gon' like that."

"It don't matter. He know he wrong. The only reason he's doing this is 'cause everybody who can stop him is locked up. But this is your fault anyway, Trez! Running your damn mouth."

Trez lowered his head and mumbled, "My bad, cuz," before returning to his ride. Chris watched him go. He started his car and thought about the gun under his seat. The .380 waited patiently; silently offering a quick resolution.

● ● ● ● ● ●

Jason invited him in graciously. "What's up, playboy?"

"What's up. You already ate?"

"Naw. You need to quit coming over here for food. Always using a nigga."

"Actually I was gon' ask if you wanted to go to McDonald's."

"*McDonalds*? I ain't finna spend no money over there. I got food in the fridge."

"I'll buy," Chris offered.

Jason's eyes lit up. "Where you get money from?"

"Kody gave it to me." Before Jason could ask, he said, "He had some money stashed. He gave me a couple of dollars for getting it for him."

"That's dirty money," Jason noted.

"Man, shut yo Sunday-school-looking ass up. You wanna go or not?"

"Yeah, let me put on some shoes."

At Mickey D's, they both ordered large combo meals. Jason noticed his friend seemed preoccupied.

"What's wrong with you?"

Chris shrugged. "I got a lot on my mind."

COLORED RAGS

Jason gave him a look. "Fool, I hope you ain't stressing over what I said about Tracy."

"Naw, I wasn't even thinking about her."

"Did you hit last night?"

Chris shook his head.

"Quit lying. You said she was on her way to your house."

"She came over for awhile."

"But you ain't hit?"

"Naw, we just talked."

Jason frowned.

Chris said, "I don't want you to think I'm soft or nothing, but–"

"But you soft?"

Chris chuckled. "I don't think I got the heart to dog no woman out."

"I didn't tell you to dog nobody out. What that got to do with smashing?"

"I don't wanna have sex with her, if I don't really wanna be with her. I'ma be real with you: When you introduced us, I thought she was just a regular chick. I didn't know she was, you know…"

"A ho?"

"Yeah, whatever. When you told me that, I didn't know how to feel. I guess I should've been cool with it. But I felt like she tricked me. When she came over, I asked her about it."

"*What*?" Jason was astonished. "You don't never let a ho know that you know she a ho!"

"I can't do her like that, Jay. I thought she was cool. I still think she cool. But I wanted to *be* with her, like a relationship. I don't know if I can do that now."

Jason shook his head. "Dog, I hook you up with some *for sho* ass, and you want a *relationship*. You too young for that shit. You can have a relationship when you get married."

Chris knew his friend wouldn't understand. And now the Tracy situation was even more complicated. If he made her his girlfriend anyway – despite her ho history – he would never hear the end of it. Did Tracy deserve a second chance? If she was serious about wanting a new life, Chris felt like he should help her, not condemn her.

The friends left the restaurant in two different moods. Jason was full and pretty damn chipper. Chris felt anxious and unsure about everything. When they returned to Jason's house, Chris found that if he avoided his problems long enough, they would eventually catch up to him.

He pulled into the driveway, and a car traveling in the opposite direction came to a quick stop behind them. Chris recognized the vehicle as the same one Trez hopped out of earlier. He wondered why he was back so soon, but it was Croc who stepped casually from the Crown Vic.

Chris gave his friend a concerned look. Jason fixed guarded eyes on the man approaching his house.

"Yo, Chris! What up? You got my issue?" Croc asked.

Chris stood his ground as the man approached. He wondered how the Crip had found him, but guessed it was only a matter of luck. If you're going into hiding, it's probably best to go further than just two blocks away.

Croc looked clean this afternoon, which was a rarity for him. His jeans were new. His sneakers were sparkling white. Even his hair was freshly plaited, with eight neat cornrows snaking from his forehead to the back of his neck. The one thing Croc couldn't pretty-up was his scars. His face and forearms showed signs of a life Chris could only imagine. He didn't think Croc would try anything in front of Jason, but those scars said a lot about his tenacity.

"You got it in the car?" Croc asked, less than five feet away now.

"Naw," Chris said. "It's put up." His heart pumped adrenaline through his veins. He didn't like his chances in a fist fight. Croc would kick his ass handily. Jason would try to help, but there were two other people in the Crown Vic. Croc was serious enough to bring backup.

"Where it's at?" Croc smiled. "Let's go get it."

Chris had never noticed before, but Croc had perfect teeth. He doubted anyone had invested in braces for the young statistic, but it was hard to imagine he was born with such a nice grill. It's funny the things you notice in times of high drama.

"I can't get it right now," he lied, hoping to buy himself a day or so.

"Why not?" Croc asked. His smile dropped a few degrees.

COLORED RAGS

"Man, what's this about?" Jason asked.

Croc's expression changed then. He fixed a prison-hardened glare on him.

"This ain't got shit to do with you, cuz." When his eyes returned to Chris, they were no longer friendly. Not at all.

"Where my motherfucking money, nigga?"

Chris swallowed hard. "That's Kody's money."

He felt like there was something he should do right then, but there was no time. Croc closed the distance between them with cat-like speed and delivered a clean shot to Chris' temple that sent him falling to the ground. Dull sparks flashed before his eyes. The world tilted as Chris rolled and tried to rise to his knees. He heard Jason shouting in a loud, angry voice. Croc said something back to him, and the two men stepped out of the Crown Vic.

Chris looked up, and his eyes focused in time to see Croc stomping towards him. Chris was ready for a kick, but the thug didn't strike again. He stood over him and issued a warning laced with blood and violence.

"Bring my motherfucking money back to the apartment *today*, nigga! Don't make me come looking for you."

From his defeated position, Chris watched him return to the Crown Vic. All three Crips got in the car and drove away slowly. They turned south at the first intersection. Jason hurried over to help his friend up. It took Chris a moment to steady his legs.

Through angry, stinging tears he decided that keeping the .380 in his car was not as effective as he thought it would be. This incident would've gone a lot differently if he had the gun in his pocket. Croc gave him plenty of chances to reach for it. Next time he would be ready.

Yeah, I got yo money right here...
BAP!BAP!BAP!

Chris could see it so clearly, it felt like he had already shot the man.

KEITH THOMAS WALKER

CHAPTER TWENTY-SEVEN
THE TALK

Some niggas is good at that uplifting shit
That's probably 'cause they ain't never loaded a clip
And wiped each bullet with a handkerchief
So even the shells wouldn't show fingerprints

Some niggas is good at shouting out peace
But they ain't out here on these streets
They don't wake up every morning and see defeat
They never had to shoplift for something to eat

Some niggas can handle this wheelchair shit
But I can't roll around like I ain't hating it
So I'ma take myself out of this predicament
'Cause I ain't down with living like this

    Dre was not as apprehensive as one might expect as he followed his dead brother through their quiet neighborhood. A few cars passed them as they marched on, giving the teen awkward glances, but Dre didn't notice. He was too busy watching his brother's strange gait.
    It was clear that Will had not returned from hell to harm him physically. That was good, but Dre had no idea what his brother wanted. He tried to broach the subject a couple of times, but Will was in no condition to talk. The walk alone took every bit of his strength. Will stepped with the unsteady stroll of a drunkard. He stumbled twice, once falling to his knees. Dre watched from behind but did not move to help his zombie brother up.

Will had looked back at him with an odd smile that exposed more teeth than normal.

You like this. Don't you, Dre?

Dre didn't answer, but he knew Will could read his mind. Plus Will saw the smirk on his face. It was all very strange, this role reversal. In life, Will had been a rock. All brawn with no compassion, Dre couldn't remember his brother ever hugging him or offering to lift him up when his spirits were low. Will never told Dre he loved him or even liked him for that matter.

But now that Will was at his lowest, Dre was supposed to feel sorry for him? Fat chance.

Will nodded and managed to rise from the sidewalk on his own.

"You ain't gon' make it," Dre informed him.

Will's eyes blazed with an ethereal quality Dre couldn't get used to. He flashed his toothy grin.

Don't worry about me, lil bro. Just keep yo head ready for what you gotta do.

There was nothing about their situation that made sense, but that comment added another layer of weirdness. Dre had never been on the winning end of a fight. He never sold drugs, packed a weapon, or did anything worthy of Will's appreciation. What in the world did he expect his little brother to do for him now? Dre predicted he would only let him down again, but he went along with the plan, just to get it over with.

Sycamore Park seemed much farther away than it did when they were younger. Dre thought it was only a five minute hike from their house, but it took twenty minutes before the community center and the small forest surrounding it came into view. Dre wiped perspiration from his forehead as they waited to cross an intersection.

"What we gon' do over there?" he asked. He was winded, but his brother was worse for wear. Will slouched, bent over with his hands on his knees.

We gon' talk, he said.

He squeezed his eyes closed as thunderous coughs racked his frame with such ferocity he couldn't catch his breath. Dre thought he sounded terribly unhealthy, even for a zombie. The coughs turned into wet, gagging spasms. Dre rushed to his brother's side.

"You alright?" he asked as Will vomited 20 ounces of gastric acids mixed with mucus and blood from what should have been a depleted stomach.

Most of the bile landed on his feet, soaking his exposed sock and one shoe. Will straightened himself with Dre's help and wiped his mouth with the back of his claw. Dre had to fight off his own wave of nausea as he watched him.

"What you want with me?" he whined, his eyes filling with tears. "Why I gotta be here?"

Will looked up at him, smiling again; his pearly whites now coated with a slimy residue.

We almost there, he said and then darted into the street without warning.

Dre watched with wide eyes, knowing one of the cars would smash into him. But of course no vehicle hit his brother. A moment ago Will could barely stand up straight. Now he sprinted across the street without any limp at all. No one had to slow or even honk their horn at the defeated gangster.

Once on the other side of the road, Will did not wait for his brother. He continued towards the dense tree line without looking back. Baffled, Dre never considered leaving him to his own demise. He kept an eye on Will while waiting for his chance to cross the busy street.

● ● ● ● ● ●

By the time Dre made it across, Will had reached the park and was headed for the community center. The building was Sycamore's main attraction. The center offered daycare for small children and was open for all ages after five pm. There were plenty of activities inside, from pinball, to arts and crafts and roller skating. They had even started a midnight basketball league to lure potential misfits from a criminal lifestyle.

At high noon the daycare kids were all locked inside, and it was too early for the older kids who came to beat the heat every summer. Dre had to break into a jog to catch up with his brother, who had disappeared around the corner of the building and was headed for the creek, some fifty yards away.

Will had only a slight lead the last time he saw him, but when Dre rounded the corner, his brother was so far ahead he

COLORED RAGS

could barely see him. Will did this despite staggering on legs that were twitching and unsteady.

Dumbfounded, Dre broke out into a full run, but his brother's awkward canter was still too much to overtake. Will reached the creek and disappeared behind one of the Sycamore trees near the bank. Dre charged after him, but there was no sign of his brother when he darted past the same tree.

The creek hadn't changed much over the years. Landscaping crews rarely mowed past the trees that lined the waters, leaving the grass and shrubs to grow on their own accord. There were a lot of weeds, most more than knee high or taller. Dre stomped through them, getting a nice coat of itchy cocklebur seeds on his pants and socks.

Will was nowhere to be found, but Dre trudged on. He steered clear of the muddy bank and fought to keep his balance on the grassy slopes. From the looks of it, Sycamore Creek had once been a modest tributary. The water was still twenty feet deep in some parts, but recent droughts had reduced other areas to stagnant ponds that were capable of floating a construction paper boat but little else.

Under the canopy of trees, deceptive shadows were everywhere. Dre looked around for his brother in vain. Beer cans and bottles in varying stages of decay littered the area. In one of the more shallow spots, Dre saw that some unlucky sap had tried to cross the creek on moss covered stones that protruded from the water. He lost one sneaker and left it half submerged God knew how long ago.

A large dragonfly zipped between Dre's eyes for closer examination. He spotted a sunbathing snapping turtle with only its snout poking out of the water. A cloud of gnats buzzed around his face. He shooed them away but was sure he inhaled at least one of them. Feeling abandoned, Dre called out to his brother.

"Will? Where you at?" His tone was low and conspiratorial, but it reached the dead ears it sought.

I'm over here, nigga. The voice came from close behind.

Dre spun and saw his brother sitting on the embankment no more than five feet away. Will's forearms rested on his knees, and his head hung low. He looked up with low, sad eyes. His rough breaths were audible now, but Dre was certain he hadn't heard them a second ago.

"Why you leave me?" he asked, not sure why he was concerned about such things.

I wasn't trying to, cuz. I just wanted to hurry up and get here. I ain't got that much time.

"You keep saying that," Dre noticed. "You ain't got time for what? What's gon' happen?"

Will looked up at him with a strained smiled that quivered around the edges. *You know what's going on, Dre. I'm dead. I can't stick around too much longer. I gotta go.*

"Where you gon' go?" Dre asked, knowing full well where people like OG motherfucking Will went when their number got called.

That's not even cool, Will said.

Dre nodded. "Sorry. So what you want with me? You said you was gon' tell me when we got here. We here…"

Will looked around. *You remember this creek, Dre?*

"Yeah."

We used to come here when we was little. Before all the bullshit.

Dre spotted a large rock across from his brother and planted his rump on it.

I don't know what it is about this park, Will admitted. *I guess it's like, a peaceful place for me. It reminds me of when we were young and innocent. This place is a refuge for my soul. It's beautiful.*

Dre disagreed. He remembered how he and Will were taken to the community center for daycare when they were youngsters. One day Will met an older kid, and they decided to sneak out. Dre was only six at the time. He traded his crayons for adventure and tagged along. When they reached the creek, Will's friend talked them into following the waterway, to see where it led.

Afraid to go back to the center with wet, muddy sneakers that would expose their caper, the boys took their shoes off before jumping into the creek. Less than a quarter mile in, Dre stepped on a broken bottle and sliced his foot so badly, the wound required twelve stitches. Will and his new friend had to help Dre make it back to the community center. Once there, Will had to confess to breaking out as well as injuring his little brother.

What was a refuge for Will's tormented soul, was a reminder for Dre of the first time he let his brother down. Rather

COLORED RAGS

than express sympathy for Dre's foot, Will had cursed him all the way back to the center. Dre was clumsy. He was a punk, a mark and a crybaby. At the age of eight, Will understood that his reputation could be compromised by his klutzy brother.

Dead Will chuckled. *You remember that time you cut yo foot, huh?*

"You brought me all the way over here to talk about that?" Dre felt the first pangs of embarrassment tweaking his tear ducts.

Naw. Will shook his head. *But I do need you in that mind state, lil' bro.*

"What mind state?"

That innocence, Will said. *Honest and innocent. I'm not gon' torture you, Dre. I'ma be real with you. I only got two things I want from you today, and I'm out.*

Dre looked skeptical.

I'm serious, nigga. Just two things. And the first one is easy. All you gotta do is talk.

Dre was eager to get it over with. "What you want me to say?"

I wanna know why you let them niggas kill me. All of the humor left Will's eyes in an instant.

Dre didn't expect him to start with such a heavy question. "I didn't, they, there was nothing I could do, Will. I couldn't do nothing to stop that."

Will shook his head. *Nope. See, that's not gon' do at all. Uh-uhn. That's just not gon' do.*

"What?" Dre cried. "What you want me to say?"

Tell the truth, lil' bro. I ain't gon' do nothing to you.

"I *am* telling the truth," Dre protested.

You think I don't know? Will asked him.

"Know what?"

Why can't you keep it real? It's over now.

"I don't know what you want me to say."

You had my gun in your hand, Will prompted.

"I, I didn't—"

You saw them niggas pull up. You was sitting right there. You knew what was finna go down, cuz. That's why you grabbed my pistol. Shit was in your hand, Dre. You had that shit in yo hand.

Dre felt a mild sense of comfort in his tears. "There wasn't nothing I could do," he insisted. "I tried..."

You tried what? What you try to do? You tried to cock it? You tried to shoot at that nigga? What you try to do, Dre? Tell me! I really need to hear this shit!

"They was, they had guns, Will!" Dre was fully sobbing now. "There was somebody else in the car. The one that got out, he, he... They would've saw me."

What? So you saying you was too scared, nigga?

"I *was* scared!" Dre blurted.

But that ain't why you didn't do nothing! You ain't that much of a pussy! You still would've did something if...

Dre looked up, hoping his brother would finish the sentence. Will stared back at him. He didn't look particularly angry about what he was hearing, just disappointed.

"If what?" Dre asked meekly.

Naw, Dre. You gotta say it.

"Why you want me to say it, if you already know?"

That's how it's gotta be done. You gon' feel better, watch. Go ahead. Get that shit off yo chest.

Dre wiped the snot off his lips. "You just want me to say it?"

Yeah. Go ahead.

"Then what's gon' happen?"

I'm not gon' kill you, bro. Shit, look at me. I can't bust a nut right about now.

Dre remained doubtful, but he knew he didn't have a choice. *I only got two things I want from you*, Will had said. *The first one is easy. All you have to do is talk.*

"I hate you," Dre said before better sense could stop him. "That's why I didn't do nothing."

Will was wrong. Dre didn't feel better at all.

You wanted me to die? Will asked calmly.

"No, I didn't want you to die. But I used to think about it sometimes. Sometimes when you went out and was gone for a long time. I used to watch the news, and when they said somebody got shot, I used to wonder if it was you."

You wanted it to be me?

"Sometimes," Dre confessed. "But it still wasn't nothing I could do. I don't know nothing about guns."

COLORED RAGS

You know about my gun, Will said. *I showed you how it work when I first got it. I let you shoot it, Dre.*

"I was scared of it, though. I wouldn't have hit nothing."

You didn't have to shoot the nigga. You could've shot towards them. Hell, you could've shot in the air. They still would've run off. You hate me that much not to even try?

Dre never thought they'd have this conversation. Now that it was happening, he found it surprisingly easy to divulge. "I didn't know I hated you," he said honestly. "I guess I did. But you hate me too."

I don't hate you, bro.

"Yeah, *now* you don't. But you did when you was alive."

You really believe that?

"You know it's true."

Dre, you been real with me, so I'ma keep it real with you. I don't hate you, nigga. I love you. You my little brother, cuz. I know I fucked with you a lot. You prolly think I dogged you 'cause I didn't give a damn about you. But that ain't true. I did it 'cause I didn't want you to be no ho, cuz. You feel me?

Look where the fuck we live. I figured you wasn't gon' make it like that; all soft and shit. Getting whooped every time you had a fight. Maybe I was wrong. I ain't never took no class on how to make people strong. Maybe I did treat you bad sometimes. But it wasn't to be mean, Dre. Whatever I did, I did it 'cause I love you. Look how we was raised. Look at Uncle Ray. That's all I know how to do. I didn't know no better way.

Dre was surprised by how comforted he felt, even though the words were coming from a spook. "Why you didn't never tell me you love me?" he asked.

Fool, what the fuck I look like telling another nigga I love him?

Dre smiled. "I'm sorry," he said.

Will nodded. *You feel better, don't you?*

Dre thought for a moment. All things considered, he did feel a little better. He hadn't enjoyed a genuine smile in days.

That's good, Will said. *That's good, 'cause you through with one of the things I needed you to do.*

Relieved, Dre asked cautiously, "What else you want me to do?"

This one gon' be a little harder, cuz. But I know you can do it.

Dre watched his brother's face. It felt good to be with Will again. Not the scary Will or the brutal Will, but just Will; with all of the fences broken down.

You did what you did in that car, cuz. We through with that. You said why you did it, and I can accept it. I don't love it, but I'ma deal with it. Most of that shit was my fault, so I'ma let it go. But one thing I can't let go is how you fucked up my legacy. You fucked up my name, cuz. Seeing as how I'm dead, you the only one who can fix that for me...

COLORED RAGS

CHAPTER TWENTY-EIGHT
SCHEMING

I bought a gun for five dime rocks
I smoked the fool that took my spot
I drove by my homies blasting my gun
I shot another crab just for fun
The police put me six feet deep
Looks like I found the place for me

    At Walmart, Mike went to the electronics department and picked up a Tracfone. It only cost forty dollars, and the minutes were sold separately. Tracfones were pretty cheesy, compared to the ones major networks provided, but Mike knew it was nearly impossible to trace the cheap cellular back to the owner. He didn't even have to give his name before purchasing it. He picked up more gauze and pain pills before he left the store.
    Outside, Mike was surprised to see his cab waiting for him. For two hundred bucks, he would have left his customer hanging, if he was behind the wheel. But his driver wasn't the shiesty type. Mike got in and directed him to a boy/girl house on the west side of town. It took nearly twenty minutes to get there. Mike hoped the dealer who answered the door wouldn't recognize him, but his reputation preceded him.
    "Damn, nigga. I ain't seen you in a long ass time. I thought you was dead."
    "Naw, just shot," Mike said.
    "I heard they killed some of yo niggas. OG Shaun and somebody else."
    "Yeah. I need a couple eight balls," Mike said, eager to get on with his business.
    "A'ight. I would hook you up, but it's been slow."

"It's cool," Mike said, producing two bills.

"Who you rolling with?" the dealer asked, looking over his shoulder to the cab idling on the curb.

"Who the fuck it look like? It's a motherfucking cab." Mike didn't mean to be testy, but he was starting to feel light-headed again. He didn't have time to answer a bunch of asinine questions.

The dealer narrowed his eyes and said, "Hold on."

He took the money and closed the door, leaving Mike on the front porch. Normally, he would've invited him inside. Mike didn't know if he was being punished for snapping at him or if the dealer was wary because of the recent murders.

When he returned with the product, Mike stuffed it in his pocket without inspecting it first. That was usually a big no-no, but it was okay if the bags were a little short. It usually took him and Spider a whole day to go through only one eight ball. Mike thought his heart would explode if he tried to snort both bags all by himself.

"Y'all gon' get them rips?" the dealer asked as Mike headed to the cab.

"You know what it is," he called over his shoulder.

● ● ● ● ● ●

For the last stop, Mike told the driver to head east. He didn't know if the cabbie knew who he was or what he was involved in, but he couldn't risk getting dropped off right in front of a motel. He directed him to Lancaster Avenue and told him to pull over at a random convenience store. When the car stopped, Mike asked the driver how much he owed him.

"Is this the last stop?"

"Yeah. I'm getting out here."

"So far we got, um, seventy-five dollars."

"They gon' ask you where you dropped me off?" Mike asked.

"Why? You planning on robbing this store?"

"Naw, man. I just wanna know if you gotta tell them where you dropped me off."

"Well, I'm supposed to," the cabbie said. "What's the problem? Is somebody looking for you?"

"I don't know. Maybe. When they find out who picked me up from them apartments, they gon' wanna know where you took me."

The driver listened quietly.

"If I let you keep that other hundred, you can tell them you dropped me off on the south?" Mike asked.

"If they catch you over here, they gonna know I lied," the man noted. "I could lose my job for that, especially if you're talking about the police."

"They can't prove nothing. I could've got a ride over here from the south."

The driver checked the store and saw a surveillance camera in clear view. If the kid was dumb enough to think he could travel undetected in this day and age, he had a hard lesson coming. "Alright," he said, just to get the boy out of his car.

Mike gathered his things and stepped out gingerly. He waited for the cab to pull away before he backtracked ten blocks, made a right at a busy intersection and another right on the next street. He walked twelve more blocks before he reached the Valley View Motel. He paid for a room for one night. He was required to provide a photo ID, which he produced casually. Attempting to conceal his identity at that point would be counterproductive. He knew the motel manager wouldn't get nosey unless he gave him a reason.

Mike held his breath as the man wrote down his information. He blew out a sigh of relief when he returned his ID with no recognition. He gave Mike a room towards the back of the motel and told him, "Don't open up a dope house. If you get too much traffic, I'm calling the cops."

"I'm not trying to open up a dope house," Mike promised. "You won't have no trouble with me."

● ● ● ● ● ●

The Valley View Motel was no place for honeymooners, light-hearted affairs or hard-working Joes down on their luck. There was only one type of person that came to this place and one activity they indulged in. There were lighter burns on the curtains and carpet, pipe burns everywhere, and small, burnt-black wads of Brillo swept under the bed.

The patrons at the Valley View were dopefiends. They bought crack, smoked crack and propositioned the crack whores who were always loitering outside. Mike dropped his bag on the bed and fished the 8 balls from his pocket. In his zest to get to the room so quickly, he was disappointed to find that he had purchased no razor blade to break down his cocaine. Undeterred, he tore one of the baggies open on the end table and used his ID to scrape together a humungous line. He rolled one of his father's bills and snorted like it was his birthday.

The cocaine was good, hardly stepped on. It delivered complete euphoria almost immediately as it blazed through his nasal cavity and numbed the back of his throat. Mike backed away from the table and sat on the bed, totally zoned out. Cocaine had always been his favorite drug. He thought that particular line was the best ever. He enjoyed his high for a few minutes before he grabbed his new cellphone.

He placed the first call to a familiar number. He told the woman who answered to let him speak to Karl.

A gruff voice came to the line. "Hello."

"What's up, Blood," Mike greeted him. "What's popping?"

"Who this?" Killa Karl wanted to know.

"This Mike."

"Nigga, what the—"

Mike grinned, happy to catch him off guard.

"Where you at?" Karl asked.

"OG Shaun dead?" Mike asked him.

"Nigga, you know Shaun dead! What the fuck you calling me for? Them folks looking for yo ass, nigga. You better hope they find you before we do. We got Amanda Street and Evil's set down with us now. You fucked up, Mike. You gon' get wet up for real!"

"I'm already wet up. I got shot too, nigga. Remember?"

"You got yo nigga Spider killed. Got me shot. I don't know why y'all did that dumb ass shit. It's a wrap for you, Blood. It's over."

"Don't worry. I'm finna get it over with. I'ma turn myself in. I just got one mo' nigga to body before I go."

"One *mo* nigga? Man, who the fuck you think you is? You ain't finna body *nothing*! You got the laws, them rickets, *and*

COLORED RAGS

some OG Blood niggas on yo ass! You started a war, Mike. You understand me, you dumb ass nigga? You started a fucking war!"

"Yeah, well, the war ain't over," Mike boasted. The cocaine flowing through his system made him feel like Tony Montana. "It's gon' keep going till I get that nigga who killed Spider."

"What? You talking about Kody? Fool, where you been? That nigga got popped right after they shot us up. He *been* locked up."

Mike was not happy to hear that. "That's alright. Somebody still gotta die for Spider. I gotta do that for him."

"Mike, you done lost yo goddamned mind!" Karl bellowed. "Who the hell you think gon' help you with that shit? You *crazy*, nigga. Ain't nobody down with you."

"Man, fuck y'all hoes! I don't need shit from you!"

"Where you at?"

"I should come over there and get yo ass too, Karl. You think I forgot about you putting hands on Spider before them rips showed up?"

"Where you at, though?"

"I'm outside yo door, nigga! Tell yo mama to duck! I'm finna get to dumping!"

Mike disconnected. His heart was going a mile a minute. He was so keyed up, he was shivering. He didn't think he'd ever felt better. He took his father's gun out of the duffle bag and placed it on the bed, just in case.

A minute later, Karl started calling back. Mike sent him to voicemail heaven. He returned to his dope and cut up another monster line. He snorted half of it and chilled for a while, so he could enjoy the high. After ten minutes Karl stopped calling, and Mike was ready to dial another number.

Cornell Harris was a rarity for dopefiends. He got up every day, went to work, was hardly ever late, and he never called in sick on pay day. He did all of this while giving the dopeman half his paycheck each week. Mike called him because he kept his lips on the pipe and his ears to the street. Cornell was the next best thing to a ghetto grapevine.

"Hello?"

"Cornell? What's going on?"

"Who is this?"

"This Mike."

"Mike? Goddamn, nigga! You ain't dead?"

"Everybody keep asking me that. Naw, man. I'm still here. What's going down?"

"Young Blood, you got half the city looking for you. Cops too."

"They asked you about me?"

"The cops? Naw, but some of yo homeboys did. They blaming you for what happened to OG Will and OG Shaun. Spider got killed. Karl and some bitch got shot. Retaliations everywhere. They shot a crip last night. But everybody really got they eye out for one person."

"Me?" Mike asked.

"You the hot topic. Yo name blowing up out here."

"What they say they wanna do with me?"

"Well, it depends on who you ask. The police say they just wanna talk. Yo set, or what's left of them, yeah, they wanna make an example out of you. They got something going on with them crips."

"Something like what?"

"Something like giving you up to them niggas. Crips say they gon' let some pit bulls eat you alive."

Damn. Mike thought that was the most fucked up thing he'd ever heard. He could already feel the dogs tearing his skin.

"What you know about a nigga named Kody?" he asked.

"OG crip," Cornell said. "From OG Will's set. He locked up, him and about three more of them got caught that first night."

Mike was so disappointed it was blowing his high. Killing the leader of the crabs was his SOLUTION. But two sources had confirmed Kody was in jail.

"Alright, I'll talk to you later," he told Cornell. "Don't tell nobody I called you."

"You know I won't."

Mike disconnected, thinking he probably would.

He frowned and gave serious thought to his next move. His first murder shook up the city and made him a household name. It also made him a wanted man. Kody killed his homies in retaliation. Some might view the warring factions as even at this point, but that's not how gang life worked. As far as Mike was concerned, it was now his turn. He would be damned if he got

COLORED RAGS

locked up or killed without killing one more high ranking ricket first. He had to do that for Spider.

Mike snorted some more and then stretched out on the bed. The pain in his chest and back was a distant memory. He felt wonderfully numb, starting with his face and flowing to every other part of his body. He was Superman with a pistol. All he needed was a name; someone important enough to make his last murder legendary.

He turned on the television and went straight to the free porn channel. Mike wasn't a fan of girl-on-girl action, but the scene playing was especially slutty. He dug through his bag for some type of lubricant, but he didn't have any grease or lotion. He did have antibiotic cream, however, and it worked out nicely.

Yeah, it did just fine.

CHAPTER TWENTY-NINE
JUDGED BY TWELVE &
POOR FROGGIE

What is black?
It's the darkness of the heart of the black man
It's the black hands throwing gang signs
It's the smooth, black barrel of the gun
It's the bent black finger on the trigger
It's yo black wig split
It's the black smoke after the explosion
Black is the darkness of the heart of the black man
That makes the shooter smile

Black is the color of your suit at your funeral
Black is the color of your mom's mourning dress
Black is what you see when you close your eyes in the shade
Black is what you see when you never open your eyes again
Black is the color of the earth
Six feet deep
Black is the black man
Black is the darkness of the heart of the black man

Chris sat on Jason's couch and held a bag of frozen peas against his head as he told him the whole sordid story, starting with Kody's call from jail and ending with Trez telling him Croc wanted the money.

When he was done talking, Jason asked the most obvious question: "How you know it's not his?"

"Man," Chris shook his head. "Kody wouldn't send me to those apartments to steal. He wouldn't put me out there like that."

COLORED RAGS

"When you gon' get in touch with your brother, to tell him what happened?"

"He said he'd call me tomorrow morning."

"But that nigga said to bring his money *today*."

"I know what he said," Chris said with a grimace. "I don't think I can go the rest of the day without running into him. He know where I stay, and now he know where you stay. I ain't got nowhere else to go."

"What about your grandma?"

Chris checked the clock. It was a little after noon. "I can go visit her, but if I don't leave, she'll wanna know what's going on. If I tell her, she'll call my mama for sure."

"You should tell your mama," Jason suggested.

"Can't do that. She'll be mad at me for getting the money. And she gon' be mad at Kody for sending me over there. Then she'll tell me to give the money up, so they'll leave me alone. She not gon' argue over Kody losing his dope money."

Jason hummed. "How you know *some* of the money ain't Croc's? He been hustling with your brother, right?"

"Yeah, I guess."

"Maybe they was stacking that bread together. Kody got popped, and he decided to take it all."

Chris was shaking his head before he finished. "Jay, if you knew Croc like I know him, you wouldn't think like that. That's a bum-ass nigga. He ain't got paper like that. If he gets five dollars, it goes up his nose. Plus him and my brother wasn't that cool. Kody already had to whoop his ass before."

Jason thought about it some more and came back to the same thing. "I think you should just give it to him, my nigga. You don't need to have niggas riding around looking for you."

Agitated, Chris rose from his seat. "'I ain't giving it to him 'cause it ain't his money! And then he busted me upside my head, like I'm a ho or something! I can't give it to him, especially not now."

"Sit down, man."

"What?"

"Fool, sit down," Jason cautioned. "Don't be getting all crunk now. You wasn't crunk when that nigga was whooping yo ass."

"Man, fuck you," Chris said as he sat down. "That's low, cuz, even for you."

"My bad," Jason said, but he didn't look too apologetic. "Let me ask you this: If Kody whooped his ass before, and it really ain't his money, how he figure he gon' get away with what he did to you?"

"It's only one way he can get away with it," Chris replied. He had already given it some thought. "He gon' burn off. Twenty g's is enough to start over with. He can go to Houston, San Antonio – some place where nobody knows him. He can get a slab, flip it a few times and be the big man. He could lock up a whole neighborhood with that money."

"Yeah, he prolly could," Jason agreed, but he had little else to offer as far as a solution.

The conversation lulled, and the two friends returned their attention to the television. But Chris couldn't get into the Good Times reruns until he came up with a plan.

If giving the money back was out of the question, there were only two options left for him. He could go home and guard the loot for the rest of the night, or he could face his problem head on. Chris thought he could go to the apartments and tell the other Crips what was happening. But there were Crips in the car with Croc earlier. It was hard to know which ones he could trust.

The more he thought about it, the more convinced Chris was that his gun was the only way out of this. He couldn't simply murder Croc, but if he waited for another ambush, he could use the .380 in self defense. That might still get him in trouble, because the gun was most likely stolen, and Chris didn't have a permit to carry it. But like Ice Cube had said, it was better to be judged by twelve than carried by six. If it was a life or death situation, Chris decided he would do what he had to do to stay alive.

An hour passed, and Chris realized he hadn't been watching TV at all. Even Thelma prancing around in a leotard wasn't enough to hold his attention. He looked over and wasn't surprised to see his friend dozing in the love seat. Chris stood and left the house quietly.

When he got in his car, he scooped the pistol from under the seat and chambered a round. He was smart enough to keep

COLORED RAGS

the safety off before placing the gun on his lap and starting the car. He put his seatbelt on before backing out of the driveway.

● ● ● ● ● ●

Dre's eyes filled with horror as Will outlined the steps necessary for redemption.

See, this yo fault, nigga. If you would've shot at them fools when you saw they was finna kill me, we wouldn't be here right now. But you didn't. Now you gotta suck it up, Dre. Go over there and tell my niggas that you wanna get the one who shot me. You know all the locs. They cool with you.

Dre couldn't believe what he was hearing. "You, you crazy!" he blurted. "I'm not going to those apartments! They gon' kill me, Will!" His voice took on a squeaky tone he hadn't heard since puberty.

See, that's what I'm talking about! Will sneered and spat out something reddish. His eyes blazed. Gone was the friendly big brother character. Will was his old self now. It was as if Dre's cowardice brought him back to his roots. He pointed a black, gnarled finger at his little brother.

You always wanna come with that ho shit! They ain't gon' kill you, Dre! I see you still got that bitch in you. That's why I treated you like I did, cuz. You gon' get that bitch outta you **right now***. You finna man up and take care of this shit!*

Dre shook his head. "No. No, Will. You know they hate me. They know what I did. Everybody know what I did! You know they gon' kill me." The truth in his words struck a chord, and his eyes brightened. "That's what you want, ain't it? That's why you want me to go over there. You know they gon' kill me, and you wanna watch, so you can go to hell and be happy."

Happy? How I'm supposed to be happy in hell? Is you even listening to yourself? If I wanted you dead, you'd be dead by now. Believe that.

"They gon' kill me," Dre whimpered.

No they ain't, cuz! Quit saying that. Get that outta yo head. The most they gon' do is whoop yo ass, but it ain't gone be brutal. They gon' put you down, that's all. You ain't never really been in the gang, so they gon' jump you in. But ain't gon' be no killing.

"I can't, Will," Dre whined. "I, I can't go over there. I can't kill nobody anyway."

Alright, Will conceded. *I don't care if you actually kill somebody. But you do gotta go on that ride. As long as you dumping at them floods with everybody else, I'll take it. That right there is all I really want. Once they put you down, and you do that ride, it's over. You can bail out, go home. Shit, you can crawl up in bed and suck your thumb, for all I care, 'cause everything will be done changed after that.*

When people think about me, they gon' think about you anyway. Our stories are tied together like that. What I want is for them to have something **positive** *to say about you. That's all.*

That's all? Dre thought about the gang initiations he'd witnessed since Will became a member of the AGG Land set. What the Crips called *putting you down,* would be described as *a vicious beating* by most of the educated world. For the initiate, it was good to stay on your feet and throw as many punches back as possible, but remaining standing wasn't a prerequisite. Dre had seen a few kids beaten to the point of unconsciousness.

It was a brutal act he swore he'd never subject himself to – which Will was fully aware of.

"I can't do it," Dre said again, avoiding eye contact. "I'm not gon' do it," he announced more forcibly. He met his brother's eyes then. *And you can't make me,* he thought. *You can't make me do it.*

Will nodded. *I can't make you, huh?*

Dre stared, curious about what he would do. The only thing that made sense was for Will to hurry on over to hell with his mission unaccomplished. Lingering in limbo, trying to persuade Dre to man up was senseless.

But Will had no intention of leaving the park without his goal accomplished. He stood slowly and looked around the tall grasses and weeds lining the embankment.

I know what the problem is, he said. *You got yo nuts up 'cause you think I'm just in yo head, right? You think I can't do nothing but talk shit, huh, Dre? That's what you thinking, ain't it?*

Dre was about to admit that was right when Will moved faster than he ever had in life or death. He took six blurred steps and thrust his hand into a tall thicket of greenery. There was a

COLORED RAGS

momentary thrashing in the weeds. Will fixed a look of sheer evil on his brother as he pulled his arm out. He had the biggest bullfrog Dre had ever seen caught securely in his vice-like claw.

You think I can't touch nothing, Dre? Will smiled and applied pressure to the amphibian. The frog's hind legs kicked wildly, trying to locate a gripping point on the dead man's hand. Its mouth hung open, its tongue lolling. The frog's eyes bulged violently. Dre could feel the bullfrog's panic. Even worse, he could hear the frog scream. It was a faint, squeaky noise that grew louder by the second.

You think I ain't real? Will mocked. *You laying in the fucking bed all night scared I was gon' rub up against you! Ain't that what you wanna know, Dre? You wanna know if I can touch you? Cuz, I will fuck you up way worse than them niggas over there!* he growled. *I'm through playing with you! Get yo bitch ass up! We going to the fucking Evergreen, and you finna set this shit straight!* **You gon' make it right, Dre!**

Dre stared, frozen in time and place. He wanted to move but couldn't. His eyes were fixed on the frog.

Will's eyes became even more menacing. He applied a lethal amount of pressure to his captive, and there was an audible, squishing *POP* as the frog's belly split below his smallest finger. One eyeball squirted out of the socket and rolled lazily down the side of the bullfrog's head.

Get yo ass up, ho! I ain't playing with you!

Will swung fast, throwing the mangled corpse at his brother. Dre tried to dodge. He brought up a hand to deflect the carcass, but it flew past his defenses and smacked hard on his mouth, leaving a wetness Dre could only assume was frog guts before it fell to the ground.

He screamed. He shot to his feet, spitting and wiping at his face with trembling hands that would soon be used to ward off blows from Will's friends. It wasn't even an issue anymore. Dre would go to the Evergreen. He would take his whooping and point a firearm at Will's murderer too. He would even pull the trigger. Whatever it took to make the ghoul go away, Dre would do it.

If Will could really read his mind, he wasn't showing it. The sneer did not leave his face.

Come on, nigga! Get going!

Dre's heart pounded so hard it hurt. He thought he was having a heart attack. He led the way out of the creek. He made it to the street with his brother quick on his heels.

As he marched, Dre wondered why some of the movies he'd seen had such a soft portrayal of ghosts. If he ever got a chance to make his own film, he'd tell the truth. He'd tell the world how ghosts are fierce, and ugly and demonic. Ghosts didn't come back for a fond farewell or to hold you and make beautiful pottery. Ghosts vomited blood and cursed and killed bullfrogs. If they didn't get what they wanted, ghosts could be fucking brutal.

COLORED RAGS

CHAPTER THIRTY
MIKE'S CO-CONSPIRATOR
& DRE CATCHES A RIDE

In Africa
I wasn't there
When strong, black men
Sliced through their dark skin
With sharp blades
And they sang
And they danced
And their thick, pure blood
Flowed freely from their bodies
Onto the pure African soil
I wasn't there
So, I waited
In America I'm at almost every corner
With my big, cement mouth open wide
And I gobble up skateboards and garbage
Children's toys and leaves
And you
When you roll down the street with your homeboys
I see you
And I wait
And when they come for you
With bigger guns than yours
When their hot pieces of lead pierce your body
You will bleed
And your thick, pure blood will flow freely from your skin
Onto these oil-streaked American streets
And I'll take your blood
And taste it

KEITH THOMAS WALKER

And let it stain my insides
Until the rain comes
And your thick, pure blood will be washed away
With all the skateboards, garbage
Children's toys and leaves
And all other human waste

Mike made more calls and snorted more lines before his SOLUTION materialized. He was only 16, a mere BG in his set, but his murderous tendencies were generations old. His grandfather had killed a man he caught sleeping with his wife. His uncle Benny sold drugs and shot a few people. His mother stabbed two men (neither of them fatally). He had three more relatives convicted of either manslaughter or murder.

Mike's original plan for his second assassination was scratched because OG Kody was in jail, and there was no way to get to him. On a normal day, he might have left it at that. But the drugs in his system, the gunshot wound in his chest, and the memory of Spider chilling in Shaun's boy/girl house gave Mike the strength and tenacity to trudge forward.

He was beyond determined. He kept murder on his mind and was rewarded with a new, *special* target. The victim was innocent. He was not in a gang and had never done anything offensive to a Blood. For many, that would've made him off limits. But for Mike, it made him a sacrificial lamb. This murder would be unexpected and uncalled for. It would make the front page of the local paper. Community leaders would decry the killing; the police commissioner for sure, maybe all the way up to the mayor.

Mike smiled from ear to ear as his visitor scraped together a line with a real razor blade. She came prepared. The one thing she hadn't anticipated was Mike's level of hatred for OG Kody and the south side rips. Initially, she was reluctant to get involved.

"I don't understand why you gotta hide in the bathroom," she said. "I mean, if you just wanna talk to him, why you gotta hide?"

"I told you," Mike argued. "If he see me, he'll prolly take off running before I can talk to him. He don't know me. Ain't nobody finna go in a room, if they see some nigga already in there. That's stupid. You talking like you wasn't never down."

COLORED RAGS

The girl didn't say anything. She leaned over the dresser and inhaled as much of the cocaine as she could.

Once a bopper, always a bopper, Mike thought.

When he found out Kody was unreachable, Mike interrogated a few hoodrats to learn as much as he could about the fagg land set. Other than Will, OG Kody was the biggest name still living. There were other goons Mike could wet up, but slaying a random ricket wasn't good enough. That would only get him a double life sentence. Mike wanted fame and glory. He wanted to stomp into jail like El Chapo; shackled from head to toe. He wanted niggas to love him. More importantly, he wanted them to *fear* him.

He watched his guest's ass as she snorted. Tracy was thin, almost too skinny to be fine, but she had a nice-size booty that made you do a double take. When one of his contacts told him OG Kody had a little brother who was going out with one of the homegirls, Mike couldn't believe it. When he found out Kody's brother was smashing *Tracy*, he knew he had his victim.

Killing Kody's innocent, little brother would be a wakeup call for the city. The papers would read **COLLEGE STUDENT GUNNED DOWN BY GANG MEMBER**. Everyone would know about it. Everyone would know Mike's name. All he had to do was convince a bitch to set it up.

Tracy wasn't really dependable, but Mike had fucked her a few times, and he knew she was pliable. Shaun had fucked her too. Many, many Bloods had. She had been away from the gang for months, but she still lived in Stop Six and wasn't hard to find. It was harder to convince her to lure Chris to a motel, but failure was not an option.

"I need you to help me out," Mike had told her.

Once she got past the fact that he wasn't dead but was definitely in deep trouble, Mike fed Tracy the best line of bullshit he could come up with. And she swallowed it, like so much semen.

"I need to talk to him," he had told her. "His brother's gang is trying to kill me for that OG Will shit, but *I didn't even do it*. Everybody think I did, but it wasn't me. It was *Spider*. And now he dead, and won't nobody listen to me. If you can get Chris to come to the motel and let me talk to him, I bet he can talk to his brother and help get them niggas off my back. I'm *scared*, Tracy. I need to go to the hospital, but I can't go until I'm safe."

"I can't, Mike. He gon' be mad when he see you and find out I set it up."

"What difference does it make if he's mad at you? This is *my* life we're talking about. You gon' put him in front of me? You think this dude's gonna make you his woman? He going to *college*, Tracy. He can get a good girl, and you know you ain't it. Keep it real. He ain't trying to save yo ass."

Tracy got quiet after that, and Mike knew he had struck a nerve. It still took the promise of two hundred dollars and all the dope she could snort to get her to the motel. But the important thing was she came.

Mike leaned back in bed and snaked his sneaker up the back of her skirt as she snorted.

"Stop," she said playfully. "I ain't like that no more, Mike." She didn't face him, and she didn't knock his foot away. She began scraping together another line, which was fine by him.

He grinned. "Yeah, you said that. I ain't seen you around much. What's up, you too good to kick it with the homies?"

"Y'all ain't about nothing."

"What about that Chris nigga?" Mike asked.

"He a good dude. I like him a lot."

"I wanna know when you gon' call him."

"I'ma call," Tracy promised.

"You need to hurry up, girl. I wanna get this shit over with, so I can go to the doctor. You see this blood?"

She turned to observe the fresh stain on the front of his shirt. "I ain't got my money yet," she told him.

Mike grinned. "It's in my pocket. Come get it."

Tracy shook her head. "Uh-uhn. I'm not even playing that game. You get it out yourself."

Mike was chipper as he produced the two bills. He tossed them on the bed, and Tracy snatched them up.

"You sure you ain't gon' try to fight him or nothing?" she asked.

"Look at me," Mike said. "I look like I can fight somebody right now? Bitch I'm *dying* in this motherfucker. You need to call that nigga and get him over here, before you get too high."

Tracy was not the type of girl who took offense to being called a bitch. It was almost a term of endearment.

COLORED RAGS

"What if he don't wanna talk to you?" she asked as she removed her cell from her purse.

"If he don't wanna talk to me, then fuck it. At least I tried."

"What if he listens to you, but he won't tell his brother nothing?"

"Damn, girl. I can't be worried about all that right now. I still gotta try to talk to the nigga. His brother run all them crabs. You can keep the money either way. I gotta do this before I turn myself in." His voice took on a shaky quality that made Tracy more sympathetic.

How stupid can this ho be? Mike wondered.

"You sure you ain't gon' try to hurt him?" she asked again.

"Tracy, I swear to God. Fuck it, I put it on my *mama*: I just wanna tell him to tell his brother I didn't do it. I wanna explain myself. That's it. I *swear*."

She nodded. She swallowed the cocaine draining down the back of her throat and dialed a number.

As Mike watched, a giggle forced its way up his throat. He camouflaged it with a cough. Tracy didn't notice.

Mike hid his pistol in the bathroom before she arrived. But from the looks of it, he could have carried the gun openly without setting off any alarms in the hoodrat's head. The bitch was seriously clueless.

● ● ● ● ● ●

Chris made a left on Berry, and the .380 began to slide out of his lap. Panicked, he grabbed it gingerly and placed it on the passenger seat. He remembered flipping the safety on, but he still felt the gun might go off if he wasn't careful.

The Evergreen was only blocks away, but his journey already seemed to have no direction. When he left Jason's house, he planned to go home and wait to see what Croc would do next. But he talked himself out of it before he got there. He didn't want Croc to come to his house, which might put his mother in danger.

He decided that confronting Croc had been the best move all along. But he wasn't so sure anymore. What he was experiencing could be labeled as a *moment of clarity*, but on the streets of Overbrook Meadows, his thought process amounted to nothing more than *punking out*.

The more he thought about it, running up on Croc sounded too much like first degree murder. He could already hear the district attorney tearing him down on the witness stand:

So, Mr. Walters, why did you go to the apartment, if you didn't plan on giving him his money?

Well, why did you take a gun with you?

Did you not know that Mr. Turner, whom you refer to as Croc, would be upset if you came without his money?

Did you not say that you and Mr. Turner had an altercation an hour before you went to his apartment?

Is it not true that you went to the apartment with the sole purpose of killing Mr. Turner to get revenge for the fight?

*You are under oath, Mr. Walters! Tell this courtroom how you lost a fight earlier that day, you went and got your gun, and then you went to Mr. Turner's apartment to pay him back. You wanted revenge, didn't you Mr. Walters? You wanted everyone to know that you're not a punk, and you're not going to let anyone beat you up. And **that's** why you killed him. Isn't that right Mr. Walters? **Isn't that right?***

"I object, your honor!" Chris shouted in the silence of his vehicle. He laughed at himself. "This motherfucker is badgering the witness!"

It was funny now, but juries weren't funny. Prisons weren't funny, and *anal rape*, no matter how you slice that pie, was definitely not funny. It was best to keep a cool head in these situations.

Chris turned into the entrance of the Evergreen. But his bloodlust had long since faded. He decided his first plan was the best plan, and he should've stuck with it. He had to wait until the bully came to him. If Croc was stupid enough to threaten him at his own home, it would bolster his self-defense argument. He would be protecting himself and his mom.

Chris slowed to a stop in front of his brother's building but did not park the car. There was no one outside to witness his aborted plunge into manhood, which was for the best. He saw the Crown Vic Croc and Trez were using earlier. He wanted to shoot out the front and back windshields, but that was just stupid.

He was about to head home, when he saw something so out of place his foot remained planted on the brake pedal. Chris had seen OG Will's brother countless times, but he never got to know him. Even with the boy's disheveled appearance, Chris recognized Dre as he staggered around the corner, heading in the direction of apartment 4.

Chris stared in confusion. Next to the guy who actually killed OG Will, Dre had to be the most wanted man on the south side. Everyone knew he was in the car when Will got shot. People were saying he had Will's gun but didn't do anything. Chris wondered what type of reception Dre expected to receive from the AGG Land Crips. He had to know they would greet him with closed fists, rather than open arms.

Dre walked stiffly, without looking around. His eyes were glued to his shoes as he took the first unsteady step up the stairs leading to Kody's apartment.

Chris didn't consider himself a do-gooder. Only minutes ago he'd been contemplating murder. But he could no more watch Dre climb those stairs then he could watch a toddler crawl onto a busy freeway.

"Hey," he said, not loud enough to arouse any neighbors, but loud enough to stop the portly boy in his tracks.

He turned, and Chris saw that Will's death had done a number on him. Dre was uncombed, unkempt, and not all there upstairs. He had a blank, defeated look in his eyes. There was mud on his shoes, dirt on his knees, and a little blood on his face. He stared at Chris with something like recognition, but his eyes never focused.

"What you doing over here?" Chris asked him.

"I - I don't know," Dre admitted timidly.

Bitch, you know what the fuck you doing here! Get up them stairs, Dre! Will was belligerent. He screamed at the back of his head, but the boy turned towards the yellow Plymouth.

"Man," Chris said, "don't you know these niggas over here wanna kill you?"

"I told you," Dre said.

Confused, Chris looked around, thinking he was talking to someone else. He wondered if the boy had gone crazy. But demented or not, Dre didn't deserve to have his head kicked in. Chris reached over, snatched the pistol from the passenger seat, and returned it to the floorboard.

"You need a ride?" he asked. "Your name's Dre, right?"

Dre hesitated.

"Hurry up," Chris said. "Get in. They gon' fuck you up, if they see you out here."

Don't get in that fucking car, Dre. Dre! You know you hear me, nigga! Get up them stairs, fool. We right here! **We right here!**

Dre ignored his brother. He opened the door and got in the Plymouth. Chris was immediately aware of an intense body odor, but this was no time to discuss personal hygiene.

"Where you stay at," he asked.

But Dre wasn't looking at him. Something at the foot of the stairs held his attention. Chris followed his gaze but didn't see anything out of place.

Get out the car, Dre. Get yo bitch ass out the car! Will stomped and flailed his arms. *You fucking this shit up, nigga! You fucking up!*

"Close the door," Chris said.

Dre gave him a worried look. "Where you gon' take me?"

He ain't gon' take you nowhere, cuz! Get out the car!

"I'ma take you home," Chris said. "Where you stay? Just close the door. We gotta get outta here."

Dre closed the door, and Chris sped out of the parking lot.

I knew you was a ho! I knew you wasn't gon' do it! Will screamed after them, but his voice was mostly lost in the squeal of Chris' tires and the exhaust from his tail pipe.

When they got to Riverside, Chris tried again to communicate with his befuddled passenger. "Are you alright? Where you live?"

Dre didn't answer. He stared down at his hands and mumbled something. Chris didn't know what was going on, but he would take him to the hospital, if he couldn't come up with an address. Come to think of it, that was probably the best place for him. Chris didn't notice any physical injuries, outside of a busted lip, but Dre's mental anguish was off the charts.

Before he could question him again, a buzzing emanated from his pocket. He pulled out his cellphone, but not in time to catch Tracy's call. Seeing her name on the Caller ID filled Chris with mixed emotions. He was running low on gas, so he pulled into a 7-11 before calling her back.

"I'ma go pay for this gas," he told Dre as he parked next to the pumps.

COLORED RAGS

It wasn't clear if he understood, but Dre nodded. Chris turned the ignition off and got out of the car.

CHAPTER THIRTY-ONE
THE FINAL CHAPTER
THE MURDA SHOW

Hi
I'm a hollow-tip .38 bullet
Don't fuck with me
Especially while I'm in the chamber of this gun
Staring at you through a barrel pointed at your face
I'm hoping you'll do something stupid
Like reach for your pocket
Say you're a Crip or Blood
Or anything else to provoke this trigger finger
'Cause I want you so bad
I want to tear through your skin
And plow through your bones and organs
I don't care if you're young, old
In a wheelchair or a cradle
Come on
Come on
Pull the trigger, dog
Let me at 'em

    Sex was the last thing on Chris' mind, so he was a little put off when Tracy told him she was in another motel room and wanted him to come over. He didn't want to go, but he bit his tongue. He was starting to wonder if Tracy was capable of changing. Did she have anything to offer, other than what was between her legs?
    She gave him directions, and Chris said he'd meet her at the Valley View in ten minutes. By the time he finished pumping

COLORED RAGS

gas, he had decided to break it off with her. He wouldn't do it over the phone though. He would meet her in person and let her down easy. If she cried, he would console her. He wouldn't disrespect her. He would treat her like the queen she was, even if she didn't recognize her greatness.

When he got in the car, he told Dre, "I gotta go somewhere right quick."

"Where?"

Chris was glad to hear he was responsive, but the boy still looked crazy.

"I gotta stop at a motel off Lancaster," he said. "I'm only gon' be in there for a minute. You want me to drop you off first?"

"No," Dre protested. "I wanna stay with you."

Chris found that odd, but it was by no means the strangest thing he'd seen Dre do that day. "I might be in there for like, ten, fifteen minutes. You wanna wait in the car the whole time?"

"I ain't got nothing else to do," Dre said, and then asked, "Ain't you Kody's brother?"

"Yeah," Chris said as he pulled out of the parking lot.

"I like Kody." Dre's voice was eerily childlike. "I seen y'all. He like you."

Once again Chris thought that was an odd comment. He didn't ask any follow up questions. Talking to the boy was starting to creep him out.

As they rode in silence, Chris shot sideways glances at his passenger. Dre never noticed. He stared out the window – not in a casual, *checking out the neighborhood*, kind of way. Chris thought he was looking around as if he was expecting someone. Dre became more anxious each time they had to stop at a light.

By the time they reached the motel, Chris was almost eager to be in Tracy's company and away from Dre. He wondered if he should take him to the nearest police station. He was starting to think Dre had been jumped, most likely by Will's friends. That would explain his busted lip and soiled clothing.

Chris pulled in next to Tracy's Mustang and took the keys out of the ignition. He didn't think Dre would run off with his bucket, but there was no point risking it.

"You sure you wanna wait in the car?" he asked again.

Dre nodded.

Chris wore a look of uncertainty as he opened the door and got out.

Alone in the car, Dre slumped in the seat and settled in for the wait. He didn't know where this day would take him, but he knew for sure that he hadn't heard the last of Will. He had only accomplished one of the demon's objectives. He had failed his brother in death, just as he had in life.

He watched as Chris knocked on the door to room 12. Someone answered and Chris stepped inside, closing the door behind him. Dre yawned and began to stretch when a huge **WHAP!** banged the back of his seat.

Dre! Will's voice was an excited hiss. Dre! He in there! He gon' kill 'em, Dre! You gotta do something!

Dre turned and was met by his dead brother's frantic, fiery eyes. At such close range, he could smell his brother's rancid breath better than he ever wanted to. He didn't know if Will had snacked on bull frog or dead pit bull, but the stench was overpowering.

You gotta get him, Dre! He in there! He in there right now!

"Who?" Dre asked.

Mike! The nigga who shot me! He in there! He finna kill Kody's brother, cuz! He finna kill him right now!

Dre looked to the motel room and back to his brother.

This is it, Dre! This is it! This is why I'm here! I didn't know, man, but, damn, now I do! You gotta get him, Dre! Can't nobody do it but you!

"Do what?" Dre asked. This was the meanest trick his brother had pulled on him since climbing out of his coffin.

It's a gun under the seat, Dre. Get it, man. You can do it. Reach under there and get it. Hurry up! He finna kill that nigga!

Dre was confused, but he bent and reached under Chris' seat. His hand came into contact with a cold, metal object. He retrieved the .380 from the floorboard and stared at it.

Go get 'em, Dre. Get 'em. Do that shit, nigga!

"Who in there?"

Listen to me! The nigga who shot me is in there. He in the bathroom. He finna kill this nigga, if you don't do something!

Dre still felt this might be a trick, but dead-Will seemed to know everything. He knew the gun was under the seat, and he could read Dre's mind too. Maybe there was someone in the motel room. But then again, what if there wasn't? Dre didn't want to barge in on Chris and his girlfriend based on the word of a ghoul.

Dre, trust me, man. Will's voice calmed a bit, but his eyes did not. They glistened, bright red, like the blistering pits of hell. *If you kill this nigga, it's over. I'm gone. I promise you that, Dre. Chris ain't got nothing to do with this. He never did nothing but try to help you. Do it, man. Get this nigga for me.*

Dre gave his brother a hard look before getting out of the car. He didn't care about preserving OG Will's legacy. But Kody's little brother was the only friend he had at that point. If Will was lying, and Dre made a fool of himself yet again, he would use the gun to blow his own brains out. Death was a better alternative to the hell his brother was putting him through.

He took a few steps towards the motel and then turned back to the car. "How it work?" he asked. "I don't know how to use this."

It's already cocked, Will said. *Just flip the safety off.*

Dre fumbled with the gun until he found the safety.

That's it. Now all you gotta do is point and shoot. Shoot that motherfucker! Get him, Dre. **Get him!**

Dre looked down at the gun, up at his brother, and then turned back to the room. He took a deep breath as he approached the door. Back in the Plymouth, Will bounced around in the backseat like a monkey on speed.

This is perfect. It don't get no better than this. Get 'em, Dre, he hissed. **Get his motherfucking ass!**

● ● ● ● ● ●

Chris' first indication that things may not be on the up and up was Tracy's eyes. They were always big, but today they were bugging. Her pupils were dilated to the size of marbles. Confused, he stepped inside and closed the door.

If there was theme music for his life, Chris imagined the band would be playing low baselines with eerie violin strings. There was so much to take in, but he only had a second to do so. His brain processed the scene faster than a computer.

Tracy was either high or scared to death. The bed behind her had been used recently. There was white powder residue on the dresser. That would explain Tracy's eyes, but why had she invited Chris over if she was getting loaded? She knew he didn't do coke – and who the hell had been on the bed?

Half a second later, Chris was ready to speak.

"What's going–"

"Hey, baby," Tracy said at the same time.

Their words swam together, rendering both phrases inaudible. Chris was about to repeat his question when he saw something out of the corner of his eye that did not fully surprise him. A door on the far side of the room began to open. With her back to the bathroom, Tracy didn't notice it. She stepped to Chris and reached for a hug, but he wanted no parts of it. He took a step back and came into contact with the closed door.

Tracy only had a moment to register confusion before the bathroom door swung open fully, revealing a youngster Chris had never seen before. The juvenile wore a blue tee shirt and jeans. He was pale and sweating. His eyes were bugged like Tracy's. One of his arms was in a sling. In his free hand, he toted a firearm that was pointed squarely in Chris' direction. There was a small twitch on the left side of his face, contracting his jaw quickly, as if he was sneering or winking – but his trigger finger was steady.

Chris' first thought was *Croc*. Somehow he had constructed this impossible set-up with Tracy as his pawn. But how could he pull it off? Did he know Tracy? Did she sleep with him too?

Tracy followed his gaze, and she turned towards the bathroom. Her reaction time was quickened by the cocaine flowing through her blood, but it took her mouth a moment to catch up to her brain.

"Mike, what you. Why you, where you? Got that?..."

"Move, bitch. Get out the way," Mike said calmly. *Get out the way, bitch! Get out the way!*

What happened next would be ingrained in the collective memory of the survivors for years to come.

The front door crashed open, sending Chris stumbling to the side. Dre charged in, much to the surprise of all three occupants. As Chris staggered, he saw that Dre had his .380. Chris didn't have time to figure out the hows and whys before the first gunshot shattered the silence and echoed like an M-60 going off in a washing machine.

COLORED RAGS

PAP!
Tracy didn't feel the bullet slam into her skull. Bits of brain and skull fragments flew from the back of her head. A spray of fine midst dotted Chris' face. As Tracy's body fell, Dre saw the kid in the closet, and *it was him!* He'd only seen him once before, but his appearance hadn't changed in two days.

Mike was skinny, scared, and armed, just like the night at the Rainbow. He wore blue rather than red, but it was the same guy. *Goddamn if it wasn't the same guy!* Will was right. Dre trained his gun in the direction of his brother's murderer and started twisting off shots.

PAP!PAP! PAP!
If Chris was surprised by what was going on, Mike was having a fucking aneurism. His plan was perfect. Kody's brother had come. Chris was standing there. *Right fucking there.* All Tracy had to do was take a step to the left, and it would have all been over. His dreams, his life, his legacy, it was all going perfectly until the unexpected variable showed up. Mike didn't know who the gatecrasher was, why he had come or why he was shooting, but he knew enough to understand that his life was in danger. Kody's brother was unarmed. The other guy wasn't.

Mike swung the barrel of his father's .38 away from Chris, to the one who was shooting. He had six bullets. He had to take out the shooter with no more than five. The last shot was for Kody's brother. No way was college boy getting away.

Something like a bee zipped by Mike's ear, and he too began to fire at will.

BAK! BAK! BAK!
Chris took advantage of the momentary lack of attention he was receiving to make his move. Dre was standing in the only doorway out of the room, so Chris chose the main window as his means of escape. Without considering how he would manage it, what he would do once outside, or how to avoid fatal, artery-slicing injuries, Chris threw himself into the curtains headfirst. The window gave way. The crash was loud enough to alert the motel's manager, but the shattering glass was all but lost in the sound of the shootout.

Draped in the curtain like Batman in his cape, Chris squeezed his eyes closed as he flew through the air, seemingly in slow motion. He did not see Tracy's Mustang, but he felt his head impact the bumper. The pain was intense, but it was dulled by a curtain of stars that cloaked his vision and rendered him unconscious. Chris continued to hear gunfire as his world faded to black. Beautiful black.

Mike kept squeezing the trigger past his fourth and fifth shot because the other guy was *still standing*, and the other guy was *still shooting*. With Mike's sixth shot the stranger finally faltered, his arms flailing wildly. Dre fell backwards, out of the open door, but not before letting off two last rounds.

PAP! PAP!

Mike savored a split second of victory before something hard and hot slammed into his stomach, sending him reeling back into the darkness of the bathroom. As he fell to the floor, and his body reacted to the trauma of his second gunshot in as many days, Mike kept his eyes on the other shooter.

The interloper was on his back now, lying in front of a yellow Plymouth. Beyond him, Mike saw something in the backseat of the car that was only fit for horror movies or the blood-filled dreams of bullet-riddled gangsters.

Mike saw OG Will. He saw that he was smiling. His black skin had faded to gray. His sharp teeth were smeared with reddish-green bile that glistened in the sunlight. Will's eyes glowed like lava, beckoning Mike to join him in the afterworld. As the echo of the gunshots began to fade, Mike saw that the demon was not only smiling. He was laughing. Will stared at him and laughed and laughed.

A deep darkness fell over Mike, and he gave in to unconsciousness or death, he wasn't sure which.

COLORED RAGS

EPILOGUE

Do you prefer a driveby
Or are walk-ups more your style?
Do your ears ever burn
From the screams of an innocent child?
Or is anyone really innocent
In your rule-less, macho game?
Do you mourn for any victim
Who's not a member of your gang?
This genocide has gone on for years
Ain't it getting kind of old?
Brothers put down your guns
You still have time to save your souls

Our people are being wiped out
By the nine millimeter disease
But still you cock your weapon
When I throw up two fingers for peace
They'll spray your name on vacant walls
For getting took out of the game
And your homies will pour out liquor
Six feet above your rotting remains
You see death around the corner
Because of the ruthless life you're in
Brothers put down your guns
The prisons have too much black skin

You front him at a club
So now he's looking for where you hang
But you take him out first
You say you did it for the gang
His boys take out your brother

'Cause you're always on the run
Did you really think those boys
Would keep their vengeance one-on-one?
Do you think your brother knew
It was your fault he faced their guns?
Now you gotta tell your mama
How you killed her youngest son
I bet you didn't feel so bad
When it was someone else's kid
Brothers put down your guns
You're making Otis Pinkey rich

You don't even stick around
To see your target hit the street
To watch his body jerk and spasm
Eyes transfixed as his soul leaves
You don't inspect your fallen prey
You don't watch that black man bleed
You don't watch his last breath form
As a spit bubble between his teeth
You don't stay until he's stiff
Until your adversary turns cold
Brothers put down your guns
Please try to save your wicked souls

    When he was done reading, the room was completely silent. It had taken Chris longer to finish his essay than expected, much longer than the fifteen minutes he'd allotted for the activity. According to the clock mounted on the wall above the students' heads, he had been reading non-stop for nearly half an hour. The bell would ring in less than five minutes.
    Chris' students weren't all "bad kids," but they were labeled "at risk" by the school district. They weren't the type of students who would purposefully interrupt their teacher during a lesson – for the most part. But they also weren't the type of kids who would sit idly by while their teacher read for thirty minutes, either. Yet, there they were. Every set of eyes was focused on the instructor. No one had spoken while he read. No one dropped a pencil. Even real coughs were muffled in anxious palms.

COLORED RAGS

     Chris surveyed his group. Quite a few mouths were ajar. A few of his more sensitive students were tearing up.
     The lesson was to instruct the class on how to write a personal essay. Yesterday Chris gave them the basics on what the essay should include, namely a personal, significant event that changed their life in some way or made them see things differently. Today Chris brought his own personal essay to class as an example the students could relate to.
     The events that occurred ten years ago following his college registration had never faded from his mind and were easy to capture on paper. The hard part, Chris found, was compacting his experience into five single-spaced pages.
     Chris thought the first question they would ask upon completion would be, "Do ours have to be that long?" He was surprised by the maturity of his students' responses. Well, most of them.
     "*Daaaang!*" Cordell, his favorite cut up, broke the silence with the elongated word. "Mr. Walters, they tried to kill you?"
     "They tried," Chris said.
     "But you didn't even do nothing," a short, Hispanic boy named Felipe said. Raising hands wasn't always a pre-requisite when speaking in his class.
     "That's right," Chris agreed. "You don't always have to do something to get yourself in trouble. Sometimes the people you consider friends will get you in trouble."
     He thought it was a bit corny to tack on a preachy message, but as a teacher, it was expected of him.
     An apt pupil named Taylor raised her hand.
     "What you got?" Chris asked her.
     "What happened to the other people? The ones who was in there with you?"
     Chris knew the question was coming and had thought long and hard about the information he would give his class. They were only seventh graders, but they lived in a war zone. According to recent surveys, fifty percent of them had someone in their family who had killed someone or were murdered themselves. But just because they were accustomed to violence didn't give Chris the green light to educate them on blood and drugs.

"Well," he said, "Dre died. Mike shot him, more than once. Dre died at the scene before the police showed up. Tracy died too."

He paused, to make sure no one was freaked out by that.

"When Dre barged into the room, I'd like to think he was trying to help me. But he was shooting blindly. I was standing right next to Tracy when he shot her, so I don't know if he was going to shoot me or not. I know Mike wanted to kill me, and Dre stopped him from doing that. I think Dre was my guardian angel that day. He saved my life."

"What about Mike?" another student asked. "Did he die too?"

Chris didn't immediately respond. Since the shootout, Mike had visited him many times in his dreams. During his waking hours, Chris found himself worrying about closed bathroom doors in small rooms. Even today, he thought of Mike when he saw ghetto youths draped in red. He hated Mike, at first. But time heals all wounds, physical and emotional. Chris learned to forgive the man who tried to take his life.

"No," he said. "He's still alive. He's in prison now. They gave him a life sentence for Will's murder. He got ten more years for conspiring to kill me – that means you can get in trouble just for planning to hurt someone. He didn't get any time for shooting Dre. They said it was self defense."

Taylor's hand went up again. "Are you scared of him? Do you think he'll get out?"

The bell rang, but no one moved.

"I never want to see him again," Chris said, "but I don't have nightmares about him, not anymore. I'm more afraid of nuclear bombs, perverts around my daughter and all of you being tardy to your next class. Now get going."

The students gathered their possessions and began the exodus out of his classroom. A few stopped at his desk to congratulate him on his essay, which was a little strange, considering he was the one who should dole out adulations. He shooed them away with a smile and told them to bring an outline for their own essay tomorrow.

Chris left a lot out of the story he read to his students. He didn't tell them how much time he was starting to spend with Kody's gang or about Croc and the twenty grand. He didn't tell them how Kody, even from county jail, was able to orchestrate a severe beat down that left Croc in ICU for a week.

He didn't tell them about Dre and Will's legacy. Chris thought it might inspire some of his pint-sized misfits, if they knew Dre's role in the shooting solidified OG Will's status as a south side legend. After ten years, it was mostly forgotten that Dre didn't actually kill the guy he was after.

Kody beat his murder charges and banged for six more years after that fateful summer. He eventually left the gang and settled down with a good woman. He was a surveyor now, making a little more than Chris, as a matter of fact.

Chris certainly did not tell his students, or the police for that matter, that the gun Dre used to save his life was actually his. The detectives believed Dre had the gun already, when Chris picked him up at the apartments. Kody still didn't know the .380 came from his gray coat.

By the time Chris' fourth period began to stroll into the classroom, the students were already buzzing about "a really cool story" Mr. Walters was going to read today. Passing period only lasted five minutes, but that had been enough time to spread the word.

"Alright," Chris announced when the tardy bell rang. He was pleased to see his pupils seated and unusually attentive for a Friday afternoon. "As some of you have already heard, today we're going to learn more about personal essays…"

KEITH THOMAS WALKER

ABOUT THE AUTHOR

Keith Thomas Walker, known as the Master of Romantic Suspense and Urban Fiction, is the author of nearly two dozen novels, including *Life After, The Realest Ever,* the *Brick House* series and the *Finley High* series. Keith's books transcend all genres. He has published romance, urban fiction, mystery/thriller, teen/young adult, Christian, poetry and erotica. Originally from Fort Worth, he is a graduate of Texas Wesleyan University. Keith has won or been nominated for numerous awards in the categories of "Best Male Author," "Best Romance," "Best Urban Fiction," and "Author of the Year," from several book clubs and organizations. Visit him at www.keithwalkerbooks.com.

CPSIA information can be obtained
at www.ICGtesting.com
Printed in the USA
FSOW01n0055210416
19438FS